TRUTH
AND
JUSTICE

Books by Fern Michaels

Fearless
Spirit of the Season
Deep Harbor
Fate & Fortune
Sweet Vengeance
Holly and Ivy
Fancy Dancer
No Safe Secret
Wishes for Christmas
About Face
Perfect Match
A Family Affair
Forget Me Not
The Blossom Sisters
Balancing Act
Tuesday's Child
Betrayal
Southern Comfort
To Taste the Wine
Sins of the Flesh
Sins of Omission
Return to Sender
Mr. and Miss
   Anonymous
Up Close and Personal
Fool Me Once
Picture Perfect
The Future Scrolls
Kentucky Sunrise
Kentucky Heat
Kentucky Rich
Plain Jane
Charming Lily

What You Wish For
The Guest List
Listen to Your Heart
Celebration
Yesterday
Finders Keepers
Annie's Rainbow
Sara's Song
Vegas Sunrise
Vegas Heat
Vegas Rich
Whitefire
Wish List
Dear Emily
Christmas at
   Timberwoods

The Sisterhood Novels:

Truth and Justice
Cut and Run
Safe and Sound
Need to Know
Crash and Burn
Point Blank
In Plain Sight
Eyes Only
Kiss and Tell
Blindsided
Gotcha!
Home Free
Déjà Vu
Cross Roads

Game Over
Deadly Deals
Vanishing Act
Razor Sharp
Under the Radar
Final Justice
Collateral Damage
Fast Track
Hokus Pokus
Hide and Seek
Free Fall
Lethal Justice
Sweet Revenge
The Jury
Vendetta
Payback
Weekend Warriors

The Men of the
Sisterhood Novels:

Hot Shot
Truth or Dare
High Stakes
Fast and Loose
Double Down

The Godmothers
Series:

Far and Away
Classified
Breaking News
Deadline

Late Edition
Exclusive
The Scoop

E-Book Exclusives:

Desperate Measures
Seasons of Her Life
To Have and To Hold
Serendipity
Captive Innocence
Captive Embraces
Captive Passions
Captive Secrets
Captive Splendors
Cinders to Satin
For All Their Lives
Texas Heat
Texas Rich
Texas Fury
Texas Sunrise

Anthologies:

Home Sweet Home
*A Snowy Little
   Christmas*
*Coming Home for
   Christmas*
A Season to Celebrate
Mistletoe Magic
Winter Wishes
*The Most Wonderful
   Time*

Books by Fern Michaels (Continued)

When the Snow Falls
Secret Santa
A Winter Wonderland
I'll Be Home for Christmas
Making Spirits Bright
Holiday Magic
Snow Angels

Silver Bells
Comfort and Joy
Sugar and Spice
Let It Snow
A Gift of Joy
Five Golden Rings
Deck the Halls
Jingle All the Way

FERN MICHAELS

TRUTH
AND
JUSTICE

ZEBRA BOOKS
KENSINGTON PUBLISHING CORP.
www.kensingtonbooks.com

ZEBRA BOOKS are published by

Kensington Publishing Corp.
119 West 40th Street
New York, NY 10018

All Kensington titles, imprints, and distributed lines are available at special quantity discounts for bulk purchases for sales promotion, premiums, fund-raising, educational, or institutional use.

Special book excerpts or customized printings can also be created to fit specific needs. For details, write or phone the office of the Kensington Sales Manager: Attn.: Sales Department. Kensington Publishing Corp., 119 West 40th Street, New York, NY 10018. Phone: 1-800-221-2647.

Zebra and the Z logo Reg. U.S. Pat. & TM Off.

First Kensington Books Hardcover Printing: June 2020
First Zebra Books Mass-Market Paperback Printing: September 2020
ISBN-13: 978-1-4201-4606-6
ISBN-10: 1-4201-4606-8

ISBN-13: 978-1-4201-4607-3 (eBook)
ISBN-10: 1-4201-4607-6 (eBook)

10 9 8 7 6 5 4 3 2 1

Printed in the United States of America

*I would like to dedicate this book to the real Jeff
Josell and the real Scott "Bones" Kimball.
It was fun watching you guys grow up and become
the parents you are today. Thanks for the memories.
Mike's Mom*

Prologue

"I pronounce you man and wife! You may now kiss the bride, Major Nolan," Pastor Leonard Bryant said, smiling from ear to ear.

Major Andrew—Andy to his friends—Nolan, planted a lip-lock on his new bride, making the pastor blush a rosy red and clear his throat to move things along. After all, he did have three other couples waiting to enter into the state of marital bliss.

Pastor Leonard Bryant cleared his throat a second time while the three waiting couples stomped their feet as they hooted and hollered their congratulations to the newlyweds. It was obvious to the pastor that they didn't mind waiting a little longer.

Breathless and breathing hard, the just-married couple broke apart and ran from the small chapel, shouting their thanks over their shoulders.

"We're down to forty-seven and a half hours until this honeymoon is over, Mrs. Nolan. How do you want to spend it? Sightseeing in my new truck, eating breakfast, or hitting the sack?" Andy shouted exuberantly.

The new bride, Bella Ames Nolan, tilted her head to the side. God, she loved this guy standing next to her with his arm around her shoulders in an I-am-never-going-to-let-you-go hold. He was better looking than any movie star she'd seen on the big screen. He was funny, witty, and charming, and did this thing with his tongue in her ear that drove her absolutely nuts. And most of all, he loved her. Her. He had told her how he loved her from the very first time they met, and her love for him had only grown stronger over the three years they had been seeing each other: FaceTiming while he was away and in person on the occasional leave.

"How about this? We climb into your new truck and drive someplace for a breakfast we do not want but pretend to eat; then we spend the rest of our forty-eight hours in bed. That's a trifecta if I ever heard one. Will that work for you, Major Nolan?"

"It absolutely will, Mrs. Nolan, unless you'd like to help me christen the bed in the back of the truck. You know, every truck has what they call a bed."

Her new husband's expression was so hopeful, so earnest, Bella burst out laughing, and quipped, "I thought you would never ask." Like she really wanted to spend even one second of their forty-eight-hour honeymoon in the bed of a pickup truck with no blanket. Anything for Andy even if her ass was black-and-blue for a month. She consoled herself with the thought that no one was going to see her ass unless she took some selfies to send to Andy once he landed wherever he was scheduled to be deployed. If she did do that, would it be considered porn? She decided that yes, it probably would be. Well then, no selfies.

"Hop in, Mrs. Nolan. We need to find a secluded place to christen this here fine vehicle. Tell me the truth, Bella, did you ever see a better-looking truck?"

In all the time she'd known Andy, she had never heard such excitement in regard to herself in his voice. Say the word *truck* and Andy was over the moon.

Bella forced herself to smile. She hated trucks. What she hated even more was the $65,000 in payments that went with "this here fine vehicle." Payments she would be making once Andy deployed. She smiled again as she tried not to think about her soon-to-be-bruised rear end.

And christening the truck was exactly what they did after pulling into an abandoned strip mall whose parking lot was secluded and in back of the tight strip of nine stores. The christening lasted eleven and a half minutes, two of which were used up with Bella tangling up the strings of her bikini panty. In the end, Andy just ripped them apart, and that was the end of that.

To say the christening was even close to pleasant would be an outright lie. Bella didn't even bother to pretend. Andy was so engrossed in the horsepower of his brand-new truck, a wedding present to himself, that he didn't even notice Bella pouting in the passenger seat as she stared out the window at the traffic and whatever scenery she could home in on.

The remainder of the forty-eight hours passed in a blur for Bella. She sobbed and hiccupped against Andy's bare chest when he said it was time for them to shower and dress because he had exactly thirty-seven minutes left on his leave. Bella cried even harder, and Andy literally had to pry her arms from around his shoulders. He beelined for the bathroom and took the shortest shower in history.

In what seemed like the blink of an eye, he was dressed and ready to go when the room phone rang. It was the desk clerk, telling Andy that his ride was waiting in the lobby.

Bella sat up in bed, stunned at what was going on. She hadn't showered. There was no way she could get dressed because she reeked of sex. What that meant was that Major Andy Nolan was going to walk out the door, and she wouldn't see him again until . . . whenever. No, no, this was all wrong. The goodbye at the end of her honeymoon was not supposed to be like this.

Bella could feel the anger start to build in her gut. She sat up, the sheet up to her chin. "Is this where you say, great honeymoon, all forty-eight hours of it, and hey, babe, I'll see you when I see you?"

Andy laughed, his head bobbing up and down. "See! I told you you would get it. You really are a good little soldier. I'm proud of you. The answer is yeah, pretty much." He ran over to the bed, his eyes on his watch. He kissed her on the nose before running out of the room. He had two minutes to make it to the lobby and his ride or they would leave without him. He decided on the stairs because he didn't want anyone to see the tears in his eyes. He felt like a jerk, a real heel for the way he'd exited the hotel room and left his new bride crying her eyes out. He knew that was the only way to play it or he would have lost it and cried right along with her *and* missed his ride. Discipline.

Andy barreled through the revolving door right on the heels of Colonel Paul Montrose and hopped into the Jeep in front of the hotel. His honeymoon was over. Now he had a war to fight.

Back inside the hotel room, Mrs. Bella Nolan stared at the door until she felt like she was going cross-eyed.

Now what was she supposed to do?

Pitching a hissy fit sounded good, but that took a lot of energy, energy she was totally lacking.

Shower? Wash away all traces of Andy? *I can't do that,* she thought, sobbing.

Roll over and go to sleep. The room is paid through tomorrow.

The Nolan honeymoon was officially over.

Chapter 1

It was three weeks since the horrendous rain. Andy's truck was still sitting in the now-dry parking lot because she didn't have the money to have it towed anywhere. He didn't have towing or truck replacement on his insurance. In fact, he had skimped wherever he could to save money. As far as she was concerned, the finance company could come and take the damn thing. She wasn't paying another red cent on that monster Andy loved and adored. She'd written him the day the rain stopped, but of course there was no response, something she found not only strange but even weird considering how Andy loved the Ram 2500.

He hadn't even acknowledged the e-mail that said she was filing for divorce.

Bella parked her Honda Civic, which was several spaces away from her two-year-old Nissan Sentra, in the same parking space she'd been issued when she had rented the apartment. The Nissan had been brand-spanking-new when she bought it. By the time the claims adjuster had finished his work, she had enough to buy the Civic with only a $66-a-month car payment. The Civic was also better on gas. The seventy-eight–year-old woman who had sold it to her swore that the 20,000-mile reading on the odometer was true and accurate, and the reason she was selling it was because she was going to move into an assisted living village and didn't need a car. Bella had bought it on the spot and never regretted it for a second.

Bella stepped out of the elevator and made her way down the hall to her apartment. She didn't run these days the way she had before. Before as in, before hiring Mitchell Jones. She played with the three apartment keys in her hand before she inserted the dead-bolt key into the lock.

Bella tossed the mail on the little bistro table in the kitchen without looking at it. What was the point? Bills, bills, bills. She could look at them anytime. Her theory was that if she opened them, she had to pay them. If she ignored them, then they didn't exist until she was ready to open and pay them.

Just the other day, she'd separated the mail into two piles. Her pile was on the left and Andy's was on the right. When she moved next week, her plan was to leave Andy's mail right where it was. Let the new tenant forward it or take it back to the post office. She grimaced when she saw the bill from Mitchell Jones in the stack of mail she'd carried in. It bothered her that she owed him money, but he'd said he would work with her and take whatever she could pay over time as she got paid. To date, she had paid him the munificent sum of $60.

Next week.

Everything was next week, when she was moving into a smaller one-bedroom apartment in the next complex down the road. She'd start her new part-time job next week. She was going to be a cashier four hours a night, six nights a week at a health-food store, earning $15 an hour plus a forty percent discount on anything she wanted to buy. It was time to start eating healthy and living a healthier lifestyle. Maybe she would meet some nice people and start to get a life for herself. She wished she could get the four years she'd devoted to Andy back, but that was impossible. The best years of her young life. How foolish she'd been to be so devoted to Andy that she took nothing in return but a ring on her finger and a pile of bills. Then again, she'd fallen in love.

Right now, right this minute, she was convinced the marriage hadn't stood a chance from the get-go. Maybe if Andy was a nine-to-five, work-at-Home-Depot kind of guy, it might have stood a chance.

Bella warned herself to turn off that kind of thinking by telling herself that you can't un-ring the bell. When she'd told her boss and some of the people that she worked with at the small graphic design company that she was filing for divorce, they had started to distance themselves from her, asking her how could she do that when Andy was fighting for his country, and calling her a spoiled brat for thinking only of herself and not what Andy was going through. It was cruel and inhuman what she was doing, they said. When she ran crying to Mitchell Jones to tell him, he'd just looked at her and lowered his eyes. It was clear he was of the same opinion as her employer and her coworkers, but lawyer that he was, he wasn't going to say anything. And besides, she was his client, and it was not his place to judge. She'd come to him seeking help, and he was providing said help. End of his story. That very night, she had a dozen résumés updated and ready to mail. So far, she had only one scheduled interview on the horizon.

Bella poured herself a glass of wine. No more running to the computer the moment she was inside. Those days were long gone. She kicked off her shoes, made her way to the sofa, and flopped down. She turned on the six o'clock news and settled down to find out what had gone on in the world while she labored all day at work.

An update on the road repairs from the hellacious rain of three weeks ago. Two United States soldiers wounded in Syria. Two senators and one congressman suddenly on the hot seat for fooling around with young pages and hotly denying the allegations while their colleagues were urging them to step down. In the next ninety days, a chain of Midwestern supermarkets would be shutting down after ninety-nine years of serving their communities.

Bella turned off the television and curled her legs up and under her as she stared off into space, her thoughts scattered. She realized she was crying when her vision started to blur. How had it come to this? How? Last week, she had gone way out of her way to contact one of the military wives of one of Andy's best friends. In the course of the conversation, she'd asked how she dealt with not hearing from her husband on a regular basis.

Evelyn Morris looked at her like she'd sprouted a second head and asked what she was talking about because James e-mailed at least three times a week. She even said they had FaceTimed at least once every two weeks. Bella explained, and the woman had looked at her with such pity that Bella thought she was going to get sick. Then she blurted out that she'd just filed for divorce the previous week.

Evelyn gave her another pitiful look and simply walked away, but she did call over her shoulder, "You're not someone I want to admit I know."

Bella hadn't cried then. She was too numb to cry. But now the tears came.

Chapter 2

Bella stood rooted to the concrete walkway as she stared at the building in front of her. It was a beautiful day in the District, crisp and unseasonably cool for this time of year. Birds perched overhead on an electrical wire chirped to one another, probably commenting on the beautiful weather. She was aware of people jostling her, muttering obscenities and other unflattering terms as they surged around her. They wanted her to move, that much was clear. She wanted to move, too, but she felt glued to the walkway. She knew she should apologize to the steady stream of people behind her, but she couldn't get her tongue to work any better than she could get her feet to move. She was on her lunch hour, as were the people around her, so it stood to reason they were all in a hurry, and still she couldn't make her feet move. *What is wrong with me?*

The reality was, Bella knew what was wrong with her, so there was no use in pretending. She was standing in front of the building that housed Mitchell Jones's office to finalize the divorce she had started almost a month ago. Mitchell had called her yesterday and told her to stop stalling or he was going to drop her as a client, and she would have to find another attorney to work with her in obtaining a divorce.

Mitchell had been more than nice to her. He said it was okay to change her mind about wanting a divorce. People did it all the time, he'd said. He'd gone on to say he had too many cases that needed his attention and he couldn't keep babysitting her, and he said that if she canceled one more appointment, he would be forced to cease to represent her.

With those threats hanging over her, not to mention the money she'd already paid out to him, she was here, now, at this red brick building with ivy crawling up the walls and fresh paint on the window frames. She could even smell the paint and see dabs of it on the shiny ivy leaves. The door she had to walk through was a beautiful, dark, rich mahogany surrounded by a lot of shiny brass on the ornate door handle, the brass plate, and, of course, the lanterns on each side of the magnificent door. She squinted harder and realized it wasn't brass at all but copper, polished to a high sheen, so glossy she could see her eyelashes.

"Move it, lady, or I'll lift you up and move you myself. I have business inside, and time is money. What's it gonna be?" a deep rough voice behind her demanded.

"Yeah, move already, will you?" a young woman who was barefoot and wearing ragged cutoff jeans called out. "I'm already ten minutes late. C'mon already!"

Bella finally moved, or maybe she was pushed, she didn't really know, and at that moment didn't care as she went with the flow. She was finally inside, with people walking all around her. All she needed to do was turn right and walk down the long hallway to suite 111. Suite 111 belonged to Mitchell Jones, and she was here to sign her divorce papers. Period. End of story. She wondered how many pages it took to say she was filing for a divorce from Major Andrew Nolan because he refused to e-mail or Skype her. And then she wondered if she would cry when she signed her name to the legal document. Even if she did cry, the world wouldn't end if she cried one more time, she told herself. Once she signed her name, she could move on and forget Major Andy Nolan and his Ram 2500 truck. She would be Bella Ames again, the name she had been born with.

Finally standing at Mitchell Jones's door, all

Bella had to do was turn the knob and walk into the small waiting room. It was tastefully decorated with comfortable furniture, and healthy, glossy ficus trees stood in the corners to fill up the dim corners where there were no lamps. Luscious green plants on the little tables that were scattered among the chairs, along with a varied assortment of magazines for men and women, and, of course, the daily paper pretty much took care of the furnishings. Despite all the stuff, the room did not appear to be crowded. Someone, probably Cheryl, the receptionist, had a green thumb, she thought. All in all, a pleasant enough place to relieve any anxiety one might feel while waiting for the help the lawyer would hopefully provide. Today, though, there was no delay for Bella. No more stalling. The waiting room was empty, and Cheryl told her she should go right on back to Mr. Jones's office since he was waiting for her. Seeing the bright unshed tears in Bella's eyes, Cheryl offered up a weak smile. Divorces, as she knew from experience, were painful.

Fifteen minutes later, Bella was walking to her car, the checked tears finally rolling down her cheeks. She looked at her watch. She had enough time to grab a sandwich and a drink of some kind before reporting back to work. Her boss was a great boss and wouldn't say boo if she was an hour late, but she tried never to abuse his generosity. With that thought in mind, Bella steered her car into the parking lot of the Burger Palace, also known as Will's Shack, which made burgers to order for its customers. Will, the owner, was working the drive-through today. Short of help again, she surmised. She tucked away the thought in case she had to get a part-time job to pay off Mitchell Jones. Unlike Andy, who didn't care how many bills he racked up, she hated owing money. When Will spotted her, he grinned and waved.

"The same, or are you feeling dangerous today?" he joked. The same meant a burger with crisp bacon, lots and lots of crisp bacon she paid extra for, a slice of tomato, and a slice of purple onion with a sour pickle on top and Virginia Gray's potatoes on the side. Virginia was Will's father's sister. Dangerous meant a cup of coffee, heavy on the sugar and cream, along with a raisin-filled cookie for dessert.

"The same, Will."

"You okay, Bella? You look sad." The two were on a first-name basis because Bella had been Will's very first customer when he had opened his little food haven a couple of years ago.

"Headache," she muttered. The moment the words were out of her mouth, Bella realized it was true, she did have a headache. She realized something else, too—she wasn't hungry. Why she had pulled into Will's Shack was something she'd have to figure out later. She paid for her food, placed the bag on the passenger seat, and drove home to her new mini apartment. The minute she parked the car in her allotted space, she called her boss. She fibbed and said she had a migraine and was going home. Nice man that he was, her boss told her to take two Advil and a nap, and, if she didn't feel any better tomorrow, to stay home, and not to worry, he'd pay her for her time off.

Inside the small apartment, Bella kicked off her shoes and tossed her purse and messenger bag on the recliner. She padded out to the minuscule kitchenette and opened the food bag. The smell of the onion and the hamburger made her gag. She quickly tossed it all into the sink and let the garbage disposal do its magic.

Coffee. That's all she needed. Maybe a cookie to dunk in the coffee. Then again, maybe not. She turned on the little twelve-inch TV that sat on the counter next to the toaster. She turned it to the channel she used to watch years ago, when she was hooked on soap operas. She watched it for ten minutes and felt as if, even though she hadn't watched the soap for over two years, she was caught up. And it had taken only ten minutes.

The sound of a knock on the door almost caused Bella to jump out of her skin. She did not know anyone who lived in the neighborhood. Why would someone be knocking on her door in the middle of the afternoon? Some scammer maybe. Someone who robbed apartments in broad daylight. A bill collector. Someone who wanted payment for Andy's Ram 2500? She'd called the finance company and told them where the car was and that the key was under the back wheel cap. She'd told the woman she spoke to that her name was Delilah Brucemeister just so they wouldn't know where she was currently located. Answer the door? Don't answer the door?

Why, she asked herself, *am I hiding or pretending to hide? I didn't do anything wrong. All I did was file for divorce, something thousands of people do every day.* So who was knocking on her door? She hadn't even put her name on the mail slot yet, so who would even know that she lived here?

The knock sounded again. Louder this time. More serious-sounding. Well, of course they would continue to knock because they could hear her TV. She knew in her gut that whoever it was knocking on her door was going to keep knocking until she opened it, which just went to prove it had to be a bill collector. The previous tenant must have owed someone money for something.

Bella started toward the tiny foyer, not believing that hypothesis for a minute. Well, the only way to discover if she was right or wrong was to open the damn door.

Which she did.

"Oh my God! No! No! Go away! Don't ever come back here! Nonononono!" Bella shrieked at the top of her lungs as she reached for the doorframe to hold her upright. Her hands slipped. She felt herself falling, then strong arms, two sets of strong arms, were carrying her into her tiny as-yet-unpacked new apartment and setting her down in a chair.

Bella stared at the two military officers kneeling at her feet. Both had their hands on her arms to steady her. How young they were, she thought. Captains in rank, both of them. Spit and polish all the way. She could smell ivory soap and something vaguely menthol. She wished someone would say something. Maybe they were waiting for her to say something. Like what, she wondered crazily. Maybe something like, hey, I know why you're here, my husband was killed in the line of duty. And then I say, well, guess what. I just signed divorce papers today, so why should I care what you have to say.

She was dreaming and hoped to wake up any minute. *This is not happening. It's just too surreal,* Bella told herself, *like something out of a really bad grade B movie.*

Things like this happened to other people

or in movies. Not to people like her. She wondered if they had arrived in a brown car. In the movies, the chaplains always arrived in a brown car. Two chaplains. Always two. She wondered why that was.

The taller of the two officers, the one on the left, said, "Ma'am, I'm Captain Jeffrey Josell, and this is Captain Scott Kimball. Is there anyone you want us to call? We can take you to a family member or a friend if you like. You shouldn't be alone right now."

"I've been alone since the day I got married," Bella screeched at the top of her lungs. Tears streamed down her cheeks. Good Lord, did she just say that? Maybe she should tell them about the divorce papers she had just signed. Would they care? Who would they tell? No, no, she had it all wrong, this wasn't a bad dream, this was a frigging nightmare. "You can leave now, Officers. I'll be fine." Bella knew she had said the words out loud, but she didn't recognize her own voice.

"Ma'am, we have orders. We have to obey them. We have people who will come and stay with you. You can't be alone right now. Do you understand?"

"I do understand. I want you to leave. Please, it's important for me to be alone right now. I'm not going to do anything silly or stupid, but I am going to show you something to prove my point." Bella wobbled her way over to the recliner, opened her purse, and pulled out the blue folder Mitchell Jones had given her. She wondered why divorce sleeves containing the actual divorce papers were always blue. The final divorce paper was always blue, too.

"See this?" Bella said, waving the blue folder in the air. "I filed for divorce today. That's why I'm home in the middle of the day. I just came from the lawyer's office. So you can see, I'm sure, why I need to be alone right now, can't you?" she announced in a voice that sounded like a dozen firecrackers going off all at once.

The two young officers looked at each other. Captain Josell shook his head; Captain Kimball nodded. Captain Josell pulled out his cell phone, stepped away from Bella, and placed a call to a female officer back at headquarters to come join them. "This is a tough one," he whispered into the phone.

Captain Kimball transferred the manila envelope he'd been entrusted with, the one he was supposed to hand to the grieving widow, from one hand to the other. No one said what he was supposed to do if she refused to accept it. Somehow, he just knew that if he did hand it to her, and she did take it, it would slip right through her fingers, and he didn't want that to happen. Thus, he wasn't sure what he should do with it. Hand it to her? Would she even accept it? Place it on one of the tables? He'd never been in this exact position before. He couldn't even remember if there was a rule in the book for a situation like this. For sure, nothing like it had ever come up in his training classes. He looked over at his partner and raised his eyebrows. What now? Captain Josell just stared at him blankly. It was obvious that he didn't know what to do, either.

Bella blinked away her tears and wiped her eyes on the sleeve of her shirt. She looked around, and said, "You look uncomfortable. If you aren't going to leave, you might as well sit down. Are you supposed to talk to me? Are you going to tell me how my husband died? Or is a shrink on the way to do that for you?

"I don't know what to do here. I've heard stories, seen movies, but I never thought I would turn out to be a leading character in one of those stories," Bella said, her voice cracking with each word that came out of her mouth. "I guess I am now one of your statistics. Is there some special protocol we need to follow?" She knew that she was babbling, but she couldn't seem to stop herself.

"Actually, Mrs. Nolan, there is a protocol of sorts. We usually follow the bereaved's lead and do what they want, and go from there. Personally, ma'am, I think you should talk to the psychiatrist when she gets here. I think you'll feel more at ease with a female," Captain Kimball said.

Bella didn't know what to say, and she didn't know what to think. What did gender have to do with anything? Dead was dead. A man talking about it or a woman talking about it couldn't bring Andy back to life. Maybe what she should do was call Mitchell Jones and ask him what to do. Lawyers usually had the answer to everything, or at least they would have you believe they did, and that's how they justified billing you out the kazoo. Maybe Mitchell could undo the paperwork and recall the whole sorry mess, and she could go on with her life and pretend she didn't file for divorce the very same day she was notified of her husband's death.

She nixed that idea immediately because she realized that, papers or no papers, it was impossible to divorce someone who was already dead when the divorce papers were filed. Bella Ames Nolan was, for all eternity, the widow of Major Andrew Nolan, not the ex-wife of a man who had died serving his country.

How could this be happening? How? You file for divorce the same day you find out your husband is dead. All within the space of an hour. And all it took was a single hour. *An hour,* her mind screamed silently. *Good God, how am I supposed to live with this? This is wrong. I need to sit down somewhere in a dark corner and howl my head off,* Bella thought, as she knuckled her eyes to keep more tears from spilling down her cheeks. She needed to say something. Ask questions? Why? You couldn't fix dead just like you couldn't fix stupid.

Bella knew she had to do something, like right now, or these men were going to be in her apartment like mother hens forever.

"Did you . . . has anyone notified Andy's sister? I know almost nothing about her, just that Andy told me he had a sister." Something niggled at her concerning the sister, but she couldn't put her finger on it. "I think they were estranged but that they had patched up their . . . whatever it was that caused a problem, and I didn't want to . . . you know, invade his . . . personal life, I guess, is how I should put it. We were so into ourselves, there was no room for anyone or anything else those last few days. We only had two days to . . . to spend loving each other.

"I'm not even sure I know her name. Susan, Samantha, maybe Sara. I'm just not sure. Andy never talked about her to me. I think the estrangement had something to do with his sister's spending his inheritance plus her own when their parents died, but that might be all wrong. I'm sorry, I just don't know very much about her."

Whatever it was, it was right there on the tip of her tongue, but it wasn't coming. *Damn it, what is it?* "Then, like I said, they patched up their differences. She was all he had in the way of family as far as I know. I guess that doesn't help much, does it?"

"You had part of it right. Major Nolan's sister's name is Sara Nolan Conover. She indicated to us that she and Mr. Conover are divorced. She now goes by the name Sara Nolan. From what we can tell, she moves around quite a bit. She is listed as the beneficiary on Major Nolan's insurance and also as next of kin. Her name is . . . was on Major Nolan's bank account. For some reason, he never removed her name from the account. His pay went into that account. The account was drained and closed by Ms. Nolan once everything was turned over to her as next of kin. Major Nolan was a little lax on updating his personal information. There was nothing in his personnel file about his . . . your marriage," Captain Josell said.

"It was only a month ago that we found out that Major Nolan was married. I'm sorry, ma'am. When we found out about you, we went back and took another look at the sister but were unable to locate her. She had cleared the bank account, moved, and is no longer on our radar. I'm sorry, Mrs. Nolan."

Bella reacted to the news like she'd been slapped in the face. And then kicked in the gut for good measure. Andy hadn't thought it important enough to change his insurance or to list her as next of kin, to put her name on his bank account, to provide for her. How could he not tell the military he had gotten married? How? That was the first thing she'd done at work when they returned from their two-day honeymoon. She'd told everyone, even the janitor, as she flashed her plain gold wedding band. She'd added Andy's name to her savings and checking accounts. She'd listed him as her next of kin and made him the sole beneficiary on her insurance. She couldn't wait to go to HR and do everything she needed to do.

And now these military people were telling her that he had not bothered to do any of the things expected of a military man who had just gotten married. And even as he had failed to provide for her, he had thought early on that it was important to nag her until she agreed to harvest her eggs and store them in a fertility clinic in case he didn't make it back. Even back then, when she'd done what he asked, she'd thought there was something ominous about the whole thing. But she had not been able to pinpoint any one thing that made her think such a thing. She chalked it up to something she did not want to think about, much less do, but she did it anyway because her husband had asked her to do it. How had all that gotten by her? Was she that much of an idiot? The obvious answer was yes—but no, not really, she was just head over heels in love with her handsome husband, Major Andrew Nolan, who looked like a movie star in his dress uniform.

It always came down to money in the end. Or the lack thereof.

Always.

The small group in the tiny living room looked at one another. Both officers jumped to their feet and ran to the front door when they heard the doorbell ring.

Bella swiped at the tears on her cheeks as she watched the hushed conference taking place at the doorway with two women in military dress. The shrink and another woman. Another shrink? She waited as both officers returned to where she was sitting, offered up their condolences again, then shook her hand. When the door closed behind them, it sounded like thunder to Bella's ears. She looked up at the two women, tears streaming down her cheeks.

"Mrs. Nolan, I'm Colonel Laura Atkins. I am also a psychiatrist. I should have come here with Captain Josell and Captain Kimball, but I was on another call and running late. I'm sorry. I got here as soon as I could. This young woman standing next to me is Lieutenant Carol Gibson. She is . . . was your husband's nurse."

Bella stared at the two women and simply nodded. She just didn't have it in her right now to say even one word. She wished they would leave so she could go to bed and sleep around the clock, then wake up and find out this was all just a bad dream. That wasn't going to happen, and she knew it. She motioned for the two women to sit down, which they promptly did.

"Do I call you Doctor or Colonel?" Bella asked. There . . . she finally asked a question that made at least a little bit of sense. Like she really cared how she should address the woman sitting across from her. *This is all about me right now, and I simply do not give a good rat's ass what you want or expect. All I want is for you all to go and leave me alone. Damn it, just go already,* she pleaded silently.

"Whatever you're comfortable with. I imagine you have some questions."

Bella felt herself nod. No, she really didn't, but knew she had to ask something. As it was, it was bad enough, they thought she was some weirdo. She wished she had a rule book and that she had read it. "Where . . . how?" she asked in barely a whisper.

"Major Nolan was the only survivor of a roadside bomb. His whole team was killed. This happened eleven months ago. Major Nolan was paralyzed from the neck down on his right side. He had partial use of his left arm and leg at first; then he couldn't use either his arm or his leg. He deteriorated very quickly. In the beginning, he could talk coherently. He knew how badly he was wounded. He could more or less feed himself finger food with his one good arm; then his voice gave out, he couldn't swallow, and he had to be fed through a tube. He was flown to Walter Reed Army Medical Center here in the area within days of being injured," Colonel Atkins said, then let loose with a heavy sigh as she heard Bella shriek.

Bella jumped to her feet like she was spring loaded. "Are you telling me my husband has been at Walter Reed, practically within walking distance from me, and no one in the goddamn army thought I had a right to know! Is that what you are sitting there telling me? Do you have any idea, any idea at all what I went through not hearing from my husband in all that time? *Well, do you?*"

No one responded verbally; however, they all bobbed their heads up and down.

"Damn it, say something," she shrieked again, the sound vibrating off the walls.

"It . . . it's complicated, Mrs. Nolan. We . . . the army . . . didn't know about you. As we said earlier, Major Nolan did not update his status after you got married. As far as his sister, his relationship, his bank account where his pay went, that was his personal business, we had no control over his affairs. Just so you know, Major Nolan's sister had his power of attorney. All of that information is in the packet Captain Kimball gave you. Right after his leave, when I assume you were married, Major Nolan deployed. You can't blame the entire United States Army for his failure to change what needed to be changed," Colonel Atkins said gently. "I understand your being upset, but—"

"When, exactly, did my husband die? You say he was injured eleven months ago. The officers said that his sister claimed his benefits, but when they found out about me, they tried to find her but couldn't since she had apparently moved. So how long ago did he actually die? A few weeks? A few months?" Bella asked through clenched teeth.

Colonel Atkins took another deep breath. "Eight months ago."

"Eight months! Is that what you said? Eight months?" Bella started to wail and scream at the top of her lungs. The nurse, Lieutenant Gibson, rushed to put her arms around her. Bella shook her off but allowed the lieutenant to lead her to the sofa and sit down with her.

"Andy, and he asked me to call him Andy since I was his full-time nurse, talked about you all the time in the beginning, when he had the strength. He didn't want you to know how badly he was injured. He hoped, and we in the medical field encouraged the hope, that something could be done for him. He said you were too young to be burdened with what he called his condition. He never called you by name until the very end. He would just refer to you as the love of his life. Or his soul mate. One time, he said that the minute he laid eyes on you, he knew you were his destiny. He loved you, Mrs. Nolan, heart and soul."

Bella sniffed. "Not enough to trust me. I would have been at that hospital twenty-four/ seven, doing whatever I could. I filed for divorce today because I could not understand how and why he couldn't get word to me when the other wives had FaceTime and shared messages. I thought all kinds of crazy things during all those months. I didn't know. How could I not have known, felt something? How? Now I have to live with that.

"I had mean, evil thoughts during those months. There were days when I hated Andy for not getting in touch. The truck he loved so much has not been repaired. I can't pay for it. I don't have any money except my salary. And now you're telling me I won't even get his insurance.

"How did you find me? For eleven months you couldn't find me, when I was living in the same place I had been when we got married, then suddenly, after I move, you show up. How goddamn convenient. This smells like a cover-up of some kind to me. Well?" she screamed again, only this time it sounded more like a frog croaking. Clearly, she was losing her voice.

"It wasn't easy, I can tell you that. Like I said, your husband's entire team was killed. All we had to go on was his military personnel file, an absentee sister we couldn't find at first, and what little Major Nolan shared with Lieutenant Gibson. The last week, when Major Nolan's condition deteriorated, he asked me to write you a letter or, if possible, to go and see you. I said I would. But before he could tell me where you lived, he died. All he told me was that your name was Bella. He did not even tell me that you were his wife. It was not until one of his buddies told us that he had gotten married on his last leave that we knew a wife even existed. Once we knew, we went back through his file and discovered the letter I had written, the one that was addressed to Bella, but we could find no one named Bella Nolan until you moved and changed your telephone listing."

"My God. I changed everything else, but the one thing I did not do was notify the telephone company of the name change, never dreaming that it could make a difference," Bella said, the anguish clearly heard in her tone of voice.

"All those months he . . . I didn't have a clue . . . he really was trying to protect you and didn't want you worrying about him. I guess it never occurred to him that not hearing from him was worse. Sometimes, men are not . . . not as . . . intuitive as women. Sad to say. The letter . . . the letter is inside the packet.

"If it is any consolation to you, Mrs. Nolan, I made sure I visited your husband twice a day when possible. I was with Major Nolan when he passed. I was holding his hand. I went to his funeral. I prayed for him. I just want you to know that. He didn't die alone. If I had known how to find you, I would have defied him and broken my promise to him and fetched you to his side."

Bella nodded, tears streaming down her cheeks. "I believe you," she whispered. "Is Andy . . . is he buried in Arlington National Cemetery?"

"Yes. Everything is in the packet, all the information you need. Major Nolan's body arrived here with no belongings, so there is nothing to turn over to you. I'm sorry."

Bella nodded again. "Thank you. I really would like to be alone now if you don't mind. And before you can ask, no, I am not okay. I won't be okay for a long time to come, but I do know how to cope, and if I feel I need a shrink or a therapist, I will get one. Right now, I think I've earned the right to wallow for a while. You all don't need to see me bang my head on the wall or hear me cussing up a storm. So, please, just go now and leave me to myself. I have your cards, and I will call you if I feel the need. I am being as truthful as I can be right now."

Bella literally jumped to her feet, ran to the door, and threw it open. Her guests had no other choice but to get up and leave. There were no hugs, no handshakes. "Just go," Bella said.

The sound of the dead bolt shooting home once the door closed was the loudest sound Bella had ever heard in her entire life.

Chapter 3

Joseph Espinosa knew that if he walked any more slowly, he would come to a full stop in the middle of the sidewalk, which would lead to a great deal of verbal abuse. Realizing what he was doing, he moved to the right so that he was almost up against a storefront featuring men's athletic gear. He stared at it without really seeing it. He turned when a bunch of giggling girls bumped into him. They apologized and started walking again.

Espinosa blinked, looked at his watch. He grimaced. He had ten minutes to get to Bertie's Tea Room, where he was to meet Alexis for lunch.

Espinosa, as everyone other than Alexis and

Annie called him, the two of them always calling him Joseph, hated Bertie's Tea Room. In his male-chauvinist opinion, it was nothing more than a girly-girly hangout. If it weren't for Alexis, whom he loved as much as he hated Bertie's, he wouldn't be found dead inside the damned hoity-toity place. The main course consisted of tiny little lettuce sandwiches no bigger than a quarter followed by some foul-tasting hummus on the side. A green organic drink that smelled like diesel oil, served over crushed ice in a small glass, and a cookie that looked like it was carved out of the middle of a haystack, were the daily fare at Bertie's. Women, Alexis included, flocked to the establishment in droves. On none of the four occasions that Alexis had managed to drag him to Bertie's, with him fighting her every step of the way, had he seen a single person of the male persuasion inside. But he loved her, so he wanted to keep her happy, and if going to Bertie's with her made her happy, then so be it.

"Fair is fair," he mumbled to himself as he trudged along. On rare occasions, Alexis joined him at LongHorn Steakhouse, where she ate a baked potato and a four-piece cucumber salad. God forbid a piece of meat should get past her pearly whites. Alexis was a true vegan.

Espinosa saw a flurry of movement ahead and realized it was Alexis coming from the other direction. They met up, hugged, pecked each other on the cheek, and then entered the little tearoom. "I know how much you hate this place, Joseph, so I appreciate you agreeing to lunch here. I've got to be quick today. Nikki called a meeting about a new case, so I need to be on time. This was the closest place that would allow me to get back in time for the meeting. Next time, LongHorn, and lunch will be on me. Okay, honey?"

Honey. Espinosa loved it when Alexis called him honey. He nodded and offered up a sappy grin as he waited for her to order for him. While he waited, he looked around. The regular lunch crowd had come and gone from the looks of things. Two white-haired ladies were whispering to each other on the other side of the tiny room. Four empty tables had not been bussed yet. Three young women in jogging attire paid their check and left, the bell over the door tinkling merrily. He had always liked the sound of that bell.

With the lunch hour basically over, the rule was that a latecomer could sit anywhere. Espinosa chose a table to his liking, held out Alexis's chair, then sat down and leered at his dearly beloved. Alexis giggled.

It was a cozy, comfortable place to take a noontime break with a light lunch that guaranteed to get the diner back to work full of spit and vinegar. The decor was pleasant. Crisp, dotted Swiss curtains covered the two bay windows. Hand-painted nature scenes of the four seasons decorated the four walls. He vaguely recalled Alexis telling him the artwork on the walls was compliments of Bertie's patrons.

Alexis picked up a menu, not that she needed it, and said, "How's everything, Joseph? What's hot in the newsroom? By the way, how's Maggie doing? I haven't heard from her in a few weeks, and that's not like Maggie. She's always front and center." Alexis shifted her gaze as she spoke. "She looks so sad. I wonder what's wrong?"

"Maggie is out on some fluff piece Ted palmed off on her. Who is sad?" Joe asked as he eyeballed the ugly-looking green drink he knew he was going to have to consume before he could leave this eatery.

"The young girl directly ahead of us. Don't stare. I think she's going to cry. Okay, you can look now. Do you think she's going to cry?"

Espinosa looked ahead of him to see a young woman, probably in her mid-twenties, sitting alone at a bar table for two. Alexis was right, the young woman did look like she was going to cry any minute. He watched as she knuckled her eyes, then dabbed at them with her napkin. He nodded to show he agreed with Alexis's take on the situation.

"She hasn't touched her food, either. I noticed she was just playing with it, stirring it, moving it from one place to another," Alexis hissed.

"She probably had a fight with her boyfriend. He's probably off somewhere doing the same thing she's doing. In other words, regretting the fight they had. That's my best guess. Oh, goody, our food is here," Espinosa said, grimacing as he stuffed six of the tiny sandwiches in his mouth at the same time. They tasted awful. Done!

Alexis chose to ignore Espinosa's sarcasm and nibbled one of the tiny sandwiches, never taking her eyes off the young woman sitting directly ahead of her. "No, Joseph, it's something serious. I can tell."

"Oh, come on, Alexis, how can you tell? You never saw her before, so how is that possible?"

Alexis sniffed and sipped at the green drink. "Because I'm a girl. She's a girl. That's how."

Joseph Espinosa's mother didn't raise any fools. He knew when to keep quiet. He dipped his fork into the hummus and somehow managed to swallow it. He knew exactly what Alexis was going to do. She was going to get up and walk over to the young woman's table and stick her lawyer nose into her business. By the time Espinosa processed the thought, Alexis was across the room, seated next to the young woman, and was clasping the girl's hands in her own. That's when he saw the waterfall of tears that had been held in check. That told him all he needed to know. Alexis now had a mission, and it did not include him. At least for the moment it did not include him.

Espinosa motioned to a little blue-haired

lady to box up Alexis's food and take away his dishes.

When she returned, he paid the check, left the tip, and gathered up the take-out bag. He got up, dropped the bag next to Alexis, and whispered, "Call me." She nodded.

Outside, Espinosa looked right, then left. Decisions, decisions. Big Mac or a Whopper? Large fries. Banana milk shake. Yeah, yeah, that was more like it.

While he ate and drank, Espinosa let his mind roam back to the encounter in the tea-room. He wondered what was making the young woman cry to the point that Alexis felt the need to interfere. Maybe Alexis would tell him or maybe she wouldn't. Women were funny that way, as he'd found out, much to his chagrin. Experts at keeping secrets. Even Jack Emery, who professed to know everything about women, agreed with that little ditty.

While his thoughts whirled and twirled, Espinosa cleaned up his mess, left the fast-food joint, and made his way back to the *Post*, itching all the way. When he itched like this, he could feel trouble coming around the corner.

Chapter 4

Six months later

Bella Nolan looked around her tiny apartment and the minuscule paths she'd created among her packed belongings, which consisted of trash bags and boxes and piles of stuff that she was undecided about and were stacked and waiting for a box or bag or the trash heap.

She was finally, finally, going to do something constructive now that the six months of mourning she had allowed herself were over. She rather thought now that she'd been overgenerous in allowing six whole months to wallow and wail, along with hosting a pity party every day of the week. She had quit her job, packed up the apartment, and was ready to move to North Carolina, where she had a distant cousin who was around her age.

Feeling desperate, she had reached out to her for help, and her cousin had agreed to lend her a hand. Adeline Beaumont said she would be delighted to help Bella out and invited Bella to stay with her while she sought out an apartment and a new job.

Addie, as she liked everyone to call her, said she could help with that, too. She knew of a spacious two-bedroom apartment that was newly renovated, and the rent was only $450 a month. She went on to say that until Bella found exactly what she was looking for in a job, she could hire on at the company she worked for as an assistant. She'd added that Bella had gotten in touch in the nick of time because her company was sending her abroad to open and oversee a satellite office for a year. She'd just sublet her own apartment or she would have let Bella rent it.

Done and done! The only downside (if there was a downside) was that she would be starting over somewhere not knowing a single person. For the most part, she thought that might be a good thing because she would then be open to anything new and challenging.

A new life. A new beginning. Starting over. Slow and easy. One day at a time.

Bella eyed the packing boxes, bags, and the piles of junk she'd accumulated over time. Most of the boxes belonged to her, but three of the huge cartons were Andy's, which he had stored in a closet in her old apartment. To this day, she had not looked at the contents. She'd just moved the boxes from one place to the other. She knew she needed to make a decision regarding the boxes, but it did not have to be right this minute. Maybe if she could find out where the sister lived, she could send them on to her. Damn, now she was thinking about her again. She never did figure out what it was that bothered her about Andy and his sister. By now, you'd think that it would have come to her. She told herself that if she would stop thinking about it, practically obsessing over it, it would eventually come to her.

What she needed to do and do right this minute was to make an appointment at the fertility clinic where she had stored her eggs. If she was moving to North Carolina, never to return to this unhappy city, she needed to transfer the eggs to a clinic close to where she was going to live. Leave nothing behind was her motto so she would never have to come back to Washington. Never, ever!

But she had doubts. Should she just leave the eggs? Stop paying the monthly fee to store them. Maybe she needed to rethink this whole thing. She wished now, the way she'd wished a hundred other times, that she'd never allowed Andy to talk her into harvesting her eggs.

She could, if she wanted to, just walk away and pretend that it had never happened. If she didn't leave a forwarding address, the clinic people couldn't track her down. Had she given them her social security number? She couldn't remember. If she had, they could track her that way. Damn it, why did everything have to be so complicated?

Bella leaned back on the sofa and closed her eyes. She needed to think. But her only thoughts were about Andy's sister. Why? "Because I hate her, that's why!" Bella screeched to the empty room. *Damn! Damn! What was it I couldn't remember about Sara Nolan?*

Bella jumped up. "That's it! That's it! I am so done with this mess, and I am never going to think about it again. Never!" To drive home her point, she scrolled down on her phone until she found the number of the clinic and dialed the number. She was given an appointment for the following day at noon with a one-hour window of time.

Bella wondered why she didn't feel something—angst, relief, anything—now that she'd done something concrete and made a decision she was going to follow through on.

Now that the last thread binding her to this place was set to be unknotted, Bella changed the channel on the television and watched the soap opera she swore she was never going to watch again. It was either that or some silly game show. Other than that, her only other choice was one of the twenty-four-hour news shows, and all they did was talk about Afghanistan and Syria and all things war and more war. She knew in her gut that if she lived to be a hundred, they would still be fighting over there. Andy had said that at least once a day and believed it implicitly. She was done with that, too. Hopefully forever.

Bella blinked when a thought raced through her weary brain. Be careful what you wish for, because you just might get it. "Yeah, right," she muttered to herself, as she forced herself to concentrate on the drama playing out in front of her on the television screen.

At twenty minutes to twelve, anxious and antsy, Bella was walking to the boulevard, where she was more likely to be able to hail a cab to take her to the fertility clinic, which was thirty or so blocks from her apartment. It was clear and cold, with a blustery wind that bit right through her jacket. She shoved her hands in her pockets and walked with her head down so the stinging wind wouldn't make her eyes water. Three more blocks to go. Maybe she'd stop at the Taco Bell that was directly across the street from the clinic and have some lunch. She'd take a seat near the window so she could watch who went in and out of the clinic, which would be directly in her line of vision if she was lucky enough to get a window seat. She did have an hour window, so it was doable if that is how she wanted to play it. Then she remembered how much she detested that particular Taco Bell and decided just to go right into the clinic when the cab dropped her off. She finally reached the boulevard and hailed a passing cab. What would normally be a ten-minute ride turned out to take twenty minutes given the heavier-than-usual midday traffic. She wondered what was going on to account for such traffic.

The Samaritan Clinic looked just like all the office buildings on Michigan Avenue. There was nothing about it that was special in any way. A lot of plate glass, shiny gray bricks with charcoal mortar between the bricks, no fancy doors, just your regular turnstile entrance. No doorman, but there was a courtesy desk in the lobby, and one had to check in before heading for the bank of elevators.

The building had twenty-one floors. The clinic was located on the top five floors. A very, very busy place. For some reason, she had no recollection of any of this. Probably, she had blocked it out because she had hated what she was doing. And now, here she was, still hating being at the clinic.

She did stop to wonder if she would come back to the District to visit Andy's grave at Arlington Cemetery. Veterans Day, Memorial Day, laying the grave blanket at Christmas. Lordy, lordy, that was three times a year. She could never do that, torture herself like that. Obviously, she needed to do some serious thinking. In years to come, visiting might be easier, but right now she was almost certain that it would be too painful to bear. Things were too raw. Not to mention the awful guilt that still wracked her whole being.

Six sessions with a therapist told her it wasn't going to get any better, and the only person who could help her was herself, so she'd buckled down and filled every waking hour of the day with some activity. That way, at night she fell into bed, exhausted, so she could wake up the following day and do it all over again.

Transferring her eggs from the Samaritan Fertility Clinic to the clinic in Davidson, where Addie lived, was the last thing she needed to arrange before heading out. Her game plan was to do some research and maybe . . . maybe think about selling one or two of the eggs to get herself a little nest egg of money so she could start off her new life free of debt and with a purpose in life. Selling off two would leave her ten eggs. Perhaps down the road, when she was really ready to take on her new life, she would consider having Andy's baby.

Then again, maybe not. Surely, somewhere in the years to come she'd meet some nice guy who would love her and want her to bear his children. That someone might not want some other man's child, she told herself.

Tears puddled in her eyes. *Don't go there, Bella,* she warned herself. "Okay, I won't go there," she muttered over and over until she almost believed it. She really needed to think about this some more.

Having made the decision that she was not prepared to deal with anything having to do with the fertility clinic, she turned around and walked back out through the turnstile. She was lucky enough to find a cab dropping someone off at the clinic and directed the driver to take her back to her apartment. She'd come back tomorrow. This, she told herself, was just a practice run to see if she was mentally ready to sever this particular tie. And, as she had just discovered, she was not. Not today, at least. With any luck, tomorrow would work.

Back in the apartment, Bella made herself a pot of coffee, called to cancel her appointment, and made a new one for the following day. She needed to finish what she'd started earlier. Once and for all. No more waffling. While the coffee dripped, she picked up the roll of packing tape and ripped off a long piece to wrap around a box that was clearly labeled, *Andy's Stuff.* There was tape on the box already, but it was turning yellow and peeling away from the opening. She wondered if the day would ever come when she would want to look inside the box to see what Andy considered worth saving. Probably not, she told herself. Maybe when she had some spare time she would institute a search for Andy's sister and send his things to her. Then again, maybe not, since she had a hate on for Andy's faceless sister.

Bella stared off into space, her thoughts everywhere as she let them take her back in time to the day Andy told her he was going to freeze his sperm and asked her to freeze her eggs. He'd said military life, especially during wartime, was unpredictable, and he knew guys who came back all shot up and no longer able to make babies. He didn't want that to happen, but if it did, he wanted to know Bella could still have a baby, carry it to term, and continue the Nolan bloodline. He said the same was true of her. She could get sick, hit by a car, all manner of horrible things could happen to her that would prevent her from having a baby.

She'd actually believed him because he was so intense. The whole thing sounded positively ghoulish to her, but Andy was so serious, so intent, and so worried something would happen that she said yes. It wasn't that she regretted it; she didn't, not really. Because his points had some merit. What she resented was the monthly payments she'd had to pay for storage. She figured it would get better financially once Andy's military pay caught up with her, but that had never happened. And when those military officers showed up at her then-new apartment, she learned why.

Time to go to bed. Tomorrow was another day. How many times had she said that of late? *Tomorrow is another day.* "I hate that phrase," she mumbled to herself. Her appointment at the clinic was at ten thirty, and she wanted to be rested and show up on time. But most of all, she wanted a clear head and her eyes on the future.

Bella pushed her way through the turnstile, marched over to the courtesy desk, and announced her name and the time of her appointment. The receptionist used her index finger, with a four-inch sparkly fingernail that matched the sparkles in her eyebrows, to trace the day's appointments. It took her a few seconds to locate Bella's information.

"Nineteenth floor. You will be seeing Dr. Candice Petre, who is in charge of that floor. Take the elevator on the left, it's nonstop."

Bella was off like a rocket. She wanted to get this over and done with.

She stepped out of the elevator to a pleasant

waiting area, where a tall, extremely thin woman, dressed fashionably, with an elaborate hairdo, held out her hand to Bella. It felt warm and dry. Her voice was cheerful. "I'm Dr. Candice Petre. Tell me what can I do for you on this beautiful October day, Ms. Nolan."

"I want to make arrangements to transfer my . . . my eggs to another location. My husband . . . my husband passed away, and I am relocating. Tell me what I have to do on this end, or is it the new clinic that will work with you? I'm sorry to say I don't know how this works."

"Perfectly understandable, and I'm sorry for your loss, Ms. Nolan. Let me just bring your records up to date. Were you single or married when you contracted with us?"

"Single. My file should be under Bella Ames. I never came back to change my maiden name to my married name."

"Most people do that right away," Dr. Petre said. She sounded annoyed.

"I'm not most people. I'm me, and I didn't do it, and what difference does it make in the end? None, that's how much," Bella said, answering her own question. Almost done. Almost.

Candice Petre looked over the rim of her glasses at Bella, and said, "But your name is Bella, correct?"

"Yes. And my husband's name was Andrew. Why? Is something wrong?"

"It says you transferred your . . . property eight months ago. It says you came here with a technician and signed off on your eggs."

Quicker than lightning, Bella bounced up and out of her chair. "What are you talking about? I did no such thing! I haven't been in this clinic since I had the last procedure done. That's at least three years ago. I know for certain my husband wasn't here, either. Did you lose my . . . Well, did you? My God, you did, didn't you? I can see it in your expression. I don't believe this," Bella shrieked at the top of her lungs.

Flustered, Dr. Petre pressed a button and, within seconds, a man and a woman in white lab coats appeared. Petre pointed to the computer screen as Bella continued screeching about fraud and calling the police. She could barely hear the introduction Petre was making. The woman in the white lab coat was Dr. Betty Donaldson, and the man was Dr. Martin Peabody.

Dr. Donaldson whistled sharply. Bella blinked and stopped shrieking to hear the doctor say, "You need to be quiet so we can make sense of this. Please. I understand you are upset. We will straighten this out. Now, Dr. Petre, tell me what happened here."

"What happened here," Dr. Candice Petre said in a voice that could have chilled milk, "is that this . . . person standing right here in front of the three of us came here this morning to make arrangements to transfer her . . . her property. The problem is that it already was transferred eight months ago. It's all right here. Here is a copy of the release she signed and a copy of her current driver's license. When you first came here, your driver's license said Bella Ames. Along the way you got married and changed your driver's license to Bella Nolan. This is a copy of the Bella Nolan license. Everything was time stamped, as you can see. We do not make mistakes here, Ms. Nolan. So, Ms. Nolan, how do you explain this? Is this your current driver's license or not?"

Bella stared down at a very unflattering DMV photo of her face on the license. She licked at her lips and managed to say, "Yes, that is my license and my picture, but I did not, I repeat, I did not transfer my property from this clinic. I didn't even know my husband had died at that time. I was in no frame of mind to . . . to do something like that. This is the first time I've been here since I had the procedure done years ago. Do you have cameras? Of course you do. I remember them when I was here the first time. Andy and I even discussed it. Andy is . . . was my husband. I want to see your camera surveillance footage," Bella bellowed.

Dr. Peabody, a fussy little man with a bald

head and wire-rim glasses, finally spoke up. "That will take a little bit of doing, but of course we will do it. We will accommodate you in any way we can. Dr. Petre is right, however. We do not make mistakes here at Samaritan. We follow all procedures that are in place to avoid exactly this kind of situation. Our records show that you were here. See for yourself," he said, pointing to the computer that Dr. Petre turned around so she could view her own profile. Bella felt light-headed at what she was seeing. Was she losing her mind?

Bella suddenly felt sick to her stomach. "Then do it. I will sit here and wait until you prove to me I am wrong. Don't even think about asking me to move. I will call the police; I was not kidding about that. And my lawyer. So hop to it, people," Bella snarled.

All three doctors started to talk over one another as they professed not to know anything about how such a transgression could have occurred and babbling on and on about how nothing like this had ever happened and they were so very careful and had an impeccable reputation.

"I'm waiting," Bella said, stamping her foot. "You can talk this to death later, but for now, find those surveillance tapes for me to see. I want . . . no, I demand to see who you turned my property over to because it sure as hell wasn't me."

"Of course, of course," the fussy little doctor mumbled as he wiped at the sweat on his bald head. Bella wondered how he could be sweating when it felt like it was forty-eight degrees in the room. "Come with me to a more comfortable waiting area while we . . . while we review our inventory of tapes. It's going to take a while, so we want you to be comfortable. Would you like some coffee, some donuts, anything?"

Bella watched the fussy little doctor deflate like a balloon pricked by a pin. He was nervous, though all three of them were beyond jittery. The only word in their minds right now was *lawsuit* and this woman standing in front of them as the new owner of the clinic.

Bella followed along behind the trio as they ushered her into a tranquil-looking room with earth-tone-colored furniture, just enough greenery to please the eye, and a fish tank that took up an entire wall, with all manner and color of fish swimming from one end to the other. As she stared at the wall of fish, she felt herself instantly calming down. She knew without a doubt that if she kept looking at it, she would fall asleep. She gave herself a mental jerk, turned away from the wall, and sat down on a nubby oatmeal-colored swivel chair. Maybe that's what they wanted, for her to fall asleep so they could cover their tracks about the loss of her property.

Well, that wasn't going to happen. The

minute the door closed behind the three doctors, Bella was pawing through her purse for the business card of the lawyer she'd met at the tearoom six months ago. The pretty young lawyer had said to call her if she could help in any way. If Bella remembered correctly, the pretty lawyer said she worked for an all-female law firm. *What was her name?*

Five minutes later, Bella had the coveted card in her hand. Alexis Thorn. Quinn Law Firm in Georgetown. Without giving the matter a second thought, Bella had her phone in hand and was pressing in the digits to the main number of the law firm. When someone answered, she said, "I'd like to speak to Ms. Thorn, please. This is Bella Nolan. We met some months back and she gave me her card and said if I needed her to call. I need her. It's urgent that I speak with her as soon as possible. Can I please speak with her?" A sob caught in Bella's throat as she waited for the receptionist to reply.

"Hold, please. Let me see if Ms. Thorn is free." Bella didn't realize she was holding her breath until she heard Alexis Thorn's voice. She let it loose with a wild swoosh of sound.

"Alexis Thorn."

"Ms. Thorn, this is Bella Nolan. I'm not sure if you remember me or not, but we met at the tearoom a while back, and you were kind enough to speak with me. You gave me your card and said if I ever needed help, I should call you. I need your help. I really need your help." Bella could feel herself start to choke up. Sheer willpower forced the tears back. "I'm sitting here right now at the Samaritan Fertility Clinic. I stored a dozen of my eggs here several years ago. It's a little complicated. I'm going to be moving to North Carolina, so I came here to make arrangements to find out what I have to do to transfer . . . I don't ever want to come back here . . . and they're gone. They said I came here and took them about eight months ago. But I did no such thing. That's around the time I found out that my husband had died, and at the time, I would have been hard-pressed to tell you what my name was. I did not take my property. Right now, there are three doctors who are supposedly looking at surveillance tapes to see if it really was me. They have a copy of my new driver's license with my married name and a paper with my signature on it, releasing the clinic once I took my property. Everything is time stamped. But it wasn't me, Ms. Thorn. Can you help me?"

"Of course. When can you come to the office? Do you know where we're located?"

"Not exactly, but I'll find it. Can I come by when I leave here, or would tomorrow be better? I know this is last minute."

"No, no, today is fine. I'll leave word at the desk. Would you have any objection if the managing partner of the firm sits in on our meeting? She's a wonderful lawyer and has been practicing law longer than I have. It's up to you."

"I'm fine with that. What should I do or say?"

"Try not to say anything. Get copies of everything and have them make you a copy of the surveillance video. They have to give you that. If you have any problems, refer them to me. Again, Bella, I'm sorry for your loss. I guess I'll see you when you get here. Try to stay calm. Easy for me to say, hard to do, but try."

"I will. Thank you so much for agreeing to see me. I can't believe this. How did someone get a copy of my driver's license?"

"A hundred different ways, Bella. It's done all the time. We'll make this right. I'm glad you called me. You are in good hands now. Take a deep breath and wait for them to get back to you. Make sure they give you a copy of the tape."

"I will. Thanks again."

"You bet. That's why I became a lawyer, to help people," Alexis said.

Bella leaned back and closed her eyes for a moment. All of a sudden she did feel calm, and she also felt like she was in good hands.

Bella opened her eyes when the door opened. One look at the expression on the three doctors' faces told her she wasn't going to like whatever it was they were going to tell her. Dr. Donaldson had a tape in her hand. She walked over to the far end of the room and slid the tape into the slot. Bella sucked in her breath, wondering what she was going to see.

Chapter 5

Bella felt an icy chill, which had nothing to do with the temperature in the room or the October weather outside, race up her spine. She hunkered into her shearling jacket and waited for the huge television screen across the room from the fish tank to come alive. "You are going to give a copy of that tape to me, right?" She hated how tight and stressful her tone sounded.

Dr. Petre hit the Pause button on the remote control she was holding. She pursed her lips into a tight circle. Bella thought she looked like she had just sucked all the juice out of a lemon. "No, we will not be giving you a copy of this tape; it's against company policy. Unless you have a warrant, and then of course we would obey the law and turn it over to you or make a copy for you. I have to check with our legal department, but, no, you will not be walking out of here today with this tape. You do, however, have a right to view this tape since you say it involves you. Excuse me, I should have said allegedly involves you."

Bella's facial muscles tightened, and her eyes narrowed to slits when she said, "I called my attorney while I was waiting for you to come back, and she said I was entitled to the tape. She said she would have to take whatever legal action is required to obtain a copy if you refuse to give it to me."

Dr. Petre sucked in her breath, her eyes narrowing to slits. This woman was trouble; Bella could feel it in every bone of her body. The woman looked at her two colleagues and could tell by their expressions they were thinking the same thing she was. Still, she had no choice, policy was policy, and rules were rules. There was simply no way around that. She clicked Play on the remote. The sound was exceptionally loud, as well as irritating, Bella thought, too loud for this small box of a room.

Faster than greased lightning, Bella had her iPhone in hand and was recording what was playing out right in front of her. It was the next best thing to actually getting the tape, she told herself. Recording it herself was the only way to prove it wasn't her image on the tape. And she would have something in hand, not just a bunch of words to show and to prove to Alexis Thorn she was telling the truth when she showed up at her office in the next few hours.

"Stop that right now! You cannot record this tape," Dr. Petre said. Bella thought she looked like a marionette the way she was hopping about and waving her arms as she tried to block the big screen behind her. Her colleagues just stared, their jaws dropping.

"Yes, I can, and until you can show me one of your rules or something in your policy manual that says I can't, I will continue. Whatever you do, do not try to stop me. We could call the police if you want to make an issue of this; then we all get to see ourselves on the evening news. And by all, I mean not just the four of us but all your clients who watch the evening newscasts. What do you think a police investigation of your clinic, playing out on the evening news will do to your continued existence as a functioning enterprise? Do you really want to test the loyalty of your clients like that? If so, be my guest.

"Look close now. Now, look, that woman is not me! Does that look like me? *No, it does not!* The woman on the screen has to be at least fifteen pounds heavier than I am. I am five foot three. That woman is at least five foot seven, and she's wearing sneakers, not heels. You cannot dispute height. She has black hair. I have ash-blond hair. The facial shape is nothing like mine. Look! Look! She chews her fingernails!" Bella waved her own hands in front of the three doctors, with their acrylic nails and French manicure. "The last time I bit or chewed my fingernails, I was six years old. Do you hear me, that is not ME! You turned my property over to an imposter, and now it's gone. Gone! How could you be a party to something like that? Just tell me how. You are evil people. What you did was evil. Every one of you is evil. Answer me, damn it! How?"

Suddenly, the silence in the room was deafening. No one would look at her. Suddenly, it seemed, the floor and the ceiling were where the action was.

"Stop! Stop! Freeze the tape!" Bella shouted. Petre was so startled at Bella's command, she actually obeyed the order. Bella made sure she got the full-face likeness of the person on the tape onto her phone. "That's a pretty good shot of the woman. It's a full-frontal face shot, almost as if she's daring the camera to capture her. I can see defiance in her eyes. It's clear as a bell. Open your eyes and look at her, then look at me! There is nothing similar about either one of us.

"Why aren't you saying something? You damn well need to say something right now!

When I'm done with this place, I will own it.
Now I want to see the original of the release
form I signed, and don't give me any of your
crap about your policy and the rules. If I
signed my name, then it's mine. Or at least a
copy is mine. Like *now* would be good!" Bella
thundered, as she felt her insides start to cur-
dle. The time for being nice to these officious
fools was long gone.

Dr. Peabody quickly opened the folder he
had in his hand. He riffled through the papers, his hands trembling, until he found the
one he wanted. He held out the paper to Bella,
who immediately screeched, "That is not my
signature! Even idiots like you would have
known that if you had compared the signatures. You didn't do that, did you? Hell no, you
didn't, I can see it written on your faces."

Bella shook her head; she was losing it and
knew it. She had to stop with the shouting,
screeching, bellowing, and speak normally. She
needed to stay in control. "Now I want you to
compare my original signature on my original
contract when I signed on here. See, see, that
is not my signature!" Bella snapped a photo,
and snapped and then snapped some more.
She felt confident that she had enough material now for the Quinn Law Firm to start an all-
out investigation of these doctors and the
Samaritan Clinic.

Dr. Petre turned off the television and slipped the remote into the carton, along with the surveillance tape. Bella continued to video everyone's movements. "You better not lose that tape. You might want to think about doing something about your security while you're at it," Bella warned.

"You can't blame us for this insane debacle," the fussy little doctor bleated. "Nothing like this has happened in the thirty years we've been in business. We have an exemplary reputation. There were no red flags. No warnings of any kind. Your account was dormant, as most are. We had no reason to think or believe that the person who showed up to collect the materials wasn't you. Thousands of people come through this clinic on a weekly basis. Surely, you can't expect us to remember someone from years ago. Obviously, as we can all see, the woman on the tape is not you. Mistakes happen. We, none of us, can unring the bell.

"Having said that, we will, nonetheless, help in any way we can. You said you contacted a lawyer, so I guess we should let the lawyers handle matters. I don't know what else to tell you other than we're sorry. I know sorry is just a word to you right now, but right this moment, it's the best we can do. We will cooperate and do whatever we can to see this through to a satisfactory conclusion. I give you my personal word on that, and I'm sure that Dr. Petre and Dr. Donaldson will do the same." Both doctors nodded in agreement.

Bella watched as Dr. Peabody's shoulders slumped as he finally clamped his lips shut. For a few seconds, she almost felt sorry for him. She knew she was being unreasonable, but only to a point. These doctors had no way of knowing an imposter was stealing from them. Right now, the big question for Bella was, how did the imposter get a copy of her updated driver's license?

Dr. Petre looked like she was sucking on another lemon. Her eyes sparked. She'd been challenged, her authority usurped by these two ninnies who called themselves doctors. It's true, they were doctors, but not medical doctors like she was. This was all going to come back on her—now, when she'd just bought into the clinic as a partner. She had put in her ten years, saved up the buy-in money, and was now a full partner, which entitled her to a share of the profits, along with all the perks that went with a full partnership. If Bella Nolan was right, and Samaritan Clinic was sued, Bella Nolan could very well end up owning a controlling interest, if not the whole shooting match, and she'd be out in the cold. Suddenly, she wanted to slap the silly little twit for upsetting her world. She told herself to make nice, but she couldn't bring herself to do that. Instead, holding the box with the tape in a death grip, she almost ran from the room to the safety of her newly refurbished office, refurbished at the clinic's expense, where she could vent her frustration. After doing so, she had to call her new partners to apprise them of what was about to go down. She looked around at her pricey new digs and wanted to cry.

But if she cried, her makeup would be all over the place, and she would look like a raccoon. No, she had to stiffen up her lips, straighten her spine, and take a deep breath as the old ditty went. Which was just another way of saying pull on your big-girl panties and get on with it. She shivered when she remembered the name of the law firm that was representing Bella Nolan. The Quinn Law Firm. She knew all about that firm because dozens of the clinic's clients used it. As one client said, they don't come any better than the Quinn Law Firm, and then went on to say she knew for a fact that the members of the firm called in their lead hired gun for high-profile cases, the famous or infamous, as some put it, Lizzie Fox, also known as the Silver Fox, who mainly practiced in Las Vegas. Petre could feel her blood running cold. She knew without a shadow of a doubt that Lizzie Fox would be on the red-eye tonight, because no case could have a higher profile than this one was going to have. There would be no shoving this under the carpet any-time soon.

"Son of a bitch!" Dr. Candice Petre seethed. "What did I do to deserve this?"

Bella stepped out of the cab and onto the curb. The streets were busy for this time of day, but then again, tourists didn't really care what time it was when they were on vacation. The Quinn Law Firm was just five blocks from the White House, which was all the more reason for the amount of pedestrian traffic as well as road traffic.

Bella recognized the building that housed the Quinn Law Firm immediately. She'd walked by here almost daily when she lived in her old apartment, the same apartment she'd returned to after honeymooning with Andy. Her eyes welled up just as a strong, gusty October wind pushed her forward. Damn, her hair was going to look like a haystack. Like she cared.

Bella entered the pleasant lobby, made her way to the reception area, and asked for direc-tions to Alexis Thorn's office. A Georgetown University student with three open textbooks in front of her offered up directions along with a smile and a badge on a lanyard. Bella draped it around her neck as she made her way to the elevators. Her insides felt like a quivering mass of Jell-O.

Seven minutes later, Alexis Thorn was guiding Bella to a private suite of offices and introduced her to Nikki Quinn; then they all settled down in the seating area, where a fire was blazing in a real fireplace. Bella loved the space on sight. Everything was earth tones with splashes of color. *Comfortable* was the key word here. A silver tray with a coffee service appeared as if by magic.

Nikki spoke first after the introductions. "We're big coffee drinkers here, Bella. Our pot goes all day long. Since opening the firm years ago, we've gone through three units, and they're the big industrial coffeepots. I guess you could say we're all coffee junkies. You okay now, Bella? I tend to babble with new clients to try to get them to feel at ease. You do look particularly tense right now. It's just my way of saying you made the right decision to seek help, and you came to the right place to get it. We won't let you down. When we take on a client and a case, we work it till it is resolved to our, and our client's, satisfaction." Nikki's voice was light and cheerful, a best-friend kind of voice, as she poured coffee into three delicate china cups.

Bella struggled to smile and failed miserably. "Here," she blurted as she handed her smartphone with the video from the clinic over to Alexis. "They wouldn't give me the tape. I don't think the three of them, and by them, I mean the three doctors I spoke with, are deliberately hiding anything. The truth is, I think they were scared out of their wits. If my opinion counts, I think they made a mistake, but it wasn't anything deliberate. At least that was my initial thought. I hate saying this, but when it comes to doctors, you expect a certain . . . I don't know, kindness, compassion, something. I had three zombies. There was nothing warm and fuzzy about any one of them. I was expecting a little compassion, for want of a better word . . . something that showed they cared. What I saw . . . what I got . . . was three people who could have worked in the Budweiser lab. It was like they had no feelings. I wasn't a person to them. I was a file folder." Bella shrugged. "Maybe you have to be that way in that kind of a business."

The two lawyers and Bella talked for a full ninety minutes, with Bella doing most of the talking. The lawyers made notes, asked questions, made several copies of the video that Bella had on her phone. And then they had Bella sign a batch of papers. Bella questioned the cost. Both women shook their heads. "Right now, you just give us a dollar bill as a retainer, and that will do it for now. We don't want you worrying about money. What we are worried about, however, is the fact that you said you are moving to North Carolina. Is it possible for you to delay the move? Do you have a job, an apartment lease there, anything to prevent you from leaving here? Are you on a timetable of any kind? We're pretty good at taking care of details like that if you are prepared to stay on here a bit longer."

"Sure. Okay. I can do that. But why?" Bella asked.

Nikki got up and added another log to the fire. Bella noticed it was a white-birch log, the bark peeling. She loved birch logs. Andy had said he loved burning cherrywood. "Do you want to tell her, or should I?" Nikki asked Alexis.

Alexis grinned. "Settle back, Bella, I have a story to tell you. Yes, this is a legal firm. Yes, Nikki and I are lawyers. We fight for our clients in a court of law. But we also fight for them in other ways. Your case as it stands is going to be a tough one to bring to court, but we can go to plan B and incorporate it with plan A, which is going to court and having a full-blown trial. When I finish, all you have to do is say yes or no, and we'll go from there. Do you understand, and do you agree?"

Bella blinked. "Absolutely."

Bella listened; then she laughed. Out loud. "I'm in. I knew there was something about you the minute I walked into this building, and the hair went up on the back of my neck when I walked into this room with the two of you. Back in the day I donated twelve dollars to your defense fund. It was all I could afford at the time. I cheered you guys on till I was hoarse and so did my friends. And now here I am actually talking to two of the members of the infamous Vigilantes. This just makes my day. I'll do my best to pay you something, and if it takes me the rest of my life, I will do it. For now, my thanks is all I have to give. Do we have a deal?"

"We do," Alexis and Nikki said in unison.

"All right, then, tomorrow is Saturday. We'll call a special meeting at Pinewood so you can meet the others; then we'll get down to business. Alexis, text Myra and ask her what is a good time to meet up."

A minute later, Alexis said, "Ten!" She looked over at Bella.

"I can make ten. Just give me an address. I'll plug it into my GPS. I can't thank you enough for agreeing to help me."

"We live for this," Alexis said, and giggled. Nikki burst out laughing; then Bella started to laugh herself. She was certain now that she was in good hands.

Bella wondered how she could feel so breathless when all she'd done was drive here to Pinewood. She sat outside the gates and stared at the awesome, intricate, wrought-iron gates. All she had to do was press a button, look into the magic eye, and the gates would open. And then . . . and then . . .

Better not to think that far ahead. Just press the button and sally forth. " 'Yo ho ho and a bottle of rum,' " she chortled, then laughed out loud. She was in good hands now. Famous hands. If someone had told her she would be meeting with the famous Vigilantes, she never, not in a million years, would have believed them. And yet, here she was. Suddenly, she wasn't nervous anymore. She hoped the others were as nice as Alexis and Nikki. She rather thought they would be. Otherwise, how could they have . . . um . . . conducted their . . . um . . . outside activities. She laughed again. And she was part of it now.

Bella parked next to a golf cart and walked toward a back porch. Within seconds, a pack of barking dogs circled her, begging for attention. She dutifully complied because she loved animals. She looked up and saw a group of women waving to her.

Her saviors.

Bella grinned when the dogs scampered off to do whatever they did in this wonderful, magical place called Pinewood.

Alexis and Nikki hugged her as they ushered her into the old-fashioned yet state-of-the-art kitchen, where she was introduced to the others. A monster fire blazed in a fireplace big enough to roast an ox. Bella immediately fell in love with the room and loved the women at first sight as they hugged. None of that hand-shaking business for these women. A hug meant, "You are now one of us, or at least on our side." A handshake meant the jury was still out.

Coffee cups came out, coffee was poured, and everyone sat down at the old, scarred kitchen table. The centerpiece of bright yellow mums in a yellow ceramic bowl was low enough on the table so that it didn't interfere with face-to-face conversations. The coffee ritual was the get-acquainted part before they escorted their new client down the secret, moss-covered stairs to the old dungeons that were now known as the war room.

Normally, a half hour was allotted to detailed introductions like, "Hey, I'm Yoko, and I own a nursery. I'm married to Harry . . ." with the others following suit so Bella would be able to keep track of who was who.

"We'll get to the boys later," Myra said. "We don't want to inundate you with too much on your first visit." Bella just nodded. She wasn't exactly overwhelmed. It was more like being awed that she was even here. She said so. Everyone laughed, Annie the loudest as she pulled out her gun and dramatically blew smoke at the end. Bella's eyes almost bugged out of her head.

"Annie can shoot the eye of a rattler from a mile away," Myra whispered. "That means she's a crack shot. We all have our strengths and weaknesses."

Bella blinked and blinked again. "Uh-huh," was all she could think to say. The girls went off into peals of laughter.

"You'll do," Isabelle said, patting Bella on the back. "We'll clean this all up later. Now it's time to get to work. Just follow us and don't be nervous."

"Okay," Bella mumbled as she got in line.

She blinked again when she heard Myra tell Lady, the big golden retriever, "GUARD!"

Annie pressed the rosette at the top of the book and curio cabinet. She stepped back to allow the secret door to open. She pressed a switch, and a light came on over a steep pair of steps that were covered in velvety green moss. "Be careful, Bella, the steps are slippery and slick. We're used to them, but you aren't."

Lordy, lordy, what have I gotten myself into? Bella wondered as she followed behind Kathryn, with Alexis directly behind her. She knew she would find out sooner rather than later.

All Bella could do was gape and gasp when she saw the huge screen with Lady Justice presiding over what Alexis said was the war room.

"Everyone, take a seat, and we can get to it," Myra said. "Annie, call the meeting to order and put that damn gun away. You don't need to shoot anyone today."

"Oh, I forgot I was still holding it. My apologies, everyone. I am now calling this meeting to order. Who wants to go first?"

"I will," Alexis said.

Bella sighed, then leaned back in her chair as she listened to Alexis tell Bella's story. How sad it sounded, she thought, tears pooling in her eyes.

Chapter 6

It was late afternoon, almost time to start thinking about the dinner hour, when Annie called a halt to the hot-and-heavy discussion that was underway.

"Time out!" Annie said, whistling sharply, her eyes spewing sparks. "We are not getting anywhere but under each other's skin. We need to go upstairs, get a cup of coffee, and think about a sandwich or ordering in. In other words, it's time to eat. We've been at it for almost six hours, and speaking for myself, I'm more confused now than when we started. What's going on here? We've never had this problem before." The girls perked up as they recognized the irritation in Annie's voice.

Kathryn let out a sharp whistle of her own. "Do ya think it maybe might have something to do with the client sitting down here in the war room with us? We've never done that before. No offense, Bella, but this is not how we normally do things. What makes this young lady special or different? Well, someone say something, or I'm outta here. We just wasted six hours. *Six hours!* Time is money, people!" If anything, her voice was even more irritated than Annie's.

Every hand in the room went up. Time out!

The Sisters looked at one another and shrugged. Expressions were sheepish. None of them had an answer. Kathryn was right, and they knew it. And Annie had a right to be irritated.

Bella just looked confused. She looked around, wondering what she should do. She didn't know these people, not really. What did they expect from her? She'd talked for hours, told them everything she knew. She didn't ask to come down here to this dungeon; they had invited her, and now they were saying they wished they hadn't. Even she knew something was wrong. It had to be her, what else could it be? Good Lord, what had she gotten herself into? She started to feel sick to her stomach.

Even though she didn't know these women personally, she could tell that the women were out of sync all afternoon. Their tone was sharp, almost belligerent with one another. At one point, she thought they were a hair away from a knock-down-drag-out fight with one another. It was her. There was something about her and her case that was bothering them, but Bella had no clue what it was, and she didn't think they knew, either. Myra, the one who seemed to be the boss, had it right when she said they needed to fall back and regroup. And she needed to get the hell out of here. She hated the way the one named Kathryn was giving her the fish eye. That was one lady she knew she never wanted to meet up with in a dark alley. Or anywhere else, for that matter.

Bella fell into line and followed the women up to the main part of the house.

Upstairs in the kitchen, Bella cleared her throat and asked if she could speak. Heads bobbed up and down, and hands waved in all directions, urging her to articulate. She took a moment to notice how different the women were here in the kitchen. They looked calm, and they were smiling. She wondered if it was her or them, or if they were just crazy like a bunch of female foxes.

"I'm glad to be here. Well, sort of. I am happy you all want to help me, but I think that my being here in person is throwing all of you off. I have nothing more to offer right now, so there doesn't seem to be much point to my staying here with you all. You could light matches under my toenails, and I couldn't give you one more iota of information. So, having said that,

I'm going to go back to town and see if I can get my old job back—hosting nights at the lounge where I used to work—if I am going to stay in town a while longer. I appreciate all you've done, bringing me here and all. It goes without saying I will never ever divulge any of this to anyone. Your activities are sacred with me. I'm just grateful you all agreed to help me, so without further ado, I'm going to leave now. It was nice meeting you all. Oh, looks like you have company," she said, pointing to the parking area outside the kitchen.

Instant pandemonium followed.

The dogs barked and yelped and yowled as they made a beeline for the door. "It's Maggie! She's the *Post*'s star reporter and one of us. She was on assignment and couldn't get here with the others. I'm glad you are going to get to meet her before you leave," Myra said, as the intrepid reporter blew into the kitchen, tussling with the dogs every step of the way as she called a greeting to one and all.

"I swear that the wind is blowing sixty miles an hour. I really had to hang on to the steering wheel, the car was all over the road. Hi, I'm Maggie, and you must be Bella; pleased to meet you. I need coffee." She continued to babble as she surprised Bella by hugging her. "By now, you must realize that we're all huggers."

Bella laughed out loud. "Nice to meet you, too. Hello and goodbye."

"Was it something I said?" Maggie looked baffled as Bella closed the door behind her.

"It's complicated. Who wants a ham sandwich? It's all there is in the refrigerator unless we cook up some pasta, but there's no cheese. Someone needs to go food shopping," Kathryn said. The irritation was back in her voice. Kathryn had the same ginormous appetite as Maggie.

"It's on my to-do list," Myra muttered. "We'll all take a ham sandwich, dear. There's a loaf of bread in the freezer. Thaw it out in the microwave. I must say it has been a taxing afternoon for all of us. As I said earlier down in the war room, we need to fall back and regroup, and I think that will be easier once we relax and eat a little food. So let's get to it. A caffeine fix will go a long way to settle us down. I can't remember the last time we went six hours without coffee."

"Try like never," Nikki said, laughing.

Things did indeed fall into place with Myra's words, and the coffee was poured. The girls did what they always did then, worked in tandem as an assembly line. Or as Annie put it, "Now we're back in our own groove."

Within minutes, the women had all relaxed and were bantering back and forth, with Maggie doing most of the chattering as she waited to be brought up on everything that happened down in the war room. "I want to hear everything, and don't leave anything out no matter how trivial it may seem."

"This is on me," Alexis said. "I never should have brought Bella out here to Pinewood, much less suggest we take her down to the war room. It's not that I don't trust her, I do. It's just . . . I don't know, it didn't feel right. And then she was there, and it was too late. I just want to say I own it, and it will never happen again. I'm sorry I wasted all our time."

"Something other than what you all said went down in the war room seems to have a running undercurrent here. Did I miss something, or did you all forget to tell me something? What is it that's bothering you? Is it the case overall? Is it Bella? What?" Maggie demanded, as she bit down into her sandwich and rolled her eyes in delight. Maggie did love her food.

The room was silent for a few minutes while everyone stopped eating to think about Maggie's question; then they all started to jabber at once.

Nikki flexed her lips, then whistled sharply between her teeth the way Jack had taught her to do when they first met. She remembered how impressed she'd been to know she had the capability to let loose such an earth-shattering sound. "Whoa! Whoa! One at a time. Sounds to me like we're all saying the same thing with a few added words of our own. If I'm wrong, tell me, but I think we're all bothered by what Bella wasn't able to tell us. She knows she heard something she thought was important, not at the time, of course, but she knows now that she can't remember what it is. I, for one, can buy into that. We all understand how that goes, been there, done that kind of thing. She probably has information locked in her mind that we could use, but she can't remember. Eventually, hopefully, she will."

Yoko reached for a pickle spear and bit down. "It's probably the one piece of information that will really help us, but you're right, eventually she'll get around to remembering it. As we all know, the more you try to force yourself to remember, the less likely you are to succeed. With luck, we might be able to work without the missing piece of information, whatever it turns out to be. But I suspect that it would be a whole lot easier if we had it."

"I find this whole thing really sad," Maggie said.

"We all do, dear," Myra said. "First, Bella loses her husband. She is just way too young to be a widow. Imagine finding out your husband has been dead for eight months, and you didn't know it because no one told you. How cruel is that? How do you get over something like that? And then to find out your, um . . . your eggs have been stolen, which means that all ties to your dead husband are gone forever. However, we still do not know if Bella's husband's sperm deposits were taken. I don't even want to go there right now, even in my thoughts. Was there anything else that bothered anyone?"

The girls looked at one another. "We all made notes. I think we picked Bella's brain clean," Isabelle said. "Now we just have to put it all together and decide what we are going to do. Are we going to work this evening or call it a day?"

The girls voted to work through the evening, and agreed to stay over and pick up in the morning in order to get the ball rolling as quickly as possible.

They all moved quickly, in lockstep, the way they always did when it came to cleanup. "Thirteen minutes!" Yoko chortled, as the dishwasher hummed to life. She did a little dance before she skipped ahead of the others to head down to the dungeons.

As always, they smartly saluted Lady Justice before they took their seats at the huge, round table.

"First things first. We need to call Avery Snowden to see if he is available to help us out. The boys might have commandeered him since they're on a case of their own."

"I'll do it," Alexis said, as she typed out a text to send to the old spy. The return text arrived in seconds. Alexis's fist shot in the air. "He's available and on his way. He said he's in Seattle. He'll be here by late tomorrow morning. His part of the mission with the boys is over, but they may have to stay another week or two to complete the mission."

"Listen up, everyone!" Annie said. "You all understand, do you not, that we are taking on the United States Army, right?"

"Your point is, Annie—and get to it without a bunch of jabbering. But before you do that, what makes the United States Army any different than taking on the President of the United States, the Secret Service, the World Bank, and a host of other notables? Surely you are not insinuating we should be intimidated. That's not what you're saying, is it, Annie?" Myra's tone of voice clearly said it had better not be what she was saying.

"Good Lord, no. I just meant there will be miles and miles of red tape to wade through. We're talking the army here, Myra. You spell that a-r-m-y. Abner, our resident in-house hacker, is not available to us," Annie said. "Did you hear me when I said miles and miles of red tape?"

Isabelle's arm shot in the air. "What? I'm chopped liver! Did you forget that Abner has been teaching me the art of hacking for over a year now, and he actually said I'm almost as good as he is? I realize the operative word here is *almost*, but I am good. I think I can hack into the Pentagon without breaking a sweat because Abner showed me how to do it when he did it. You can apologize now, Countess de Silva," Isabelle said with a bite to her voice.

"I'm sorry, dear, I sincerely apologize. I don't know what I was thinking. I keep forgetting how talented you are. It won't happen again," Annie said contritely.

Isabelle grinned and hugged Annie. "I know. Sometimes, even I forget that I can do these devious things. Who knew!" she said, imitating an infamous commercial about cashing in one's life insurance and throwing up her arms dramatically. "Don't go pinning any medals on me yet. Hacking the United States military isn't like hacking the local drugstore to see what drugs your neighbors take. Not that I would ever do that," Isabelle added hastily.

"Now, having said that, I think I will wait for morning, when I'm fresh and clicking on all cylinders, to dive into that particular hornet's nest. And I like to map out a strategy first, the way Abner taught me. So, if you don't mind, I'll do that while you all do whatever it is you plan on doing. If you need me, do what the song says and just call my name."

The women settled down at the table and looked at one another. The silence was unnerving. Maggie bounded to her feet and spun around. "I'm not getting any of this. What's up with all of you? By now someone, usually you, Nikki, or Annie have at least a half plan of action or else the whole thing. Why do I feel like I'm swimming upstream and the water is running low?"

"Maggie is right. What is it about Bella and

her case that's got us in this funk?" Kathryn demanded, her voice so irritated, the others blinked, wondering if something else was bothering the long-distance truck driver.

"Maybe because her husband was injured and died, and no one told her for over eleven months?" Yoko said softly. "I think that might make me a little crazy, to say the least."

"Eleven months of writing letters and believing her husband was going to come home to her and they were going to raise a family might have something to do with it," Alexis said, a catch in her voice. "I know that would bother me. How do you get over something like that?"

"It's everything," Nikki said quietly. "Bella is just simply too young. To us, she's still a kid. Well, sort of. You know what I mean, young. I know it happens, but she's our . . . our first up-close-and-personal case where love is involved. I think I read somewhere that the military, the army in particular, is so careful about stuff like this. All that time Andy . . . I guess it's okay to call him Andy . . . was in a hospital almost within walking distance of where Bella lived, and no one told her. This is just eating at me. I want to . . . to *do* something to someone. I want a payback, and I want it now. I know that's impossible at the moment, but I feel better having expressed myself out loud."

"Whoa! Whoa!" Maggie bellowed. "Before we start dishing out blame, we need to look to Andy. It was his job to notify the military of his new status. I get the in-love part, the two-day honeymoon, and I get the deployment. Even so, Bella and making sure she was taken care of should have been the only thing on his mind. It was his idea to have her freeze her eggs, his idea to donate his sperm. So he was thinking ahead in that regard. Meaning he might come back impaired or not come back at all. So if he was thinking of all that, why didn't he think to do the paperwork that would see that his new wife was taken care of if something happened to him?

"I'm thinking of his military life insurance, not to mention his military pay. Where did he think that was going to go? We need to find out where it was going prior to the marriage. It doesn't make any sense to me whatsoever. Not to Maggie Spritzer, private citizen, Maggie Spritzer, Vigilante in training, and it sure as hell doesn't compute to me as Maggie Spritzer, *Washington Post* reporter."

"Maggie's right. She summed it up perfectly," Myra and Annie said in unison.

"That means we're back to square one," Nikki pointed out. "Let's do a rehash of what we know. Everything Bella told us and everything we were able to pull out of her with the exception of the one thing she can't remember," Nikki said.

"Before we do that, I want to go on the record saying it bothers me that Bella knows so little about the man she married. Speaking for myself here, Alan and I had a short courtship before we got married. And yet I knew every single thing there was to know about him, practically from the moment he fell out of his mother's womb. Just the way he knew everything about me. I get it that Bella and Andy were in love and into each other. But so were Alan and me, and yet we talked and talked, kissed until our lips were bruised, and made love twenty-four/seven, and we still talked and learned all there was to know about each other. Tell me it wasn't the same with all of you. Go ahead, I'm waiting," Kathryn said angrily. "And yeah, I'm mad as hell here, so there!"

"I for one agree with Kathryn," Alexis said.

Heads bobbed up and down in agreement with Kathryn.

"It's almost like there's some secret to Andy's past he didn't share," Yoko said.

"Then we need to find out what that secret is," Myra said. "Let's make a list of what we do know and what we don't know, and take it from there. I don't see any other way to parcel out assignments. I'm certainly up for suggestions. Right now, the only thing we know is that tomorrow morning Isabelle is . . . um . . . going to be doing some . . . um, work that none of us know how to do. What she finds out might turn out to be a whole bunch of nothing. Or it might turn out to be a treasure trove of things we need to know. Now, who wants to go first?"

Maggie's hand shot high in the air. "I'd like to take on Andy and his sister. I wasn't here when you all talked to Bella, but from what I gather from what has been said here, she knew next to zip about her new husband's sister. Right off the bat, that strikes me as strange. And she wasn't interested enough to ask questions. Don't you all find that strange? Or is it just me?"

Once again, heads bobbed up and down. "Go for it, darling girl, and leave no stone unturned. We want to know everything, every nit-picking detail," Myra said.

"I'm on it," Maggie said, a devilish gleam in her eyes. As one, the girls shuddered because they all knew how relentless Maggie could be when she was stalking prey. Whatever was out there to find about Andy's sister, Maggie would find it.

Chapter 7

"Listen up, girls. Today is a brand-new day, and we have to make it work for us. I think we're off to a good start, and you'll see why in a second. We all need to thank Nikki and Yoko, who rose early and went to the village and brought us back these lovely breakfast sandwiches and . . . they told me . . . they ordered Antonio's to deliver lunch and Pagoda to deliver dinner. Today, we are good to go, ladies. What that means is we can work straight through the day and not worry about our meals or the cleanup," Myra said happily. "I just love it when things work out so easily," she continued to babble.

An hour later, the girls looked around to

make sure they were leaving Myra's kitchen neat and tidy since Myra was extra particular about her kitchen. Sometimes she was worse than Charles when it came to, "everything has a place, and that's where I want to see it." End of story.

"All right then, girls, let's get to it," Myra announced, once everyone was comfortable and seated at the large, round table in the war room. "I've been thinking about this case all night. I couldn't sleep thinking about poor Bella. Why is it things like this happen to nice people like Bella?" Annie asked fretfully. "And yet . . ." Annie hadn't finished what she was about to say when Alexis started to talk over her.

Alexis clucked her tongue and shook her head. "Now, Annie, you know there is no answer, and even if there were, *we* are never going to find out what it is. Things are what they are, and we have to live with it. We also know that no one and nothing is as it seems. I hate to be the one saying this because I am the one that brought Bella to us, but I'm going to say it anyway. Somewhere, something is off. It's not something I know, it's more like something I feel, and I, for one, always pay attention to my gut instincts. I cannot explain it any better than to say it's just something I know. I believe you've all had that feeling at one time or another because we've talked about it on several occasions. Like I said, nothing and no one are what they seem. Having said that, I'm now afraid to take that thought any further, so I'm tossing it out to you all for your input."

No one, not even Annie, knew what to say to Alexis's declaration, so none of them spoke in response. They all knew time would prove that ditty right or wrong, and they'd deal with it when that happened.

Nikki and Alexis walked up to the dais, where Charles's wall of electronics waited for them. The two lawyers worked in tandem as Myra called the meeting down below to order. The room went silent as iPhones came out, were turned to record, and placed in front of each sister.

It was Annie's signal to say, "Listen up, girls!" It was the way she started every meeting. "We're going to do a quick rehash of what we know. Then we are going to parcel out assignments. I just want to know if everyone's decks are cleared before we commit one hundred percent to Bella and her mission. I'm thinking, and this is not based on anything in particular, that this case could go seven to ten days. Bare minimum, a week. What say you all?"

Nikki and Alexis both said their court calendar was clear for the next two weeks. "What has to be done at the office can be done by our paralegals. That means we're good," Nikki said. She quickly added, "I see five to seven days."

"The nursery is in good shape. We did our fall decorating last week for the Harvest Ball and Halloween. My pumpkins, according to

Kathryn, are on the way. At least some of them," she corrected her statement. "The college boys that work for me have it all under control. Annie was right when she told me that if I paid extra, the boys could and would assume more control. Any of the four can run the nursery in my absence, and the best part is they're all honest, really nice young men. That means I'm good, too. I agree with Nikki, I see five to seven days," Yoko said.

"I'm kind of stuck," Kathryn said. "I don't know what happened, but Mr. Hanover's pumpkins aren't ready to ship yet. I was supposed to pick up and deliver them two days ago, but he didn't have enough help to pick and load them. What that means is I am on call where he and his pumpkins and his butternut squash are concerned. I might have to leave you all if things get back on track again sooner rather than later. I'm thinking a week, but that could change if I have to bail out on you all and leave you shorthanded."

"If that happens, we'll just have to manage to work around you," Annie said. "That leaves Maggie, Isabelle, Myra, and me. We're good. Maggie?"

"Ted is due back tomorrow, so he can take over. I'm all yours and looking forward to this mission," Maggie said, as she tapped furiously on her laptop. Then she snorted. "If my opinion counts, I'm going to go out on a limb here and say ten days even with Avery Snowden doing most of the heavy lifting. But I could be wrong, which, as you all know, rarely if ever happens."

"I only have two active clients at the moment, and everything is running on schedule. I'm good, too," Isabelle said. "I am working on . . . um . . . the Pentagon. I'm thinking a week of round-the-clock dedication. I'd say five days if Abner were here doing the hacking, but with me . . . I'm not that confident."

Maggie held up her hand, her expression one of confusion. "Who is doing what, and how are we going to go about all of this?" She looked around at the Sisters, her hands fluttering in the air. "I don't even know where to start. What's with this case, why is it giving us all this angst? I'm not getting it." She looked as befuddled as the others felt. Maggie was never befuddled.

"I don't think any of us are getting it, dear," Myra said soothingly. "That's why we're here. We are going to figure out how best to handle this mission just the way we've done in the past. I think part of it is that Bella was here, here where we conduct our business. This special place we're in right now has always been sacrosanct. Our private place. For want of a better word or phrase, we all see it now as if it's been invaded. It doesn't matter if Bella can be trusted or not, she was here. We broke our own rule. That is not good. We weren't prepared for Bella because it never happened before, and I'm not blaming Alexis, we all agreed to bringing Bella down here. I think we're back in the groove now and recognize what has to be done. Technically, we are starting all over again with the information we have on hand—information Bella gave us, which is not all that much, sad to say."

"Let's get to it then," Nikki called down from the dais.

"All right, this is what we know, and we only know what we know because it is what Bella told us. Is it all true? We do not know it to be true or false with any certainty. Yet. Would Bella lie to us to gain our help? Possibly, but she did not seek us out, Alexis volunteered our help; so the answer is likely no, she did not lie to us. We need to remember that if we start to parcel out blame here. I, for one, believe that the young lady is on the up and up, so to speak," Myra said.

"We know Bella's three-year courtship, such as it was, was not basically physical for the most part since Major Nolan was deployed most of the time. E-mails, occasional phone calls, some FaceTiming whenever they could. Then they had two two-day furloughs. We're talking intimacy here, or *sex* if you prefer that word instead, then the one week of a hard and heavy courtship, when they were glued to one another the entire time and got engaged at the end of the week. That's about the sum total of their relationship. Then the major was deployed again, managed to get a forty-eight-hour leave, and they got married. They had a two-day honeymoon, and that was the sum total of the relationship after the week-long courtship. As far as we know," Kathryn said. Always the outspoken one, she added, "The whole thing sucks. What's bothering me, and I said it before, is that Bella knows next to nothing about the man she married. That absolutely does not compute for me. It shouldn't compute for any of you, either."

"You're right, it doesn't compute for any of us, Kathryn, but we aren't Bella. There is simply no accounting for love-starved people, and that's what I think Bella was. I don't have a fix on the husband yet," Yoko said.

"Well, he must have loved her as much as she loved him; otherwise, why marry her? Where is it written he has to marry her? That's because it isn't written anywhere. Major Nolan, all on his own, made the decision to ask Bella to marry him," Maggie pointed out.

"Well then, he should have damn well followed through and done what he was supposed to do, see to it that his brand-new wife was taken care of. Which he did not do," Isabelle snapped. "He did not arrange for her to receive his military pay. He did not have her named the beneficiary of his military life insurance. The blame goes to him, not Bella, and yes, I'm sorry he's dead, but he was still alive when the time came to make the life-altering decisions one expects a husband to make about his wife's welfare."

"Maybe that's the way Midwesterners do things," Myra said.

"This is what we know. Major Nolan was from Oklahoma and Bella from Kansas. They first met in San Francisco; then Bella followed the major here to Washington. I think I have that right," Annie said.

"Yes, dear, you have it right. That's what Bella shared with us," Myra said. "Bella really has no family with the exception of a distant cousin somewhere in North Carolina. She said she barely knows her. It's more of a case of she knows *of* her rather than knowing her as we think of knowing each other. I'm thinking it's a Christmas card thing and maybe a phone call once a year, something like that. That's why Bella was going to relocate to North Carolina. The cousin is all she has in the way of family, so it's understandable. Even a distant cousin is better than no cousin at all when that's the end of the bloodline."

"Major Nolan had a sister that Bella really knows nothing about. Or did know nothing about until the army apprised her of what they had on file, which we now have and which is skimpy at best," Annie said.

"Bella said Andy never talked about her other than to mention that he had a sister. I believe her name is Sara, and according to Andy's records, she was at one point married to someone named Steven Conover, from whom she was later divorced. I don't think we know the when, the why, the how of it all because Bella didn't share any of that, so it probably means she never knew. Or cared, for that matter. I have the impression brother and sister were not close. At least that's how Bella made it sound," Myra said. "I'm not sure of this, but I got the impression the sister was older than Bella's husband. Anyone think differently? Not that that means anything to the case. She's older, so what?"

Maggie let out a loud whoop. "I got it! I got it!"

"Then by all means share!" Kathryn snapped.

"Sara Nolan was married to Steven Conover for three years. But it says here that her name was Sara Windsor Nolan Conover. So either she was married to someone else or she was adopted or the siblings had a different parent. When she was married to Conover, they lived in Baltimore. He still lives there. He's a sculptor. I went on his website. His creations sell for five digits. They're quite beautiful. He's actually famous. No children. Their divorce was finalized the week that Bella and Andy were married. Sara, that's the sister's name, did not attend the simple justice of the peace ceremony in the courthouse. I'm guessing on this, but I think it doubtful that Sara even knew that her brother got married. I can't find out what she does for a living or if she ever had a job. I can't find a trail. Isabelle will have to try to find out her social security number so we can track her," Maggie said, as she shuffled the papers in front of her. "According to this army report, the only address they have for Sara Nolan is the husband's address in Baltimore. As we all now know, their records are hopelessly outdated. Back to you, Annie."

"I was up a good part of the night, couldn't sleep for some reason, so I went down to the kitchen to make some coffee and fiddle with the computer. Myra was there waiting for me because she couldn't sleep either, so we more or less, sort of, kind of, started looking into things. We decided, and of course it will go to a vote with all of you, but we think Avery should go to Oklahoma and Kansas and find out everything he can about Major Nolan and the sister, Sara. He's got the manpower, and we don't want to spread ourselves too thin here.

"We also need to find out more about Bella. Doesn't matter that she's our client. Clients have been known to gild the lily, as the saying goes, so in the interests of leaving no stone unturned, we think it's a wise move to have her checked out as thoroughly as her deceased husband is. So, later that's up for a vote, too."

"We need a tracker on the sister. That means a vehicle and her phone, and the only one I know capable of placing and monitoring them is Avery Snowden. Once we locate her, I want her under surveillance twenty-four/seven. My gut is telling me she's the key to this whole sorry mess," Alexis said. "Avery will be able to do all of that plus more depending on what he runs into for us, and that frees us up to do other things. Avery's people will be able to get the sister's early background, but we need to know what happened to her, the how, the what, and the when of it all when she left Oklahoma, probably around the age of eighteen or so.

"And, of course, we need someone to talk to the ex-husband. I'm thinking he is going to be a gold mine of information. Who's up for that? I can't go because I have to update and replenish my red bag. I'm dangerously low right now, and that's not good when we're just about to start a mission."

"I'll take the ex-husband," Nikki said, smacking her hands together in gleeful anticipation. "Maggie, you want to partner up with me?"

"Yes, ma'am!" Maggie said smartly. "I'm ready whenever you are."

Myra scribbled some notes on a legal pad. It was how she kept track of what she called "all the little and also the big details," because she hated using her laptop. More often than not, at least once a day, she professed her deep hatred for all things electronic. One of her favorite sayings was, "Just give me a piece of paper and a pencil with an eraser, and I'll see you at the finish line." Most times, her boast was on the money.

Annie held her hand up. "Yoko, how about

if you and Kathryn take on the Samaritan Clinic. I think you two look the part of prospective clients. Don't make an appointment. Go in unannounced and catch them all by surprise. You'll get a feel as to whether they're hiding something or not. Don't tell them who you represent until you are satisfied you've gotten all you can get by way of information from them. If you get the feeling you're giving off vibes, then don't admit to why you're there. I personally don't think the staff deliberately or knowingly did anything wrong. They were sloppy, yes. So, unless and until we come up with something different, I'll assume that to be the case."

"Sure, no problem." Yoko looked over at Kathryn, whose head was bobbing up and down just as fast as Maggie's fingers were flying over the mini keyboard.

"All right then, that's settled." Myra scribbled on her pad. "I thought, if you all have no objections, Annie and I will take on Walter Reed, the hospital where Major Nolan was cared for, and see what we can come up with?"

"Are we voting?" Nikki queried. "I vote yes to everything." The others seconded Nikki. Myra scribbled some more.

The morning passed quickly. At noon, Annie called a halt to announce that it was time for lunch. "I hear Lady barking, so that has to mean Avery is at the gate, just in time for lunch. Let's hop to it, girls, I'm anxious to get this mission underway."

The greeting over, Myra ushered Avery to a seat at the counter while the Sisters set the table and warmed up lunch. By the time Kathryn removed the crusty bread from the oven, Avery had been brought up to date. He was busy tapping out instructions to his operatives as the girls set his plate in front of him.

"I hate to eat and run, but I just got a booking on a two o'clock flight to Tulsa. I'll be back in touch sometime late tonight. Does that work for everyone?" Avery asked. The Sisters said they were good with his decision.

"Then let's eat!" Maggie said, as she dived into her spaghetti and meatballs. "Eat hearty, Nikki, because when we're finished here, we are heading off to Baltimore. I'll sign out the *Post* van and we hit the road. I can't wait to meet Mr. Steven Conover."

Annie looked at Myra and smiled. "I think that means we are officially on the case. Everyone has an assignment, including you and me, so I say we all split up and do what we have to do. We report back here tonight. I realize dinner will be whenever anyone wants to eat. Nikki, if you and Maggie feel the need to stay in Baltimore, by all means do so. Just check in."

The gang ate with gusto, then tidied up with their usual thoroughness. They all said goodbye to Avery and split off to do their own thing.

And then it was just Myra and Annie.

"I think we need to dress up a little more, don't you, Annie? I don't think these schmata dresses will work at Walter Reed. A little make-up, too. Fifteen minutes, and I'm driving."

Both women literally flew up the stairs, Lady and her pups hot on their heels, to do Myra's bidding. They recognized a mission was about to commence, and they were scheduled to go on guard duty.

Just another exciting day at Pinewood.

Chapter 8

Maggie typed Steven Conover's address into the GPS before she drove out of the underground garage at the *Post*. "Forty-seven minutes to Baltimore once we hit I-95, if we do it nonstop. Then we have to find Steven Conover's place, and that could take us a little time. I feel safe in saying we'll need another thirty minutes, so, technically, we're looking at an hour and a half until we lay our eyes on Mr. Steven Conover."

Nikki nodded as she settled herself more comfortably by adjusting the seat belt across her chest. "Maggie, do you remember Bella's telling us, or maybe you weren't there yet, but she said something was bothering her that she couldn't remember. She said it was something she either heard or read, and she couldn't remember what it was. I have that same feeling. It's something I must have read in the paper or something I saw on the Internet. Whatever it was, it had to do with the military. I must have glanced at it or skimmed through it, but because it was of no particular interest to me at the time, I just forgot it. You're in the newspaper business. Do you recall anything about the military? It was recent, I'm thinking. Something in the last six months that's ringing a bell in my head. For the life of me, I can't think what it is. Now, wouldn't it be something, and lucky for us, if Bella and I are on the same page and neither one of us can remember the same thing. Crazy flukes like that happen all the time," Nikki said fretfully, her brow furrowed in thought as she struggled with her memory.

"Nothing comes to mind, Nikki. Do you have anything else to go on? If I did see it, I probably did what you did, glossed over it since I don't know anyone in the military these days."

Nikki slapped at her forehead. "Actually, I do, Maggie. I think it was something about signing a petition. I just can't remember if I did or not, but if I was thinking about it, it must have seemed important at the time. Damn. I hate when I can't remember something." Agitation rang in Nikki's voice as she yanked at her seat belt in frustration.

Maggie took her eyes off the road for a second to look at Nikki. "In your opinion, in your gut, do you think it's important to this mission?"

Nikki didn't have to think about the question. "Yes, I think so, but if you ask me why, I can't tell you. This is my gut talking, but my gut has served me well both in and out of court all these many years. I always pay attention to my gut feelings. Jack says I scare him because, as he put it, it's uncanny how I'm right ninety percent of the time."

"Ted says that about me, too." Maggie laughed. "I think it's a female thing, to be honest with you. Probably has to do with our hormones." She looked over at Nikki, wiggled her eyebrows, and giggled.

"Okay, then." Maggie waited for a break in traffic before she moved into the right lane and steered off the road to the shoulder. "You drive, and I'll see what I can dig up on my laptop. No sense wasting time gabbing or gossiping when I might be able to figure out what it is you cannot remember. Who knows, we might have some answers by the time we get to Steven Conover's house. I know my way around the military archives, so it will be easier for me to do it. Might as well make use of our time on the road. I need to do something, accomplish something of value today. Everyone needs to do that, don't you think? I try to make it a goal every day. See, see, if I'm not working, I'm babbling. Just ignore me, Nikki."

Seven minutes later, Nikki inched her way back into traffic. "Have at it, Miz Reporter. I'll just pay attention to the road and all the crazy drivers out here."

"Hmmmn," was Maggie's only comment, as she tapped away a mile a minute.

Fifteen miles down the road, Maggie's fist shot in the air. "I think this might be it. Tell me if it rings any bells. I'm going to read it to you just the way it is here. Some club or organization called Change.org posted it. There is a bill called HR 553 that military widows and widowers want Congress to enact into legislation. It seems that over 65,000 military spouses are being denied their full military insurance due to an archaic law dating back to 1972. In today's time, that is forty-eight years during which Congress has failed to change this for men and women who have given up their lives for their country. That's if I'm reading this correctly. It says here that the amount is $1,000 a month for the survivor. That's some serious money, Nikki, for a spouse to lose. Especially if there are children involved. Simply put, these men and women are being denied survivor benefits because of this archaic law. There's an address here for an Offset Facebook group and, of course, instructions on contacting your member of Congress.

"There are all kinds of stories here about families and their hardships. This one lady said they handed her a folded flag and said on behalf of the President of the United States and a grateful nation, she was to accept the flag. That was when she realized the Department of Defense wasn't grateful at all. She said she sacrificed her husband, her children's father, her best friend, her sole provider, then they expected her to sacrifice financially again, and giving her that flag was going to make it all right." There's a ton of stories like this. It's really sad. I had no idea about this, I know you didn't either, and I'm sure outside of military circles, no one else knows either. I won't go as far as to say they don't care. I'm sure they do and would care, and would help if they knew. *If* is the operative word here. I guess the organization is trying to get the word out to the public. I'm going to locate the petition, and I'm going to sign it. I think I'll do an article on it when we get back. I'll run it by Annie, but I know she'll agree and sign on, too. The written word, as we know, is one of the most powerful tools in the world. Once it's printed, it's there forever. That's just my opinion," Maggie added hastily.

Nikki could feel the excitement building in her voice. "That's it, that's what I read! Damn, you're good, Maggie. I remember the 65,000 number, but what I can't remember is if I signed the petition. I want to believe I did because that is just so wrong. I am assuming Bella isn't getting that $1,000 a month. The sister got whatever the military was handing out at the time by way of insurance. I wonder why she never turned it over to Bella. I sure hope Isabelle comes up with some good records that we can run with. What's it say about why the survivors are being denied?"

"This article says there are spouses who were eligible to receive the Dependency and Indemnity Compensation, an entitlement paid from the VA to indemnify or hold the government harmless for causing the death of the spouse. It also says that there are 65,000 such spouses, of which Bella is one, who will have their Survivor Benefit Program annuity insurance benefits offset dollar for dollar by the DIC. Full SBP payment is unfairly denied to those surviving spouses. They call it SBP-DIC offset, and these spouses in this article want to fight to end that. They say it is a purchased insurance. It is not normal for one's insurance to not be paid just because the beneficiary has another policy.

"Some of these spouses lost seventy-eight percent of their income. The article goes on to quote some senators who have opinions and aren't afraid to voice them. And then people can reply to an e-mail and sign the petition, is what I'm getting out of this. I'm going to send this off to Myra and Annie, and have them call Bella to see if this is what she couldn't remember. Having said that, I don't know how a person could forget something like this, and in her case, how she's involved with how everything went down with her husband's death. This is her dead husband we're talking about here."

"Shock would be my guess," Nikki said. "She was traumatized. Anything else?"

"Just the names of some of the congressmen and senators asking them to pass HR 553 to change the law. By the way, they're up to 175,663 supporters now. Their goal is 200,000 signatures. I just signed the petition myself."

Nikki held up her hand for Maggie to be quiet. "Shhh, what's she saying?" she asked, referring to the robotic voice offering directions.

Maggie listened intently, then repeated the instructions. "Go to the next traffic light, make a right. Go five blocks and make a left turn on Westminster Avenue. Stay on Westminster for seven miles and you'll come to a cobblestone road with a sign with an arrow that says, SCULPTURES BY STEVEN CONOVER. From that point, it's three quarters of a mile to his showroom. I read on the Internet that he lives in an apartment over the showroom. The whole thing— the apartment, the showroom, and, of course, his workroom—was originally an old barn that he renovated. The barn or the showroom sits on eleven acres. I saw pictures on his website of animals he's sculpted. The grounds are like a natural habitat. Oh, you turn here, Nikki. This is what happens when you talk and don't pay attention. My bad. Sorry."

The rest of the ride to Steven Conover's sanctuary was made in silence.

"Twenty-seven minutes," Nikki said, looking at her watch. "We're here. How do you want to handle this, Maggie? Do we go in as who we are and give it all up, or do we pose as possible clients in the hope he gives up something? Why he would give up anything at all to two strangers is anyone's guess. So, I say we play it straight and hope for the best. You have your *Post* credentials, so that will help. You okay with that, Maggie?" Nikki said, as she parked the *Post* van in one of the six designated parking spots in the small parking lot. The only other vehicle in sight was a high-dollar shiny new silver Range Rover parked in the number one spot. Both women assumed the Range Rover belonged to Steven Conover.

Maggie led the way up a paved walkway surrounded by colorful, late-fall chrysanthemums. She looked around at the manicured grounds. Steven Conover had a good eye for color, style, and uniformity. It was all very pleasing to the eye. "It's nice here, but off the beaten track so to speak. You'd really have to know this place is here to get here. Too far from town for me. I'm a convenience kind of gal myself."

"Me too." Nikki giggled. "You do realize, don't you, Maggie, that's just an excuse we use for being lazy?"

Maggie didn't agree or disagree, but she did laugh out loud.

A bell tinkled over the door when Nikki opened it. Soft music, golden oldies, could be heard coming from the back of the building.

Nikki looked at Maggie. Both women shrugged at the same time. "Do we whistle, do we yell, hey you! What?"

The air moved and swirled all at the same time as a whirling swarm of Yorkshire terriers descended on the floor of the showroom. They came from all directions, yapping, barking, and yelping, stubby tails swinging furiously back and forth.

"They're my welcoming committee," a tall man with a bushy beard said, laughing at the expressions on Nikki's and Maggie's faces. "They're all from the same litter. When it was time to find them a home, I just couldn't part with them. By way of introduction," he said, pointing to each dog. "Meet Jam, Jelly, Flash, Rosie, Maxine, Charlie, Gus, and Harvey. They were the litter. The mom is Lily, and the dad is Lenny. Yep, ten dogs. Love each and every one of them. But you didn't drive all the way out here to hear about my dogs. What can I do for you? And the next question I always ask anyone who walks through that door behind you is, how did you hear about me?"

"For starters, we aren't customers. I'm not adverse to buying something if it screams my name. My name is Maggie Spritzer. I'm a reporter for the *Washington Post*. My friend is Nikki Quinn. She's an attorney with the Quinn Law Firm in Georgetown. We're here to ask for your help. The only thing I can offer you in return for said help is some free advertising in the paper and an interview or article if you prefer. In answer to your second question, I searched you out."

"Since this appears to be more social than business, let's go upstairs to my apartment and have a cup of coffee. I was about to do that when you arrived. I pretty much live by a schedule, and I tend to get a little cranky when I get behind."

"I'm kind of like that myself," Maggie said, as she tiptoed around a cluster of little dogs who were bent on sniffing her feet. "I think they smell my cat on my shoes," she said, and giggled.

Steven laughed. "For sure, those little rascals can smell a cat or a squirrel a mile away. So what's it gonna be, ladies, coffee, tea, soft drinks, or something stronger?" Steven asked, as he prepared the coffeepot. "By the way, this is Kona coffee, straight from Hawaii. Nothing better in my opinion if that will help you make a decision."

"We'll take it!" Nikki said. Maggie nodded.

"This is very nice," Maggie said, looking

around the lived-in beautiful kitchen. It was full of antique Alabama red brick, a monster fieldstone fireplace big enough to roast an ox, green plants hanging from the beams and over the windows. What looked like handcrafted chairs and a table were covered in bright red tartan plaid cushions, while matching place mats decorated the rough-hewn table.

"I inherited all of this," Steven said, waving his arms about, "from my parents when they passed away. Both my parents were world-renowned sculptors, so they pretty much paved the way for me to take over their business once they were gone. I didn't change a thing—the plants were my mom's. They were my biggest challenge, but I persevered. My dad had rigged up a watering system because Mom wasn't tall enough to reach up to water them. I just turn on the water and voilà, the plants are watered. The cushions and place mats were made by my mother. She used to sew and craft things at night during the long winter months. All these dogs I just introduced you to are descendants of my parents' dogs, the dogs I grew up with. The prize, though, is the fireplace. I like sitting here in the winter with the dogs, having my dinner and watching the evening news in front of a blazing fire. In my opinion, it doesn't get any better than that. Now, having said that, my ex-wife hated this place. She did her best to get me to go all glass and shiny stainless steel and silk flowers, to which, of course, I said no. I don't have that wife anymore." He chuckled.

Maggie and Nikki nodded to show they agreed as Steven set out delicate cups both women knew were heirloom china along with cream and sugar. "I have some cookies, but I'm afraid they're store-bought?" It was more a question than a statement. Nikki and Maggie both shook their heads no.

The minute the coffee was poured and everyone was comfortable at the table, Steven looked at both women and said, "Talk to me. Tell me how I can help you."

"We're here about Major Andrew Nolan and his wife, Bella."

Steven looked perplexed. "Am I supposed to know Major Nolan and his wife, Bella? Were they customers? If so, I don't remember them. The names do not ring any kind of bells. Please, please tell me they aren't disgruntled customers."

Nikki's and Maggie's expressions went from shock to disbelief. "Seriously?" Nikki finally managed to gasp. "You really don't know them?"

"No! Why are you looking so surprised? Who are they? I repeat, please don't tell me they are past customers who are now unhappy with something they bought from me and now want to kill me because they don't like it after paying a small fortune for whatever it is they bought." Steven laughed at his own wit, but when neither woman joined in, he grew serious. "Suddenly, I'm not feeling so chipper. I think you had better explain things to me."

The sudden anxiety Steven was exhibiting made both women rush to explain their presence. Nikki took the lead.

"It's not you, Mr. Conover. It's about your ex-wife. Major Andy Nolan was her brother. He died some months ago. He was wounded in Iraq and sent here to Walter Reed hospital, where he died. He was married to Bella Ames, so she would be your ex-wife's sister-in-law. It seems that the military paid survivor benefits to your ex-wife, his sister, and not to his wife. Bella was told that his sister had his power of attorney. Major Nolan apparently did not notify the army about his married status before he died, so when your ex-wife presented herself as his sister, they paid her his military insurance.

"It was a rushed wedding during a two-day furlough, and we're sure that filling out paperwork was the last thing on his mind before he deployed. I'm sure the major had good intentions, but, for whatever reason, he didn't follow through. Another possibility, though, is that he asked his sister to do it for him since she had his power of attorney, and therein lies the problem."

"Can you add anything to that? We need to find Major Nolan's sister. According to the army, she took the money and disappeared. You never knew about the brother? I can't wrap my head around that somehow. Do you know where your ex-wife is, so we can straighten this out. Our client, the major's wife, has been left out in the cold here. That's just not right. We can't even go after the army because the sister obviously had all the paperwork in place and was able to collect not only his military insurance but whatever funds he had in his personal bank account. I'm not getting how," Maggie said, giving Conover the evil eye, "you know nothing about any of this. She was your wife, for crying out loud!"

Conover bristled at Maggie's tone and her words. "Hold on here. I met Sara at one of my shows in San Francisco. She bought a piece of mine, and we got to talking and hit it off. I saw her every day for the entire week of the show. By the end of the week, I was in love, and so was she. At least I believed so at the time. She said she was from Oklahoma, her parents were gone, and she had no other relatives. That statement alone made me want to jump in and protect her with my life. I talked her into coming back here to Baltimore with me. I didn't have to do a hard sell. She wanted to come. Two weeks later, we got married by a justice of the peace. Sara arranged the whole thing."

Nikki reared back and stared at Conover, who just glared at her. "She actually said she had no relatives."

Conover's hands fluttered in the air. "She

said she was all alone in the world now that her parents were gone. I had no reason to doubt her. Besides, I was hopelessly in love, and I admit it."

Maggie's tone was sour when she said, "But now you're divorced. What happened, if you don't mind telling us."

Conover got up and walked over to the counter to pour himself a second cup of coffee. He looked questioningly at Nikki and Maggie, who shook their heads.

Conover was back at the table, his eyes staring off into space. "The first year was pure magic. It was everything a guy could want plus more. I thought my life was perfect. Oh, we squabbled, but we always kissed and made up. Nothing serious. Sara did hate this kitchen, though, but she wasn't much of a cook, so it really didn't matter. I like to cook, so I didn't really mind. Sara never got a job once we moved here. She liked to sleep in, go out to lunch, shop, do all the girly things you women do. You know, facials, manicures, pedicures, that kind of thing. I indulged her because it made her happy, and if she was happy, then I was happy."

"What went wrong? You said the first year was wonderful. What happened in the second year and the third year?" Nikki asked.

Conover blinked as he knuckled his eyes. "I'm not sure. Whatever it was, it was subtle and just crept up on me. It started off with her going back and forth to Oklahoma to, as she put it, settle her parents' estate during the second year. She'd stay six weeks at a time. Here's the kicker, she'd call me almost every day, and I never knew and still do not know the name of the town where she lived. She referred to the town as a pimple on the butt of a monkey, explaining it was no place anyone wanted to live and that those who did live there couldn't wait to leave, just like she had. For some strange reason, that seemed to satisfy me.

"My business took off like a rocket. I was so busy I didn't have time to worry about Sara and her trips and how distant we'd become. I guess you could say the bloom was off the rose by then. The wild passion sort of went south. I was working seven days a week, sixteen, eighteen hours a day to complete my commissions. At night, I was exhausted and more often than not fell asleep in the recliner. Sex was not on my agenda. Sara said she didn't mind. When she was home, she'd spend her time reading or watching television. Thinking back, I was content. And stupid."

"What drove you apart in the end," Maggie asked, as she tried to get a mental fix on the man sitting across from her. She thought he was just what she was seeing, a really nice guy trying to get by who got taken by a fast-talking floozie. (She loved that term, *floozie*, and used it as often as she could. It was also one of Annie's favorite terms.)

"No one thing comes to mind. We drifted apart, I guess. The beginning of the third year, I had a trade show. Sara always loved to go to them, and she actually boosted my sales with her positive pitches on my behalf, but that year she didn't want to go. It was three days in Memphis and four days in Nashville, Tennessee. I thought she'd love it there, Nashville and all that, Sara loved country western music, but I was wrong. I was away for a whole week. We spoke at least once a day, though. Usually at night, to say good night and to talk about our day. When I got back home, she was gone. She left a note that said, *This is not working for me anymore*. She signed her name, and that was it. Oh, and she cleaned me out, took every last cent in our account and even forged my name and took the money out of my IRA and my 401K. Close to a million bucks. She left me forty bucks in my checking account, plus what I made at the trade show. That was all I had to my name. I never saw her again, never heard from her either until I received papers from an attorney notifying me that she had divorced me."

"How long ago was that?" Nikki asked.

"A year and a half ago."

Maggie chewed on her bottom lip as she struggled to come to terms with what Steven

Conover was telling her plus what she'd heard from Bella and the Sisters. None of this was adding up in her mind. She risked a glance at Nikki, who seemed to be struggling with the same thoughts.

"What did Sara do, if you don't mind my asking? Are you sure she has a brother?" Conover asked.

"Yes, I'm sure," Nikki said.

"Your ex-wife claimed Major Nolan's military benefits. Right now, we cannot prove that she knew that the major had gotten married or not. The wife, Bella, even though she married the major, didn't take the time to go over his background. All she knew was he was from Oklahoma, his parents were deceased, he had a sister who confiscated his share of his inheritance. He said her name was Sara. I'm starting to think she was not a blood sister. I think, and this is just a thought on my part, but I think the major's father was married and was either divorced or widowed when he married the major's mother, and Sara was his stepchild. Meaning the sister's mother died or she ran off and left the girl with the major's father. Far-fetched, but it does make sense. The major's parents were up in years, suggesting the mother gave birth to him late in life. We think Sara is older than Andy. Do you know how old she is now? Perhaps his first wife had a child, and Sara was that child. What name was she going by when you married her?" Maggie asked.

"Windsor, and she's thirty-one I'm two years older than she is. I can't believe this. Sara is a con artist!"

"And this surprises you . . . why?" Nikki asked. "You said she cleaned you out. That should have been a clue for you. I hate to say this, but she played you. Now, please, think. Do you have any idea how we can find her? Places she might go, people she knew, that kind of thing."

Steven Conover shook his head. His eyes were bright and shiny. *Unshed tears,* Maggie thought. She felt sorry for him and wanted to make things right but didn't quite know what to say. Nikki said it for her.

"Mr. Conover, sometimes . . . sometimes things just aren't what we want them to be. It's not a perfect world, and none of us are perfect. You said you had a wonderful, magical year. That's what you hang on to, what you remember, that memory. Time will take care of everything else if you let yourself be open to the world around you. Whatever is meant to be for you will happen. Right now, at this point in time, Sara Windsor is just someone you used to know. If I can, I'd like to make a suggestion. Go to the SPCA and save an animal. Make him or her yours. They will love you unconditionally.

"Now, having said that, perhaps you should get two animals so they have company for when you are working during the day," Nikki said. "What's two more dogs? Just two more to love."

"I have a cat named Hero. He was sitting outside my door one day during a rainstorm. I have to say he is the smartest cat I've ever seen. Keeping that cat was the smartest thing I've ever done in my life. I just love that cat, and when he nestles in my neck and purrs, I about go over the moon," Maggie said dreamily as she thought about Hero curled up on her pillow.

"My husband and I have a magnificent German shepherd that is the smartest dog on the planet. He can buckle his seat belt, answer the phone, fold towels, and make his own bed. I think I am capable of killing anyone who would even dare harm a hair on that dog's body. His name is Cyrus."

Nikki spoke so vehemently that Conover reared back. And then he grinned. "Okay, you sold me on getting another animal. Unfortunately, I can't help you in regard to where Sara is or who she might know. Now when I think back to those days, I see how blind I was. I wish I could help you. If I think of anything, how can I get in touch with you?"

Maggie fished around in her backpack and pulled out a business card. She wrote her cell phone number as well as Nikki's on the back. "Call day or night, we'll always answer."

Conover accepted the card, walked over to the refrigerator, and slipped the business card under a magnet of an alligator showing off its monster teeth. "Sara got this magnet, why I don't know." He looked at it, then tossed it in the trash can next to the sink. The business card went under a magnet of purple tulips with a yellow butterfly perched on one of the petals. He laughed out loud. Maggie and Nikki smiled. Steven Conover really was a nice guy.

"I'm sorry to hear about that guy, Major Nolan. I'd like to meet his wife someday if that's possible."

"Oh, I think it is. We'll suggest it to her when we get back to town. I bet she shows up at your showroom one of these days. You'll like her. She's very down-to-earth. Nothing pretentious to her, and she is absolutely going to go over the moon when she sees this kitchen and all these dogs. She's from Kansas. Who knows what will happen from that point on," Maggie said, giggling.

"Thank you for your time, Mr. Conover. Please, if you think of anything, call one of us. We really need to find Sara Windsor. Maybe I should say Conover. I'm thinking the con in her would have her take back her maiden name, or she'd get a new name altogether. We'll find out sooner or later. Thanks for the coffee," Nikki said.

"My pleasure. I'm just sorry I wasn't more help. Not to worry, I will call if I think of anything. I'll show you out."

In the van with the engine running, Maggie threw her hands in the air. "I was so hoping he'd be able to help us. Nice guy. That chick must be really nasty to steal from her brother, then clean out the husband like that. He's well rid of her if you want my opinion."

"Just drive, Maggie. I want to get home so I can think. I need to be around my stuff when I have serious thinking to do. People don't just disappear. We need to find her."

"Before you go all silent on me, we need to find out what Sara did to earn a living before she met Steven. I know he said she didn't work when they were married, but she must have had a job of some kind unless she had a sugar daddy or something. Call Conover and ask. Knowing what she did to earn a living might help us find her more quickly. I'm thinking that, in the end, we're going to have to turn this over to Avery Snowden. Finding the impossible person is his forte."

Nikki worked her phone, talked quickly, grimaced as she listened, then ended the call. "Nothing much, Maggie. She sold cosmetics in a department store, worked as a cocktail waitress in some girly bar. She also sold time shares to condos, and that's what she was doing when he met her. He also said she had expensive clothes and jewelry, drove a really nice Jaguar, and always seemed to have a lot of money. He said he was stupid and just thought she was really good at selling the time shares. Can I go silent now?"

"Okay," Maggie said agreeably. She, too, needed to think.

Chapter 9

Annie scowled as she paced Myra's spacious kitchen. She muttered to herself, then looked at Myra. "We have not accomplished one damn thing in the last four days. All we've been doing is running around like a bunch of wild chickens. We have absolutely nothing to show for ninety-six hours of our time. Multiply that by the seven of us and the number will blow your mind. And"—she paused dramatically, throwing her hands in the air—"that doesn't count Avery Snowden and all his manpower. What's wrong with this picture?" she screeched. Annie's tirade was unlike anything the Sisters had ever seen. They stopped whatever they were doing and stopped speaking, not knowing what to do.

Myra flinched. She hated when Annie got like this. The only thing that would appease her was something positive in the way of news. And good news of any kind was the one thing they did not have. She looked around at the glum faces of the Sisters seated at the table. "Let's do a recap of what we've done in the last four days. We might have missed something the first time around. By the way, Bella called this morning before you all got here. She was, as she put it, wondering why she hadn't heard from any of us. She more or less implied that she was disappointed in us. Us as in the Vigilantes. I think she was expecting instant gratification. I could hear the disappointment in her voice. I told her Rome wasn't built in a day, and these things take time and planning, and a healthy dose of luck doesn't hurt. She didn't sound to me like she was buying what I had to sell."

"It is what it is," Yoko said philosophically.

Nikki held up the coffee carafe. Everyone nodded that they wanted a refill. Nikki poured, as Annie finally stopped her frantic pacing. She sat down at the table, held up her cup, and waited.

"Who wants to go first?" Myra asked.

"Me and Yoko," Kathryn said, raising her hand as though she was in a third-grade classroom. "There wasn't one likable person in the bunch that we talked to at the clinic. Maintaining and running a fertility clinic like that must be stressful. Everyone seemed antsy and jittery. I didn't see a smile on anyone. Yoko and I both agreed they're a bunch of snooty women. But Dr. Peabody had a high snoot factor, too, and he's a guy. As far as we could tell, he is the only male doctor, but there is one male nurse. The good doctors Donaldson, Petre, and Peabody are just what they are. The only thing we could tell that they're guilty of is not checking more thoroughly when Major Nolan's sister showed up. They showed us many requests that were on the books of women who transferred their eggs to another fertility clinic for a variety of reasons; relocation seemed to be the main one.

"Dr. Peabody said there is a procedure that has to be adhered to. One minute, they were there, then they were gone, all properly signed off on. As far as they were concerned, that was the end of the story. Until now. They are petrified of a lawsuit. It was written all over their faces. It would be a hot mess if it ever got to court. I can tell you that, and I'm not even a lawyer," Kathryn said.

Yoko looked around at the faces of the other Sisters. "Kathryn and I opted to go in as ourselves. We simply said we represented Bella and hoped to resolve the case and absolve the clinic. I thought they were as forthright as they could be under the circumstances. All of them, in our opinion, realized they are looking down the wrong end of a lawsuit, and ignorance or negligence is no defense. They must have talked to their lawyers and been told that."

"They are now aware of Major Nolan's sperm donations but were not at the time when the sister did the transfer. It is not known for certain if the sister even knew about those donations. Dr. Peabody gave us the name of the clinic to which the eggs were transferred. It's in Bethesda, Maryland. Yoko and I went there. Of course, we didn't learn a thing—the privacy act and all that."

"We waited outside at lunchtime and nailed the first person we could who looked bribable, and offered five hundred dollars if she could tell us about the major's sister. She agreed; then we met up two hours later on her break. She said more than a dozen new clients made deposits during the time period in question. No one with the name Nolan, or Conover, or Windsor is on file. That doesn't mean the sister used her real name, she could have used an alias, which I would be willing to bet is just what she did. It is certainly what I would have done in her shoes.

"We did learn one more thing, though. The young woman we bribed was a little chatty. She said an egg, as in one egg, could go for as high as $50,000. Sometimes more. The norm is $25,000, at least at her clinic. She said the bigger the clinic, the more prestigious the clinic, the starting price is $100,000 if the owner wants to sell them. She said there is one woman who became a millionaire doing just that. That, to me, is just wrong. I don't know why, but it just seems . . . wrong for some reason," Yoko said. It was hard to mistake the anger in her voice.

The Sisters batted that summary around for a few minutes. The end result was they all agreed with Yoko, it felt wrong, but people were people and for many, money was the name of the game. No one was breaking any laws except Sara whatever name she was going by at the time.

"You're up, Isabelle," Annie said.

Isabelle grimaced. "You aren't going to believe this! I found the sister's social security numbers. That's as in plural. She has, like, a dozen. Actually, eleven. With different names. I had to . . . um . . . ask Abner's friend Phil for some help. He went on the dark web, someplace Abner will not allow me to go, and he came up with the information for me. She has a number for the name Nolan, her married name Conover, and the very first one ever issued is in the name of Sara Marie Windsor, so I guess that is the name she was given when she was born.

"She has eight aliases and a social security number to go with each. And there are a dozen more identities that are in process. I have the list on my computer. She was a very busy lady, that's for sure. So far I have not been able to hack into her brokerage accounts or her bank accounts. I don't know whether she doesn't have any or she's managed to get a super-duper identity I haven't dug up yet. Plain and simple, the woman is a con artist. None of the addresses attached to the alias social security numbers are residential. Some are stores, one is a church, and one is a baseball field, that kind of thing. She covered her tracks really well. I'm still working on it. Just remember, I'm not Abner or Phil. I'm a hacker in training."

"We'll take that into consideration, dear," Myra said. "What you did manage to get is remarkable and more than we had starting out. Just do your best."

"I have nothing to report other than my red bag has now been replenished. I feel confident in saying that if anything crops up, I can handle it. I'm free now if you need me to do anything," Alexis said.

Maggie looked up. "Is it my turn?" Not bothering to wait for a response, she rattled on. "I don't have much. That chick was really good at covering her tracks, that's for sure. Right now, I am perusing her high-school yearbook and trying to see if any of her classmates are on Facebook. I have sent dozens of queries, but so far, no one is getting back to me. What I do know is she has not attended a single class reunion. That's high school. As far as I can tell, the major's sister did not go to college."

"Keep at it, dear. Eventually, something will turn up. I guess that leaves Annie and me to report in. Annie, do you want to do the honors?" Myra asked.

"Happy to, Myra. First of all, I want to say Walter Reed is an amazing hospital. It's also a very sad place. Myra and I spoke to the major's nurse, his doctors, a few of the volunteers, and several patients who knew Major Nolan. We were both convinced there was no negligence or anything like that with his care. Everything was top-notch. He had the best of the best. It just . . . it just wasn't meant to be," Annie said, a catch in her voice. "His nurse, Lieutenant Gibson, said she spent every available moment she could with him. She said they prayed together, and they cried together. Her only regret was that she didn't press him more on his background. She said when she did, he got agitated, and that was not good for him, so she just kept the conversation neutral. She did say that he only had kind, loving words for his parents. When the conversation turned to his sister, he got agitated. No details. And then the confession about his wife."

"Confession? That's a strange way to put it, isn't it?" Nikki said.

"That's what we thought. And I mentioned just that to Lieutenant Gibson, and she said it was because she asked him who had his power of attorney and he said his sister, but then he said his wife, that he changed it at the last minute and his friend took care of things for him because he was being deployed, and it cut the time too close. That was the first Lieutenant Gibson knew about his being married. The nurse who took care of him when he had first arrived at Walter Reed transferred out three days after Major Nolan's arrival, and Lieutenant Gibson took over. The original nurse might have known, but Lieutenant Gibson wasn't sure. If that was the case, then Major Nolan wouldn't want to repeat it all over again. At least that was what Lieutenant Gibson thought. In the military, I'm told," Annie said, "if you deploy, you need to designate someone to handle your affairs, hence the POA."

The girls looked at one another, understanding perfectly. Murphy's Law. What could go wrong did go wrong. Period. End of story.

Eight cell phones dinged at the same time. A text was coming in to all eight phones. The only person who could make that happen would be Avery Snowden.

Annie read the text out loud as the Sisters followed her every word.

"'Hit a stone wall. Major Nolan's parents resided in a retirement community, and these people will not look at me or my people, much less talk to us. Annie and Myra, you're up. You'll fit right in here, and these people will talk to you. I'm sure of it. Gas up that plane and get here as soon as you can. In the meantime, I am scouring the town for people who still live here who might have known the major or his sister. We are staying at the Commodore Hotel on Evergreen Avenue. Directions to follow.'"

Annie was on her phone. "Like right now, Peter," she said to the pilot. "Wheels up in sixty minutes. Tulsa, Oklahoma," she responded, when he asked for a destination so he could file a flight plan.

"Shake it, Myra!"

"Annie! Wait! I have to change my clothes, pack a bag. Hold on here."

Annie stopped in her tracks and whirled around. "Do you have your pearls on?"

"Of course. What a silly question."

"Then move your ass, Myra. That's all you need. We're burning fuel just standing here."

Myra spun around to look at the Sisters. Her expression said it all when the girls gave her a thumbs-up and made shooing motions with their hands. Myra galloped after Annie, yelling for her to slow down. Annie ignored her. Myra ran as fast as her arthritic knees would permit.

* * *

"Well, we're here," Annie said.

It was late afternoon when the Uber driver came to a stop at the gate leading into Lakemore Estates, the senior living enclave where Major Nolan's parents had once lived. Avery Snowden said they were to say they were going to the real-estate office on the property. Otherwise, they wouldn't be permitted to enter. Once inside, he said they were to drive to 74 Winchester Terrace, where Maddie and Henry Olsen lived. The Olsens had been good friends with the Nolans before they died. They did as Avery had instructed, and the guard at the gate waved them through.

"Avery is worth every penny we pay him, doncha agree, Myra? That was a piece of cake."

Myra simply nodded. Annie was on a roll, she could feel it.

A half mile down the winding brick road, the Uber vehicle slowed and pulled onto a brick-paved driveway that matched the road. A bright red Honda Civic sat in the driveway. The Uber driver handed Myra his business card and told her to call him when they were ready to leave and said if he wasn't on another ride, he would come and pick them up. Myra nodded and pocketed the business card.

Both women looked around. "Everything is so . . . so neat. Trimmed, brushed, washed, whatever. The flowers in the mini flower beds look like they'd been placed in the ground with precision. Possibly a ruler to measure the distance between each bloom, and each house appears to have a color scheme. I could never live here, Myra. It's like . . . almost too perfect. It reminds me of a set on a movie or something," Annie griped.

A dog barked down the street and an echoing response could be heard coming from another dog. She wondered if they were dog friends. Such a silly thought. Annie shrugged as she followed Myra up the walkway to a front porch with a bright yellow door with a eucalyptus wreath on it.

Myra rang the doorbell and fingered her pearls. Why was she so antsy, so jittery? So they schemed their way inside this enclave. So what? It wasn't like they were criminals, and they really did have a good reason for being here. They had done worse things than this in the past. Maybe it had something to do with the aging process.

She shook her head to clear her thoughts. Lately, she'd spent way too much time thinking about growing older. She gave herself another mental shake. She just hoped the Olsens were understanding people.

Both women looked around at the neat, tidy porch with the baskets of colorful fall flowers. They looked lush and healthy, not a yellow leaf to be seen. A mister went off on the far end of the porch with a soft hissing sound just as the dog down the street barked again. An answering rejoinder could be heard. "I sure hope this is not one of those Stepford towns," Annie hissed, "because that's how it is starting to feel to me. Something about this place bothers me."

Myra was about to make a comment, but the door opened to reveal a man and a woman standing side by side. They were holding hands. She deliberately did not look at Annie, who she knew was just itching to pull out her gun and shoot the hand-holding couple. "Mr. and Mrs. Olsen, my name is Myra Rutledge, my friend standing next to me is Anna de Silva. Countess Anna de Silva," Myra clarified. "We're here to talk to you about an old neighbor of yours, Andy Nolan. His widow Bella asked that we come here. We need some information on the family, so we can help her. We're hoping you can help us do that." She waited expectantly for the couple's response.

"How did you get in here?" the tall, bearded man barked, ignoring Myra's plea.

Anticipating that this little talk was going to go south rather quickly by Olsen's tone of voice, Annie snapped, "How do you think? We lied." And then a devil perched itself on Annie's shoulders. "By the way, my friend and myself also have another name we respond to. Try this on for size, the Vigilantes!" She reached behind her and whipped out what she lovingly called her six-shooter. She looked Mrs. Olsen square in the eye as she made her declaration.

The screen door whipped open so quickly that Myra and Annie almost toppled over. "Lord have mercy!" Mrs. Olsen exclaimed. "I've been waiting all my life to meet you ladies. You come right on in here and pay no mind to my husband. He loved Andy Nolan like he was his own son. He's just being protective of that young man. I loved him, too. We, both of us, about laid down and died when we heard what happened to him. Why it had to be Andy and not Sara is a mystery to me. I know, I know that is not nice of me, being a Christian and all, but I can't help it. And I will not apologize, either. That girl was a bad seed. Still is, I'm sure. You all just follow me into the parlor, and we can talk there. Mercy, I cannot believe this. My bingo partners are simply not going to believe this. No sirree, they are not. Can I get you something to drink before we . . . what's the term . . . get grilled? Henry, are you getting this? We're being grilled by the Vigilantes. Such an honor! I am just so beside myself. Does it show?"

Annie laughed. "Just a little. We're good," she said. She was still holding the gun and she stroked it as she eyed Henry Olsen, who was looking everywhere but at Annie.

Myra nodded. "First, let me explain why we're here and about Andy's young widow. As I said, we're here at her behest." Both Olsens nodded and listened intently as Myra shared what she and Annie knew, and what they now needed to find out. "Tell us what you can about Andy's parents."

Surprisingly, it was Henry Olsen who took the lead, but first he looked at Annie and apologized for what he called his bad attitude. Annie graciously nodded that she was okay with his apology. However, she did not return her six-shooter to the small of her back. She continued to stroke the shiny metal as she listened to him speak, almost reverently, of the Nolans.

"Maddie and I were friends and neighbors with the Nolans for thirty years. Seems like we knew them all our lives. Dan had just married Sonia when they moved next door to us. We were all young back then. Dan had been married very young to a lovely young lady who was killed by a drunk driver. Sonia was his second wife. The first wife, her name was Melanie, had a two-year-old daughter from a previous marriage. That husband wanted nothing to do with a two-year-old little girl, so Dan took her in. To this day, Maddie does not believe that Dan legally adopted Sara. Speaking for myself, I was never quite sure if he did or didn't. I think Dan thought if he said he was Sara's dad, then he was her dad. End of story right there."

"The Nolans were as poor as we were back then," Maddie said. "There would not have been any money for lawyers, and Dan was still paying for his first wife's funeral on time payments," Maddie volunteered.

"When Sara started school, she used the name Nolan. But somewhere over the years I heard, and it wasn't from the Nolans that I heard it, that Sara started using the name Windsor. It was none of our business, so we never asked them about it," Henry said.

"A year after they moved in next door to us, Sonia, Andy's mother, got pregnant, and so did I. We became even closer then. I had a baby girl, and Sonia gave birth to Andy. The children were born just a month apart. We all hoped the two of them would grow up to become a couple. That never happened," Maddie said wistfully.

"Next spring, Maddie and I are going to take a road trip to Washington, D.C., and we plan to go to Arlington Cemetery. We'll take some flowers for Andy's grave, if it's allowed. If not, we'll go, kneel, and say some prayers. I think Sonia and Dan would like us to do that. I know they'd do it for us if the situation were reversed," Henry said.

"We need to know about the daughter, Sara. What we've heard so far is not good," Myra said.

"A bad seed, that one. I know I keep saying that, but there's no other way to describe that girl. Well, she wasn't a girl anymore, a young lady I guess," Henry said ominously. "She hated young Andy with a passion, always trying to get him in trouble. She'd lie, cheat, steal. Like I said, a bad seed. Sonia was at her wits' end. Dan . . . he just couldn't control her, so she ran amuck and pretty much did what she wanted to do. She was never held accountable for anything. Wild and uncontrollable. Even knowing all that, young Andy adored her. He often told me she was the prettiest girl in school. He told me when he came back here before deploying the first time that he had given her his power of attorney. We wanted to tell him that was a mistake, but we didn't. Now I regret not doing that every day," Henry said.

"Who died first, Mr. or Mrs. Nolan?" Annie asked.

"They both died in a tragic bus accident at the same time. The root cause was a tornado that sprang up out of nowhere that day. Maddie and I were supposed to go on the senior bus trip with them, but we both came down with the flu. The trip was to Las Vegas. A big truck, one of those eighteen-wheelers, lost control, crossed the lane, and smacked head-first into the bus. Everyone on board died, and so did the bus driver. It was just awful," Henry said. "They found the bus and the bodies strewn everywhere along that highway after it was all over. It was in all the papers and on television for weeks. Maddie and I, sick as we were, had time to get to our shelter in the basement.

Months later, we saw on the news that the truck driver had suffered a heart attack at the wheel at the same time. Maddie cried for weeks, and I cried right along with her. Sara now, I never saw her shed even one tear. That's not to say she didn't. We just never *saw* a tear, I guess, is what I'm trying to say." His tone of voice was as sour as lemon juice.

"I called the army to let them know so Andy could come home to the funeral. It took a whole bunch of time because he was over there in Iraq." He pronounced it, I-RAK. "By the time he got here, his parents had been buried. Sara saw to that. She wanted them in the ground lickety-split, and there was no one to oppose her. That boy cried his heart out to us. He was here less than thirty-six hours, and he had to leave again. He said he left everything in Sara's hands," Henry said.

"Quicker than lightning, Sara put the house up for sale, and it sold quickly. She got a pretty penny for it, too. In other words, she got the inflated asking price because Dan kept the house updated and in good shape. Sonia had just gotten a new kitchen, too. All beautiful cherrywood. That helped raise the price Sara got for the property."

"How much did the house sell for?" Annie asked.

"It was $389,000. And she didn't use a broker, just put a sign in the yard. That was all clear money, and there was no mortgage on the house. Andy should have gotten half of that, but he told Maddie in an e-mail all the way from I-RAK that Sara said she made some bad investments and lost it all. By rights, if she was never legally adopted, and we think she knew that for years, she was not entitled to anything from the Nolan estate. As far as we know, neither Sonia nor Dan left a will. Since Andy is the only biological son, he should have gotten everything. Sara sold both their cars, too, and kept the money. We think she got close to maybe $17,000 or $18,000 total for both cars. Like everything else, Dan was the one who kept them maintained. Whoever bought them got a good deal. Andy didn't get any of that money, either. He excused it all by saying Sara was a novice at investing and she was just trying to double the money so they would have more to divide."

Myra and Annie both blinked at the disgust and downright hatred they were hearing in the older man's voice.

"Bella, his widow, told us Sara got his insurance money, and I guess she also cleared out his bank account. Nothing illegal about any of it. The major had given his sister his POA," Annie said. "Bella was left with nothing. We'd like to find Sara and perhaps explain to her that she needs to make things right with her brother's widow."

"That's the thing, though, ladies. Sara is not

Andy's sister. She was no relation at all to Andy. I don't see the young widow having any rights here. Andy was of sound mind when he gave her his power of attorney. While we might not like what Sara's done, and even though she is not a blood relative, she did not do anything illegal. Underhanded, yes. I don't know what you think you can do to make it right?" Henry Olsen said.

"By the way," Maddie interjected, "a month or so after . . . after our dear friends passed, Henry and I went to the courthouse and searched the family-court records to see if we could establish that Sara was adopted. The people there were really nice and helped us. We couldn't find a thing. We even had Sara's social security number because Andy gave it to us. Well . . . he didn't exactly give it to us, what he did was he showed us some paper in regard to the house, and Sara's name and social security number were on it. I said I had to get my glasses to read it and walked over to the desk and copied it down. I don't even know why I did it. Something just told me to do it. Would you like it?" Both Myra and Annie nodded. Maddie scampered over to a tiny corner desk and a minute later returned with a sticky note with Sara's social security number.

Annie and Myra just smiled. They were happy they could confirm the information they already had.

"You just shush now, Henry. These fine ladies know what they're doing, and while we wouldn't or couldn't do anything, they can because of who they are. Ladies, you have my blessing, and Henry's, too."

"Do you know how we can locate Sara. We've already talked to her ex-husband, a famous sculptor who lives in Baltimore."

"Sara was married!" the Olsens said in unison. They looked shocked to their core at the news.

"Yes, to a man named Steven Conover. He does beautiful work. The marriage only lasted three years. Sara left him and took all his money, and other than receiving papers indicating that she had divorced him, he has not heard from her since she walked out with his money. He claims he has no clue where his ex-wife might be, and we believe him.

"We thought she might have come back here to Oklahoma. To the home base, where she grew up and was comfortable knowing Steven wouldn't follow her. In fact, he said he did not even know the name of the town here in Oklahoma where she lived. He excused it all by saying he was in love. Bella, Andy's widow, did and acted the same way. Being in love seems to be the standard go-to answer for everything that didn't work out. And that's why we're here," Myra said.

"I'm taking the fact that you didn't know

Sara was married to mean you also don't know anything else about her," Annie said.

"That's as true a statement as any I could come up with. We never knew any of Sara's friends. As far as we know, she never brought any home. Sonia said she thought it strange, but then she said, and Henry and I don't know how she found out, but she told us Sara was hanging with a rough crowd, motorcycle people with tattoos and piercings, things like that.

"Dan never said a bad word about the girl. That always bothered Sonia because she was a tad jealous of Dan's first wife and Sara being her child and all," Maddie said.

"Do you know if any of Andy's friends from the early days are still around?" Annie asked.

"I do know the answer to that, and it's no. Andy only had a few friends, and they scattered across the country. Andy said in one of his rare e-mails to us that he tried to track down some people named Lynus and Zack, but he couldn't find them. Do you ladies know how to work Facebook? Maybe Sara uses it. We don't do social media. I can see Sara using it. Most young people do today. Henry and I are old-fashioned," Maddie said primly.

"What's going to happen now?" Henry asked.

"I don't honestly know, Henry. We're going to try to find Sara. Right now, that is our top priority. We can't do anything for Major Nolan except try to make things right for his young widow," Annie said. She debated saying something about the fertility clinic for a moment but changed her mind. Some things were just better left unsaid.

"I'm sorry we couldn't be of more help. But we're glad you stopped by. We don't see many people around here. Sonia and Dan were our only real friends. People who live in this community are not what you would call friendly. Everyone minds their own business, and no one joins anything. Activities are nonexistent. So it's nice to have company once in a while. I wish, though, it was under other circumstances. If you like, Henry and I will try to see if we can find out anything that might help you. We have all the time in the world to do whatever will help you. If you give us an e-mail address or phone number where we can reach you, that would help," Maddie said. "And don't you worry for even one little minute, your secret is safe with us, ladies."

Myra and Annie nodded as Annie rattled off their cell phone numbers and Myra's e-mail. Maddie dutifully copied them down in a tight script.

The goodbyes were quick, with Annie expounding away about how people took thirty minutes to say goodbye when all the other person wanted was to be on their way. When Annie said goodbye it was goodbye, and that was the end of it; and she never looked back, either.

Myra called the number on the card the Uber driver had given them. He said he would pick them up in eleven minutes.

To pass the time Annie suggested a walk around the block, but then changed her mind, and said, "Let's just walk up to the corner. This place depresses me. So we're going to the Commodore Hotel to meet up with Avery, is that right?"

Myra said it was.

"Are we staying overnight or flying back home? I need to call Peter and let him know."

Myra shrugged. "I'm okay either way. I'm sure we can buy whatever we need in one of the shops in the hotel if we stay over. Seriously, though, Annie, I doubt we can accomplish anything here that Avery can't with his people. The Olsens pretty much summed it up. Sara left, and we got all there was to get of the back story, so I'm thinking we should meet Avery, share what we have, and head home. We can probably do more from our home base, anyway."

"That works for me, and I agree with you for a change." Annie laughed. "Here comes our ride, right on time. How do they do that, get it to the minute like that?" Annie fretted. "He said eleven minutes, and it is exactly eleven minutes."

"You know what, Annie. I don't know the answer, nor do I care. Do you really care?"

"I-do-not!" Annie linked her arm with Myra's. "Don't ever change, Myra," she said, opening the door of the Uber car.

"I won't if you won't." Myra giggled as she slid into the back seat, Annie right behind her.

"Please take us to the Commodore Hotel."

"Sure thing, ladies."

Chapter 10

Nina Lofton, aka Sara Windsor Nolan Santiago Bernard Conover, exited the main terminal, dragging the designer suitcase that cost more than her airline ticket from Reagan National Airport in Washington, D.C., to Tulsa International Airport. She exited the main terminal, looked around to get her bearings, and walked over to a line for Uber pickups. She took her place behind two casually dressed older women. She heard them call each other by name. Myra and Annie. Old-fashioned names, she thought to herself. They looked pleasant. Even motherly.

She missed not having a mother. Once, she was told, she had a real mother. Then, when she was older, she was told that her mother, her real mother, had died, and she was going to get a new mother whose name was Sonia. She had someone she was supposed to call Dad, but he wasn't a real dad, either. Just two people whom she lived with. She worked hard at not calling either one Mom or Dad. For some reason, she just couldn't get her tongue to work to say the words. In her mind and in her thoughts, she called them Sonia and Dan. She hated both of them even more than she hated a two-headed snake. But she had endured because of . . . because of . . . Andy.

Those people, Sonia and Dan, said Andy was her brother. It was a lie. She didn't have a brother, just like she didn't have a mom or a dad. Andy was theirs. Andy belonged. She didn't belong. She wasn't theirs. She was just tolerated. She hated that they thought she was too stupid to figure it all out. Wasn't it Plato who said, "Wise men speak because they have something to say; fools speak because they have to say something"?

She, Sara Windsor, fell in love with Andy Nolan when she was seven years old and tasked with watching over her three-year-old little brother who really wasn't her brother, little or otherwise.

Andy adored her, that much she knew. It was hard not to smile and laugh with him. She had fun playing with him, reading him stories, and pretending to be the characters she was reading about. But she did all of that out of sight of Sonia and Dan. What feelings she had for Andy were private, even way back when she was a little girl who was wise beyond her years. Of course, she didn't know that then, though she came to know it with each passing year. She wondered how that had happened because it was such a long time ago. Where did those smarts come from? Her real mother maybe. It made her feel good to think that.

A gust of wind whipped through the tunnel-like area where she was standing with the line of people who were all grumbling about the lack of, and the slowness of, the Ubers they'd all called for.

The two ladies in front of her seemed to be the loudest, calling each other by name. "We should have taken Henry Olsen up on his offer to drive us to the hotel," the one named Annie said. The one named Myra shaded her eyes against the October sun and squinted down the road. "I think you're right. I think this was an exercise in futility. What did we even really learn?"

Annie poked her friend in the arm and hissed, "Check out those shoes on the woman behind us. Louboutins, and that pair goes for nine hundred bucks. Saw them in Neiman Marcus. I wonder if she's trying to match that red hair she's sporting. You can tell it comes out of a bottle," Annie sniffed.

Myra shrugged to show she wasn't interested in the woman's red shoes or her red hair. "We should have stayed home and let Avery handle this. No one knows anything about Sara Nolan or Sara Windsor or Sara Conover or whatever name she is using at the moment."

Nina Lofton almost fell out of her red stilettoes at the mention of her name by two strangers standing right in front of her. She did a double take, then backed up carefully, a step at a time, so as not to call undue attention to herself, and ran as fast as her spike-heeled shoes could carry her back into the airport, where she called a number she knew from memory for a car service. She walked over to the service exit and waited, her foot tapping the concrete floor, her guts churning. Weird things happened to her all the time, but this was definitely one of the weirdest things ever. Here she was, standing in a line waiting for an Uber and thinking about Andy Nolan, and two women she'd never seen in her life were talking about her. Her! She told herself that was about as weird as it could get. Why? Who were they? Why did they mention Sonia and Dan's best friends, Maddie and Henry Olsen. Andy called them aunt and uncle, but they weren't blood relatives. She never called them anything but the Olsens.

Sara leaned against the wall and closed her eyes while she waited for the car service she'd called. Andy's dear sweet face swam behind her closed eyelids. Andy made her life bearable. Andy always knew just the right thing to say to her, knew when to give her a quick hug or take her hand in his. Once he'd kissed her tears away. If she lived to be a hundred years old, nothing would ever compare to that one minute of time in her young life. Instantly, things in her little world were made right when he was in her line of sight or near her. She questioned how that could be when Andy was four years younger, and everyone knew girls matured faster and more quickly than boys. She told herself whoever had made that observation didn't know Andy Nolan.

They told each other secrets, and as far as she knew, Andy never divulged anything she ever told him. And she'd never told anyone anything he'd confided to her. In the end, who would she tell, certainly not the Olsens or Sonia and Dan, and she had no friends to speak of. Andy Nolan was her only friend. And she was okay with that.

Until . . . until Andy discovered girls. More to the point, when girls discovered Andy Nolan. Girls flocked to him because he was sweet and cute. Sweet and cute grew into handsome, and from handsome he went to drop-dead gorgeous, and then it was look-out-world-here-comes-Andy-Nolan! He took it all in stride and didn't get serious about the adoration or admiration. Football was serious, getting ready for college was serious, and going into the military was serious. He didn't want baggage, and girls, he'd told Sonia, were baggage. In a good way. He went on to say when he left to make his way in the big, wide world, he didn't want to be encumbered in any way except by Sara because she was his big sister and he loved her. Like a sister.

Those three words were like a knife in Sara's heart. That's when she knew for certain there would be no future for her with Andy in her life. And Andy was oblivious to her feelings, which made it hurt all the more.

When it was time for college, she elected to go to the community college so she could still stay in the Nolan home while Andy finished four years of high school. When Andy was accepted to the university of his choice in California, she packed up and left with him. She used all her wiles to convince him she needed to be there so he could have what he called a big sis to talk to.

She made a joke out of flying the coop, and Andy had laughed and said he was secretly glad she was going to go with him because he was afraid of being homesick because he'd never been out of Tulsa, not to say the state of Oklahoma. Nor had Sara, so that made them even closer in Andy's eyes.

As for Sara, she simply could not imagine her life without Andy close by. No way. She counted the minutes until Andy would get out of class so they could talk or grab a burger someplace. Just telling each other about the hours they had spent apart.

Sara knew and dreaded the day when Andy would start bringing college coeds to meet her. She'd be Miss Nice Lovely Big Sis to them, and later, when she was alone with him, she'd pick the coed to pieces and Andy would then move on to the next girl. Just the thought of Andy kissing a girl and maybe . . . just maybe . . . doing other things with her made her violently ill. So ill she would throw up. Andy Nolan was hers. Andy Nolan belonged to her. And no one was going to take him away from her. *No one!*

Sara's life revolved around Andy. People always commented on how close the brother and sister were. She always beamed with pleasure. Andy just . . . what Andy did was stare into space at their comments. She never did figure that out. She worked two part-time jobs so she could have free time on Andy's schedule. She told him she was taking night classes, but it was a lie. He said he was so very proud of her. She remembered how she'd about gone into orbit at his praise.

He, in the meantime, was easily pulling down a GPA of 4.0. Andy was incredibly smart. He constantly joked that he was going to leave her flat and go to England to attend the London School of Economics. Then he laughed and so would she because they both knew it would never happen. Because, as Andy put it, it rained all the time in England, and he hated rain. He liked sunny, warm days. He was going to live forever in the sunshine state of California.

Weeks, months, years passed, with Andy completing his college education in three years and one month. He immediately signed up for the military, enlisting in the army.

Boot camp. Six weeks of nothing. Then OCS on the horizon. Sara wanted to lie down and die right then and there. How could she exist for six weeks without seeing or talking to Andy? How?

Sara had to stay behind. Communication between the two of them dropped to nonexistent. She stayed in bed for days at a time. She couldn't cope. She literally could not function. Sometimes, she didn't eat for days. She lost weight. She started to think she might die.

Then, suddenly, the magic began. Five weeks into boot camp, Andy found a way to call her on the phone. His voice was hoarse, choked up when he said how hard boot camp was, but he was going to make it because he was determined. The word *failure* was not in his vocabulary. A career in the military was something he hungered for, and he wasn't about to give it up. He said he just worked harder, doubled down, and made it all happen. He told her how much he missed her. The reason for the call was to ask her if he could bunk with her for a few days before he headed back to Tulsa to see his mom and dad before being shipped out to God only knows where because suddenly he wasn't sure about Officer Candidate School. She remembered how she had literally swooned at his request.

Her response was, "Yes, yes, yes, a thousand times yes." Andy made a smacking sound with his lips and she did the same before she hung up. Long-distance kisses. If only she could experience the real thing. If only.

Sara bounded out of bed as though her feet were spring loaded. She had her life back. She headed for the refrigerator and ate everything edible that didn't have something mysterious growing on it. Then she showered and washed her hair. After that, she cleaned her tiny apartment from top to bottom and ran to the store to buy more food. She needed energy and stamina.

She went back to bed and slept deeply for six straight hours. A wonderful, restful, happy sleep. She woke full of spit and vinegar, ready to take on the whole world.

Andy Nolan was coming home!

Sara shook her head to clear her thoughts. She cleared her throat and wiped at her eyes. She knew Bella's last name. Ames. She'd find a way to locate her through her driver's license. Or hire a private detective.

Sara stepped through the door when she saw the town car pull up to the side door of the

Tulsa International Airport, where she was waiting. She gave the driver the address of the Commodore Hotel on Evergreen Avenue. She was here for two days; then she was heading back to Virginia. Finally, she would be free of the Nolans once and for all. Just one more meeting with their lawyers, sign another batch of papers, accept the generous check, and she was done with this hateful place. She made a promise to herself never to return. This place, this entire state, was going to be erased from her memory.

Sara stared out the side window as the driver skillfully steered the town car past the line of Ubers waiting to pick up their fares. She spotted the two ladies ahead of her in line who had been talking about her. Who were they? Why were they here? she wondered.

She felt frazzled now, out of sorts. When she got like this, she knew she had to find a quiet place, a place with a Zen-like atmosphere, where she could zone out and think and project. For some reason, she felt frightened, uneasy. The last time she'd felt like this, she'd been eight years old. She knew she needed to find that space as soon as possible before she lost control.

Annie looked over at Myra just as she stepped into the waiting Uber. "I think this is a big mistake. What's wrong with the two of us? We don't seem to be able to make up our minds about anything since we got here. I thought we came to the airport to get on my plane to go back to Pinewood after deciding not to go to the hotel. I even called Peter. Then we decided to go to the hotel instead to talk to Avery Snowden. What we know, which is not all that much, we can tell him in a phone call. I think we should go to the plane and head home. What do you think?"

"I'm okay with that, Annie. I was more or less thinking the same thing. Tell the driver to take us to the hangar where your plane is instead of the hotel." Annie did just that; then she called the pilot and told him to get the plane ready. She listened to him gripe and grumble about the cost of fuel and sitting on the runway and then canceling and the tower bitching at him in five different languages.

Annie grinned at Myra, and said, "Not to worry, Peter, we'll sit in that crummy lounge and wait for you to call us. Things happen, you know how it is," she said airily.

"I hope he doesn't quit on you. No one likes a show-off, Annie," Myra said.

"Peter won't quit. He's been with me forever. I'm his son's godmother. He hates burning fuel, he's very frugal, and maintaining a plane is a high-dollar enterprise. He's just a little too conscientious sometimes."

It was the Uber driver who started to snipe and snarl when he realized how very close his destination was and that he wouldn't make any money on the ride. Annie apologized and slipped him a fifty-dollar bill. The driver looked at the crisp bill and grimaced. "We're not permitted to accept tips." Annie rolled her eyes and dropped the bill on the front passenger seat when the car came to a full stop at the private hangar.

Annie bounced out of the car, Myra hot on her heels. They headed for the lounge, where Myra ordered two double Kentucky bourbons on the rocks.

"Attagirl, Myra!" Annie held her glass aloft. "Cheers!"

Chapter 11

Myra and Annie ran from the car, the ferocious October wind propelling them forward. They could hear the dogs inside barking an early greeting.

"No place like home," Myra gasped, as she tried to hold down her skirt and fight the wind at the same time. She was struggling to take a deep breath when she finally managed to open the door.

"You got that right, my friend. Thanks for letting me stay with you. I hate staying in that big house all by myself when Fergus is away. I think I spend more time here than at home," Annie grumbled, as she did her best to finger-comb her wiry curls.

"When are you going to marry that man, Annie?"

Annie mumbled a response that the wind carried away. It didn't matter, since Annie's answer was always the same. "When the time is right I'll know it, and the time isn't right yet." And that was the end of that, so Myra didn't bother to ask her to repeat her mumbled answer.

Inside the kitchen, the dog-sitter moved to the side so the dogs could go through their welcoming routine, which was to drop to the floor and roll around so they could lick the women to unconsciousness before they responded by tickling them in all their sweet spots. The dog-sitter, Artie, who happened to work for Myra's veterinarian, timed the reunion. Ten minutes to the second.

Myra clapped her hands for the dogs to settle down, and handed out treats. She listened to the dog-sitter's report, which wasn't really a report because all he said was, everything is and was fine, and there were no glitches. He accepted his pay and waved airily, calling over his shoulder, "Call me if you need me." Myra said she would.

"It's only seven thirty, Myra. Coffee or wine. Or how about two fingers of that fine Kentucky bourbon you have stashed in the cabinet."

"I'll get the ice," Myra said.

"Attagirl, Myra."

Once they were seated at the kitchen table,

Annie leaned forward. "I think we're slipping, old girl. We came home with nothing. How can that be, Myra? I hate it when we draw a blank the way we did. Makes me start to doubt our capabilities, and yet we covered all the bases."

"There wasn't anything else to get, Annie. What there was to get we got. You can't get information, facts, details out of a rock. We did our best. You talked to Avery. He's not doing any better than we did, and he's a *spy*. And his people are trained investigators. I know this is going to sound . . . oh, I don't know, maybe crazy or bizarre, but you don't think she, meaning Sara, would . . . you know . . . go after Bella and maybe try to . . . to . . . do something to her, do you? She has to know by now that Bella either found out or would find out about the transfer of eggs and start to question the military about her husband's insurance and his back pay and . . . and everything that goes on when there's a death."

Annie drained her glass of the hundred-proof bourbon, topped off Myra's, then poured more into her glass. "I've more or less been wondering the same thing, Myra, but I didn't want to say it out loud. Maybe we should have her move out here to the farm until we can resolve this. The question is, how do you feel about that? This is your house. She was a sweet girl. I don't think she'd give you an ounce of trouble."

"I'm more than okay with that," Myra said. "We should run the idea by the others, but we can't do that until tomorrow. We'll call a mid-morning meeting. Maybe by then, we'll have heard something from Avery. I'm going to go upstairs and take a shower. How about you call Isabelle and the others to see if she found anything in her hacking. Maggie, too. I won't be long."

Annie nodded agreeably as she reached for the bottle of bourbon. She was feeling no pain, as well as downright happy, which always happened when she drank good bourbon. She pressed the number 4 for Isabelle's number on her smartphone and waited for her to pick up.

Outside, Annie could hear the wind whistling in the eaves over the kitchen. She felt a moment of panic as Lady got up and walked over to the door, stood still, and listened, then lay down on the carpet. She gave a soft woof to let Annie know things were all right. Annie sighed with relief as she waited for Isabelle to pick up, which she did on the fourth ring.

"You're back home already! What happened?" Isabelle queried.

"Nothing. At least nothing that can help us. We met the Nolans' best friends. No help there. Couldn't find out anything on Sara that we didn't already know. Avery might have found out something since we last spoke to him, but he has had as much luck as we did.

We just decided we weren't needed, that Avery could handle whatever there is to handle by himself. We'd just be in the way. I was hoping you would have something to report."

"I want to go on record right now and say this whole thing is out-and-out crazy. I hate dealing with the military. They do not like the way civilians look at things or do things. They're very rigid. And . . . they are not cooperative, but I had Abner's friend Phil help me. He zipped through those records and files in nothing flat. How about if I bring it all out to the farm in the morning. Maggie called earlier and said she had some stuff, too, so we thought we'd come together once Myra sent a text saying you two were on your way home. I'm bushed, Annie, I just want to go to bed now, okay?"

"Absolutely. I'll call the others and we'll meet up around eleven. I'll have someone bring lunch. Does that work for you?"

"Right now it sure does. Glad you and Myra made it home safe and sound. Annie, that woman Sara, she's bad news. Really bad news. Don't laugh at me and don't call me paranoid, but I think we need to put Bella in protective custody. In other words, our protective custody. I just have a bad feeling, and I can't shake it. So that has to mean it's serious."

"Dear, I would never laugh at you. Myra and I just had that very discussion not ten minutes ago. We agree with you about Bella. We'll take care of it."

"Okay. Good night then."

"Good night, Isabelle," Annie said softly. "Sleep well."

Bella looked around her tidy apartment before she slipped into her navy-blue blazer. Taking Myra and Annie's advice, she had gotten herself three part-time jobs, just to keep busy and help with the bills until she could move to North Carolina. Today was her day to work a three-hour midday shift at the Guest Quarters hotel chain. She actually liked the job and the interaction with the guests, and the time passed quickly. The pay was decent, too, for a part-time temporary job. None of the three part-time jobs gave her much time to think about her life and her current problems. She still cried herself to sleep every night, but she knew that eventually her crying jags would stop and her pillow would be dry in the morning. Time. Everything took time. She blinked away the threatened tears just as her doorbell rang.

Alarm coursed through her body. No one knew where she was. No one. Well, that wasn't quite true. Her new best friends who were helping her knew, but they also said they would never seek her out without calling first. And then at nine this morning Myra Rutledge had called and said she wanted her to pack her things and move out to the farm for the time being, which meant she was going to have to give up her three part-time jobs with little to no notice. She had agreed to do it, and her bag was packed and sitting by the door. She explained that today she couldn't leave the hotel on such short notice and would drive out after her shift was over.

So who was knocking on her door?

Bella tiptoed over to the door and looked through the peephole. Her eyes widened in shock. Dr. Martin Peabody from the fertility clinic!

Open the door? Don't open the door?

Bella threw caution to the wind and opened the door. She didn't say a word, she simply stared at the fussy little man with the owlish glasses standing in front of her. Finally, she found her voice. "Give me one good reason not to call the police right now."

Peabody shook his head. "If I could, I would, but I can't. I'd like to talk to you for a few minutes if you have time. Please, I want to help you and myself at the same time. Won't you at least hear me out?"

The man was whining. If there was one thing in this life Bella couldn't stand, it was a whiny man. So unmanly. "All right, ten minutes. I have to go to work. Why are you here, what do you want from me? Haven't you and your people made my life miserable enough? Tell me what you want before I decide if you are harassing me."

"I came here to talk to you on my own behalf and on behalf of my partners. I'm here to ask you to please not initiate litigation proceedings. We really did nothing wrong. And even you must admit that. There was no way for any of us to know your husband's sister was impersonating you. No way on this earth. She had your driver's license. She had a copy of your electric bill with your name on it. She had a library card with your name and address on it, plus two of your credit cards. She also had a copy of . . . of your husband's death certificate. That was the clincher for us. That woman even showed us canceled checks that you wrote to us for storage. No one ever looks like they really look on their driver's license. The picture on the license was close enough to the license we had on file from when you first came to us. As I said, the likeness was satisfactory. Wigs, makeup these days can alter anyone's appearance."

He blathered on, then took off his glasses to wipe them on a tissue he pulled out of his pocket, at the same time taking a long, deep breath. "Well, not the actual checks but photocopies. As Dr. Petre said, giving her the eggs was a no-brainer.

"Everyone knows going to court is a crapshoot. You will have the sympathy of the court and a jury because your husband was killed in the line of duty. They won't care that we did it all by the book; their sympathy will be with you. We know this. That means you could very well end up owning the clinic we've all worked and slaved over for the last thirty years. We have an impeccable reputation. Please don't do this to us. If it's about money for you, we talked it over and we're all willing to take out bank loans to pay you."

Bella shook her head. "I don't want your money. This was never about money. I can't believe you're asking me to just drop this. Just drop it! I. Don't. Think. So!"

"If I could tell you where your eggs are currently stored, would you consider changing your mind? If I could tell you what kind of car your impersonator drives and give you the license plate of her car, would you reconsider?"

Bella bounced to her feet, her face full of rage. "Are you sitting there on my sofa, in my apartment, telling me you have this information and you withheld it from me? That is out-and-out blackmail. Is that what you're telling me? Why? Why would you do such a thing?" Bella was screaming at the top of her lungs.

Dr. Martin Peabody closed his eyes and sighed. "Fear mostly. Some greed if we're being honest. A lot of people would be out of a job. Dr. Petre just bought into the business, using her life savings. She would be wiped out, just as we all would if you won your lawsuit, which we all think you would. I'm being as honest as I can be here. Like I said, a jury would be sympathetic to you and we know it. I came here to ask you to please, have your lawyers reconsider. They're bound by law to do whatever you tell them to do. We can't unring the bell, Mrs. Nolan. What's done is done, and we did go by the book. We really did."

"You knew, and you never said anything," Bella screeched.

"No! No! Good God, no! I just happened to be looking out my window the day the woman posing as you followed the specially equipped van that transported your eggs. I've seen that same scenario dozens of times. I didn't think anything of it. I was actually thinking about taking my grandson fishing the next day because it was my day off. It barely registered at the time. At the time," he repeated. "Then when you showed up and told us your story, the fear kicked in, and I just kept quiet. I will admit to that and own it. I'm sorry for that. I really am. No one knows about this but me. I came here on my own."

Bella wanted to scream again at the top of her lungs, but her throat felt scratchy from the last time she'd let loose. She bit down on her tongue and warned herself to remain calm. She took a giant deep breath, and said, "So now you're here to blackmail me. You'll give me the information you withheld if I don't sue you. Do I have that right?"

Peabody nodded miserably. "Sadly, yes. But if you don't agree, then I'll deny it."

"I could turn you over to the police right now."

"Yes, you could," Peabody said. "And I would still deny it. Where is your proof I said any such thing to you? I'm desperate, Mrs. Nolan. The entire staff, the partners are desperate. And our clients . . . I shudder to think what they will think or do.

"At least think about it and get back to me. I don't want to keep you; you did say you had to go to work. I appreciate your talking to me at all. I thought for sure you'd slam the door in my face. I would, however, just like to leave you with a thought. The people who work for me at the clinic, most of them have been with me since we opened thirty years ago. They depend on their jobs, they have families. They have kids in school, kids in college, two of my staff have severely challenged children, and taking care of them is costly. They need their jobs. What happened was an honest mistake, no one person's fault. That woman had everything she needed to steal your property. Please be honest with yourself even though you are hurting right down to your very soul. Please, get back to me once you speak with your attorneys. Thank you for your time; I can see myself out."

And then he was gone, and Bella was alone to ponder the man's words. He knew how to get in touch with the woman who stole her eggs, most likely Andy's sister. It wasn't the money, she didn't care two figs about that, she just wanted her eggs, and Dr. Martin Peabody knew where they were. Give a little, get a little. Just the thought of a lawsuit was like a kick in the gut. She knew she didn't have the stomach for that, and she did sympathize with the staff at the clinic.

Bella looked at her watch. She was going to be late. She sent off a text and asked the front-end manager if he still wanted her to come in since it would take her a good thirty minutes to get there depending on traffic, and she was already late to begin with. She was told to come in as soon as she could get there.

The urge to Lysol her tiny space engulfed her, but she shook away the urge and left the apartment, careful to lock the door. And then she put a loose thread at the bottom of the door. She'd read about that once in a spy novel. This way, if the thread was disturbed when she got back, she'd know someone was either in her apartment waiting for her with harm in mind, or someone had already been inside and robbed her. She wished she had done that at her old apartment before Sara Windsor Nolan had obviously invaded her space to obtain copies of all those documents she used at the clinic. Somehow, Sara had entered Bella's apartment, probably picked the lock, then went through all her things and took what she wanted. God in heaven, how did Andy ever get a sister like Sara Windsor? That was the thing, though, she wasn't a blood sister.

Bella shook her head to clear her thoughts. She did a final check of the hallway to make sure no one was lurking about, and walked to the elevator. The fine hairs on the back of her neck were standing on end, she could feel them move. Don't think. Don't think about anything. Just get through the day, then drive out to Pinewood, where she would be safe. Her safety right now was paramount. She didn't know how she knew that, but she knew it as surely as she knew that she was standing on the corner waiting for the traffic light to change from red to green.

Bella stepped off the curb, thinking, My God, that's why Myra Rutledge wanted her to move out to Pinewood. Myra and the others also believed her life was in danger.

Chapter 12

Avery Snowden stared out the window of his rental car, wondering if he was doing the right thing by showing up unannounced at the Nolan family attorney's office. What was he going to learn here? The Nolans had passed quite a while ago, prior to the death of their son. Surely, probate was over and done with, settled, and all things pertaining thereto taken care of. If he'd had his druthers, he would have gathered up his people and headed for the airport, but Annie had called, and said, "Not so fast, Avery. Go talk to the lawyer. Lawyers know secrets, and with all the Nolans gone now, he may very well share some of those secrets with you."

Avery didn't believe it for a minute, but Annie signed his checks, so whatever the boss wanted, he was duty-bound to comply. It wasn't that he had something to rush home to anyway; he didn't. He just hated wasting time and walking away empty-handed.

He pressed the button to raise the car window just as the door to the red brick building opened. A tall, striking redhead sashayed through, wearing bright red stilettoes. Avery always marveled at how women could keep their balance, still walking and looking regal to boot at the same time. One of the Sisters, Kathryn Lucas, called red stilettoes slut shoes. He grinned, although the woman exiting the building that housed the Nolans' lawyer didn't look like a slut. She was dressed conservatively and was carrying a very pricey ostrich briefcase. Probably an attorney. He waited another minute or so until the woman passed him and got into an equally pricey, high-end set of wheels: a Mercedes-Maybach. Yep, he decided, she had to be a high-dollar attorney to afford a set of wheels like the sleek vehicle he was looking at. He waited another second to appreciate the generous expanse of leg and thigh as she got behind the wheel. He sighed. The days were long gone since his imagination took him to passionate places.

His knees protesting mightily, Avery climbed out of the car and walked up to the stand-alone brick building with a small parking lot on the side. A simple plaque adorned the door, polished to such a high sheen to match the other hardware on the door that he could see his reflection clearly, even the pimple on his chin: BRADFORD AND SONS LAW FIRM.

Avery looked at his watch; it was a quarter to five. Almost quitting time unless they worked till six o'clock. It was already six forty-five for Annie back East. He looked around. Now that the redhead with the great legs was gone, there were only three cars in the lot in addition to his own. He speculated that Bradford Senior, if there was still a Bradford Senior, was retired, and two of the cars, both Beemers, belonged to two sons, and the other car, a Saab, probably belonged to a secretary or receptionist.

Avery opened the door. Directly in his line of vision was a desk with a middle-aged woman sitting behind it, stamping envelopes. She looked up, smiled, and said, "I do hope you are not going to tell me you have an appointment I forgot to log in the books. My boss would be very unhappy if that were so."

Avery grimaced. "No, I'm not going to tell you that." He showed his credentials, and said, "I just need five minutes, possibly ten. And I have no problem paying for your boss's time. I'm headed back to Washington, D.C., in another hour, and I have to get back to the airport as soon as I leave here."

"Washington, D.C., is certainly popular

today. The client who just left here was also headed back to Washington, D.C. I've never been. One of these days," she said with a sigh.

"Go through the door on the left, walk down the hall, and Mr. Bradford, that would be Ellison Bradford, Mr. Bradford Senior's oldest son, he's packing up to go home a little early today so he can go to his daughter's basketball game. Just tell him Julie, that's me, said it was okay for you to see him."

Avery smiled and nodded as he started off. Loose as a goose. From the looks of things, the Bradfords ran a loose ship, which was good for him. He liked places like this, with actual wood, worn carpets, scarred furniture that was old and comfortable. Kids' pictures plastered on all the walls with Scotch tape, along with their framed law degrees. Outdated magazines that were falling apart and a candy dish with only three mints left were on a messy oak coffee table that looked like it had come over on the ark completed the picture of an old family law firm that had been practicing law since dinosaurs roamed the Earth.

Ellison Bradford snapped the lock on his briefcase just as Avery tapped on the frame of the door. "Julie said it was okay to come back here. She also said you were leaving early for your daughter's basketball game, so I'll make this quick. I'm Avery Snowden. I worked for MI6, for Her Majesty. I'm retired now and living here. I wonder if you would mind talking to me a bit about Sonia and Dan Nolan. Andy, too, if you know anything about him. In a manner of speaking, I represent Andy's widow, Bella." He waited while the young attorney digested all he'd said.

"I have some time. Please, sit down. If I have a stupid look on my face, it's because Sara Windsor Nolan just left here not fifteen minutes ago. We finally settled and signed the last of the probate papers. You just missed Sara by a few minutes. She's probably the one you want to talk to. I have to warn you, she is . . . a bit edgy. I don't know her all that well. Sonia and Dan Nolan, before their demise, were my father's clients. My brother and I inherited all of Pop's clients. I knew Andy quite well, we played football together our senior year. Sara . . . like I said . . . I didn't know her, still don't. She's . . . um . . . I guess *difficult* would be the word to use. I tried to get more background on the family after they passed, but Pop has dementia and would get frustrated with the questions, so Tony, that's my brother, and I just gave up.

"When we heard about Andy's death, we were beside ourselves. Sara showed up and all she wanted to know was what the estate was worth and when she would get the money. She produced Andy's power of attorney. For a while, it was a hot mess."

Ellison Bradford picked up a dark brown accordion-pleated envelope and waved it at Avery

Snowden. "This is the Nolan file. Andy's paperwork is in here, too. I asked Sara if she wanted a copy, and she asked why she would want that crap? Then she said, 'Just write me the check, and I'll be out of here. My brother and I were the executors of the estate.'

"I could almost feel Andy breathing down my neck and saying don't do it, don't do it, but I had no choice. I talked it all over with Tony and Dad. Sometimes he has lucid periods, and we got him on one and he said we didn't have a choice. He also said Sara was bad news. Andy was different. Andy was a great guy. He constantly made excuses for Sara. I'm not sure if he liked her or not. Even though she wasn't a blood sister, he treated her like one. I don't know what else to tell you, Mr. Snowden."

"Would you consider letting me take that folder if I promise to return it in the same condition you give it to me? I would like to study it. I'm afraid that Sara Windsor Nolan is trying to cheat Andy's widow. I don't want that to happen. How much was in the estate?"

"It was quite robust. Dan was a very savvy investor. He made Andy a wealthy man in his own right by investing his salary from the early days in the military. Round numbers, close to $10 million of Andy's money alone. In addition, the Nolans owned some really pricey property in Montana that they sold to a conglomerate to build a ski resort. They bought it way back in the day for $75,000, made payments on it for years, and planned to retire there one day. They finally sold it for $25,000,000. They left everything to Andy. They did leave a token amount to Sara—$5,000. And now she has it all. And do you know why she has all of it? Years ago, Andy came into the office and made a will. He was being deployed at the time. He left everything to Sara. I am the one who drew up his power of attorney. It was the first one I had ever done. Dad stood over me. I wish to God that that had never happened. Water under the bridge, as they say.

"But to answer your question, sure you can take the folder but be sure to return it. I hate to rush you, but I have to leave now."

Avery looked up at the tall, lanky man with the infectious grin and thanked him. Ellison laughed out loud. "You're wondering how someone my height, my weight could have played varsity football, right?" Snowden nodded. "Speed. I was also on the track team. Fleet of foot and all that. I wanted to go the pro route and I had a good chance at it, but then I blew out both my knees, and that's how I ended up being a lawyer. Listen, call me and keep me updated, okay? I feel like I owe Andy my best, so if there is anything I can do to help you, I will, and there will be no charge."

The two men shook hands; then Snowden was sitting in his rental staring at the accordion file. He'd actually seen Sara Windsor and hadn't even known it. He wondered what he would have done had he known it was her when he first laid eyes on her. He made an ugly sound in his throat at where his thoughts were taking him.

Snowden warned himself not to go there, not yet anyway. Soon, though.

Chapter 13

Sara Windsor Nolan, also known under dozens of other aliases, sat down at the kitchen counter on one of the tufted, luxurious stools she'd bought on a whim for $900 a pop. Were they worth $900 each? Probably not. The only reason she bought them was because she could. These days, she could buy anything she wanted anytime she felt like it. She had what she believed was unlimited money, so why not spend it and try to make herself happy? Why not indeed.

But the money did not make her happy. She knew that even if she were the richest person on the planet and had a trillion dollars sitting in a box next to her, she still wouldn't be happy. The only thing that would or could make her happy was Andy Nolan, and that was never going to happen because Andy Nolan was dead and buried.

Andy had shared his body, his love, his passion with that twit Bella Ames. How was Sara supposed to forget that? There had been other twits before the twit he had married, but they didn't matter. A series of one-night stands didn't mean a thing to him, and that's precisely what Andy had told her. And she believed him. Andy had never lied to her. In fact, Sara doubted that Andy even knew how to lie. He had gone on to explain that every guy had one-night stands. Everyone knew that. Here today and gone tomorrow. They meant nothing.

She let her mind take her back to that week when Andy had visited her in San Francisco and how wonderful it had been. Until the last day when Andy went out to buy some shrimp to cook for dinner and forgot to come home because, as he put it, he'd met the girl of his dreams. She was the one for him. The one he was meant to meet. In a fish store, no less. His soul mate. And wouldn't you know it was on the day before he was to leave to go to Oklahoma. He was devastated.

All he kept saying was, "You have to meet her, sis. You'll love her. I love her already, and I just met her a few hours ago. I got her phone number and address. I'm going to try to get back this way before I get my final orders." He kept gushing about Bella, and all she could do was paste a sick smile on her face as she prayed for Bella whatever her name was to drop dead. That night, though, after Andy fell asleep, she went through his wallet and copied down Andy's new love's address, name, and phone number. Information was power.

Even though she had not planned to go to Oklahoma with Andy, she changed her mind at the last second after she learned about Bella from the fish store. Together, they left San Francisco for Oklahoma because there was no way she was going to let Andy out of her sight for even one little minute. She regretted it almost immediately because all Andy did was talk about Bella. It was Bella this and Bella that, and how Bella wasn't into makeup like Sara was or fancy clothes like Sara wore. She worked hard, was frugal, and she was an orphan, and on and on he blathered until she finally snapped at him, "Enough already, Andy! I had no idea my clothes and makeup offended you," she screeched. Something she'd never ever done.

Because Andy was good-natured, he took Sara's comment in stride and toned down his comments, but he did say, "I'm not letting this one get away. We're meant for each other. I know it, I feel it in every bone of my body. Soon as you meet her, you'll know what I'm talking about." Then he added insult to injury, and said, for the umpteenth time, "Sara, my dearest darling sister, you need to find a boy-friend who will love you like I love Bella!" Right then she wanted to throw up and scream at him. *I did find him, he's standing in front of me! It's you, you fool! Why can't you see it?*

And then the magic was gone. Just like that. That quick, the love was gone to allow hate to seep into her pores. They went to Oklahoma, where she pretended to be glad to see Sonia and Dan, who smiled at her but hugged and kissed Andy till he cried for mercy. Then they returned together to San Francisco, and Andy sought out the faceless Bella for a brief few hours. When Andy returned to her tiny apart-ment to gather up his things and head to the airport, she knew from the look on his face that he had cemented his relationship with Bella.

Andy had sex written all over his face. How she kept it together she didn't know, even after all these years. She did, though, and somehow she even managed to smile and wave goodbye and not show how devastated she was when Andy didn't kiss her goodbye. He did, how-ever, stop in the doorway and blow her an air kiss that she did not return. She knew he didn't even notice.

Sara tried every trick in her arsenal to find out Bella's last name from Andy even though she already had the information. She wanted to see what he would say, but he was having none of it. He made it clear that Bella was off-limits, even to her. What she took that to mean was that Andy was saying "I'm not telling you because I don't want you screwing it up for me." The realization hurt so bad, Sara thought she was going to bleed.

Andy left, and Sara continued to do what Andy told her to do so many times—she found a boyfriend. After ten years of going from rich boyfriend to rich fiancé to an occasional rich husband and back again to rich boyfriend, she'd lost count of the number of boyfriends and fiancés—dozens. All of them meaningless. Two, she married early on and never bothered to divorce. Both as meaningless to her as her other relationships.

But all of them had money. Which she helped herself to, to line her nest egg. She always made sure to clean out their bank accounts before moving on. Always with a new name and identity.

Until Steven Conover. He was the nicest of all the men she'd filled her life with. She actually liked him. But he wasn't Andy Nolan. And yet he was by far the richest. Which meant she was now rich. She knew to the penny what her portfolio was worth. High seven figures.

Sara let her mind go back further to Sonia's and Dan's deaths, which didn't bother her in the least. She'd tried to whip up some tears for the benefit of the Olsens, but she simply could not squeeze them out of her dry eyes. She did her duty. She sat in the metal chair in the funeral home, shaking hands with the Nolans' friends. Andy had been notified but didn't arrive until after the funeral. He'd cried on her shoulder. Sobbed, actually. She had closed her eyes and let her dreams take hold as she stroked his head and wiped at his tears and kissed his cheek. He'd burrowed against her chest. It felt so good, she thought she was going to black out. Then he'd jumped up and run out of the house.

When he said goodbye to her hours later, he told her he'd gone to the park and called Bella and spent his last hours talking to her. A quick kiss on Sara's cheek was all she got. Plus his words. "I hate leaving you with this, but I have to get back. You have my power of attorney, do whatever you think I would do. It would be nice if you could magically double my bank account while I'm gone, because when I finish this tour, I'm going to ask Bella to marry me. We'll need to buy a house for the kids we plan on having and a truck for me and an SUV for Bella to haul the kids around in. Bella asked me to ask you if you would be her maid of honor. You're the only family I have, and by extension, Bella's also. I said you would. My buddy Paul is going to be my best man. If I can get him here, that is." Andy blew her a kiss, and yelled, "See ya, sis. Pray I get back in one piece."

She didn't pray, though. She was too distraught to do that. Andy was going to marry the faceless Bella. Hate blossomed quickly. She had to find a way to get rid of her once and for all. If they got married, then she'd get a Christmas card once a year. Andy would forget about her. He'd have kids. Bella would require all his time. And there she was, not belonging again, left out in the cold, her life as empty as a grocery sack after the groceries were put away. She had money, but money couldn't make her happy no matter how much she had. She was smart enough to figure that out. The only thing that could ever make her happy was Andy taking her in his arms and saying, "I love you, I love you, I love you!"

Now it seemed like it was never going to happen.

More time went by. Sometimes, it was fast and other times tortoise slow. Communications from the other part of the world were sparse. Sara understood that Andy was fighting a war. He had the rank of major now. He'd risen quickly in the army. She'd tried to find out whatever she could about Bella, but Andy wasn't sharing anything. He did mention her on occasion. He said she'd moved east and that she liked Washington, D.C. Then he threw what Sara called the mother of all bombs at her. He said he'd wrangled a ride on a cargo plane that was coming Stateside and would be here for two days. He didn't tell her the dates and there was no way for her to find out, either. Andy said he was calling and apologizing ahead of time for not being able to see her, but he was dragging Bella to a justice of the peace the minute he got off the plane. "We're finally going to get married, and I want to spend every second with the love of my life."

"What are you saying, Andy? Are you really saying you don't want me at your wedding?"

The answer was an explosive, "Yes, that's what I'm saying!" It was the ultimate put-down that Sara knew she would never recover from. Andy must have realized his words hurt her, so he hastened to say, "It's just us, sis. Don't be upset. Next leave, we'll all go out to dinner, and you'll get to meet Bella. I know you will love her like I do. Just be happy for me, okay. Gotta go. Love ya!" Sara's hate was in full bloom now. She went out and bought a gun.

And those were the last words she'd ever heard Andy speak. Sara told herself not to go there because she couldn't handle the grief. She told herself to think about other things, secrets Andy had told her, confidences he'd shared, like his donating his sperm to a sperm bank to freeze. How two visits ago, he'd convinced Bella to freeze her eggs in case something happened to him. Things like that.

Sara looked around the beautiful kitchen but barely noticed it. She knew it was considered beautiful because she'd read in the real-estate brochures that this kitchen was crafted for every homemaker in the world, not someone like her. It had everything. Everything.

And it was all built-in and flush with the wall—clean, stark lines. She looked at the top-of-the-line names on the appliances. Wolf, Sub-Zero. When something came with red knobs, the price was two grand higher, which made every woman in the world want to have the red-knobbed appliances in her kitchen. It makes no sense, but that's the way it was. Andy would have shaken his head and dragged her off to Sears or Walmart, where his parents had always shopped. Andy was frugal, and she had always admired that. He had always had money to lend her when she used up her allowance ahead of time. He never asked for it back, but she made sure she paid him exactly when and what she'd promised. Andy told her more than once that she was the only one he could trust.

That particular day, they'd made a pact with each other to never, never, ever divulge a whispered secret. She'd been so thrilled, so giddy that Andy thought that much of her, she felt like she was walking on air. Even though Andy never said the same thing to her, she assumed he felt the same way. Otherwise, why even bring it up or discuss it. No, they were always on the same page. She was sure of it.

Sara uncorked an outrageously expensive bottle of wine and poured it into a flute that looked like it would shatter if you even breathed on it. She found a package of stale crackers and a chunk of cheese that had a corner with no mold on it. She devoured it as she finished the wine, then poured another full glass.

While she was up and moving, she opened the china buffet, which was where she kept all of Andy's mementoes. She rummaged until she found the eight pieces of paper that Andy had entrusted her to take care of, which she had. She looked down at the sheaf of papers that looked wrinkled and ready for the shredder. That would never happen, not on her watch.

They were from the fertility clinic. Seals in place. Andy's signature where it said "donor." While it said donor, the word that should have been on each piece of paper was *client*, along with an assigned number. Only it wasn't Andy's name on the eight pieces of paper even though it was his signature. Because he didn't want anyone to know what he was doing or why he'd chosen to use an alias. He'd even asked for her input. In the end, he had chosen the name Windsor for Sara's last name and Andrews for his own first name. All eight pieces of paper bore the signature Windsor Andrews, with an *s* at the end. They had laughed like two lunatics at their antics.

Sara remembered the discussion they'd had over what they were doing. She'd said she just heard guys donated their sperm for money. Why didn't he take the money? was her burning question. Andy's answer was simple. He was going into the military. Things happened, things went wrong. Andy said he wanted to be sure if anything went awry that he could have a bloodline to fall back on. She'd accepted it all because it actually made sense to her.

And now . . . she was the sole owner of eight slips of paper saying she could be inseminated and deliver eight children that would all look like Andy and her. Assuming, of course, that all donations, contributions, or whatever they were called were swimmers. And that was exactly what she was going to do. The best part, though, was knowing that the snot Andy had married knew that he had made eight donations or contributions.

Sara had no doubt that Bella Ames was searching for Andy's progeny. That's how she thought of them, even if they were just sperm cells. And if she, Sara, the woman of many aliases, had anything to do with it, Bella Ames would never find them.

Sara fanned out the eight pieces of paper and stared at them and the dates. Andy had made his deposits to the fertility clinic on the same day of every month for eight months; then he'd asked Sara to create a checking account under the name Windsor Andrews and pay the storage fee every month while he was deployed, a duty she relished and happily performed each and every month.

As she stared at the signed receipts, she couldn't help but wonder if Andy ever shared their secret with snotty Bella. While she wasn't sure, she didn't really want to know if Andy's wife knew how close Sara and her husband were. She had never been sure if Andy viewed their shared secrets as sacrosanct the way she did.

Sara shook her head. She had no way of knowing if she and Bella Ames were anything alike. She hoped not. She didn't want to be anything like anyone but herself. What she did know for certain was if she was in Bella Ames's position and knew about those eight pieces of paper, she would be turning the world upside down to locate those eight specimens—progeny, Andy's sons and daughters. She loved the way those words rolled off her tongue.

If Andy had shared his best-kept secret with his new wife, then Bella surely would have contacted Andy's parents' lawyer, or at the very least tried to find her, Sara, to ask for help. Then again, maybe she was spinning her wheels because Bella didn't like kids, Andy's or anyone else's kids. Not everyone was cut out to be a parent. She ought to know, she thought sourly.

Sara plucked a magnet off the refrigerator that said Alfonso would deliver a pizza with the works along with a quart of sweet tea in twenty minutes for the princely sum of $20 plus $5 for delivery and a $10 tip. Total $35. Cash only. No credit cards. No checks.

Sara dug around in her purse. She had forgotten to go to the ATM today. Tomorrow, for sure, she would need to hit one up. After pawing through the contents of her purse, she came up with the full amount, with the last two dollars being in change. She shrugged. Money was money. That's when she realized how hungry she was and that she hadn't eaten anything today except for that little chunk of mold-free cheese.

While she waited for the pizza delivery, Sara uncorked another bottle of wine, this one more costly than the last bottle she'd opened. She swirled it around, sniffed it, then sipped the wine. She was no connoisseur, that was for sure. It was dry and sweet, and that was the way she liked it. Knowing next to nothing about wine, she decided it was probably worth the money. You could get a buzz on with cheap wine just the way you could with expensive wine. Had she been smart, she would have chosen Bud Light. Beer went with pizza more so than wine. But . . . the crowd she was running with these days preferred wine with pizza. When in Rome . . .

Alfonso was as good as his word. The doorbell rang exactly twenty minutes from the time she had made the call. Money changed hands. Sara was careful to lock both locks and slide the dead bolt into place.

The pie smelled heavenly. Sara dived into it with gusto and gobbled four slices so quickly she could feel a bad case of heartburn coming on. Like she cared. She reached for the fifth slice and chomped down. It tasted just as good as the first bite had. She finished the wine in her glass and knew she needed to take a nap. She reached for the tea bottle and chugged with gusto. Cold and frosty, tongue-numbing. She loved it. But yes, a nap was definitely in order. She'd wake up refreshed and, she hoped, full of spit and vinegar and ready to take on Andy's widow, Bella Ames Nolan, the little snot.

To Sara's wooly, woozy mind, a two-day marriage counted for nothing. Not when she had access to, at the very least, six hundred years of the Andy Nolan–Sara Windsor bloodline sitting right in front of her.

Sara rolled over on the couch. She reared back when her face brushed against the scratchy brocade of the sofa. It took her a full two minutes before she realized where she was. Normally, she slept in a king-size bed in a bedroom bigger than most people's houses. She did like lots of room. At the moment, it simply didn't matter. The only thing that mattered now was that she get up, wash her face, brush her teeth, and get down to work.

Sara returned to the kitchen thirty minutes later wearing a silky, slithery hostess gown, a gift from her third husband . . . maybe the second one, she really couldn't remember. Nor did she care. The only thing she really liked about it was all the different shades of purple that went into the swirling mass of material. She felt like a fairy child when she wore it, a feeling she liked very much. Magical. A feeling that she never had growing up in the Nolan household.

Sara sat down and immediately went to work. She kept shaking her head as she tried to come to terms with the fact that she'd taken a five-hour nap. Five hours! She couldn't remember if she had ever slept five hours straight in her whole life. She shook her head again to clear it before she opened up her laptop and her phone. In the blink of an eye, she made three medical appointments. A heartbeat later, she had an appointment for an extensive blood work-up, compliments of her OB-GYN.

Two hours later, satisfied that everything was on schedule, Sara finished the online shopping spree that left her positively giddy as she tried to imagine the weight gain from her pregnancies and how she was going to look in her swanky, designer maternity clothes. She'd take a lot of selfies and stick them up on the wall in what would be the baby's dressing room. Maybe what she could do was have a really good picture of Andy blown up and put on a cardboard mount with a back to it so it could stand alone. She wouldn't call it Andy. "No, I'm just going to call the lifelike cutout Daddy," Sara squealed happily. "Maybe I might

even get one of myself and call it Mommy."
Sara giggled. Mommy and Daddy looking after
their brood.

Sara's thoughts meandered down another
road. What to name the firstborn. Andy, of
course. And if it was a girl, it would be Andrea.
She also needed to think of another, better
name for the second child if it was a girl. She
sucked in her breath. She knew she had to be
careful. Sara and Andy . . . Someone might put
two and two together and come up with Sara
Windsor and Andy Nolan. She could absolutely see that happening at some point. Well,
she had all the time in the world to think
about names, disguises, and ways to blend in
and ways to hide out.

All the time in the world.

Sara filled her glass with a new batch of ice
cubes. The night loomed ahead of her. She
needed to work on her various lists. Put things
in order so that her plans flowed flawlessly.

The first list had only one task on it. More
like a question. Not caring what time it was,
Sara dialed a number she knew from memory,
certain she would get a robotic message direct-
ing her to leave a message at the sound of the
tone. Instead, she was surprised to hear a grav-
elly voice say, "This is Clint Aldrich. What can I
do for you at this ungodly hour of the evening?"

Sara cleared her throat. "Hello, Clint. This

is Jackie Pope," Sara said, using one of her many aliases. "I'm sorry about the time. I lost track of it today for some reason. I think the weather might have something to do with it. Supposed to rain. Barometric pressure and all that. Before I retire for the evening, I wanted to know if you have anything new on Bella Ames."

"Her name is Nolan. Not Ames. You keep mixing it up, Miz Pope."

Sara giggled. "I do, don't I? I'm so sorry. I'll try to be more careful. Do you have any news? Do you know where she is?"

"Well, of course I do. I am a detective after all. Mrs. Nolan left today to go to Virginia to visit someone named Myra Rutledge. She's married to a veddy veddy British gentleman named Sir Charles Martin. He once worked for the queen. That would be the Queen of England. Scuttlebutt has it that they were friends in the sandbox. You aren't paying me for background material, so I keep it to a bare minimum.

"I followed Mrs. Nolan to Pinewood, but once she drove through a security gate, I could not enter without proper credentials, so I drove back around, parked, and took up a position in a small, well-tended forest. From where I was hunkered down, I could see directly into the courtyard and the parking lot, and I could also see the contents of the kitchen through the kitchen window. I stayed till four o'clock, when it became obvious to me, Mrs. Nolan was not going to leave."

Sara bristled angrily. Her voice was just as angry when she said, "How can you be sure she wasn't going to leave?"

"Because at three thirty she opened the trunk of her car, took out two suitcases, and carried them into a very quaint little cottage. The day had been overcast, and it looked like dusk. She turned all the lights on and settled in for what looked to me to be a mini vacation. Is there anything else you want to know?"

"I would like a report around noon tomorrow. You can e-mail it to me."

"Okay. You're the boss. Anything else, Miz Pope?"

"No, I think that's it. Thank you for your help, and I apologize for calling so late. It's been one of those days if you know what I mean."

"I do. I have them on a regular basis. Good night, Miz Pope."

Sara ended the call without saying another word.

Her eyes looked from one end of the table to the other, to the lists, to the pictures, to the legal papers. What to do with the whole mess? Should she get rid of what she didn't need? Or would this turn out to be one of those cases in which the minute she discarded something she would discover that she needed it, but it would be too late to retrieve it because she'd gotten rid of it? Perhaps what she didn't want or need right now, at this point in time, could be put in a box with a whole lot of tape. A whole lot of tape because it would take too much time and trouble to cut it all away. Yes, yes, a whole lot of tape, maybe even a whole roll. She did have three rolls because that's how they were sold.

Sara clapped her hands. It was a plan. Everything always looked better when you were following a plan. She took a deep breath, then another, and still another. She suddenly felt incredibly powerful. She was here in Kalorama, one of her favorite places. She loved this particular house.

Too bad that Andy had never seen it. He'd spent considerable time at her previous house in Lorton when he was going to some kind of special school that raised him in rank. He'd been so proud of himself. One day, they were driving through Kalorama and he remarked that when he was ready to settle down and raise a family, he would buy a house there, in Kalorama. She wished there was a way for her to tell his spirit she'd done just that for him. Maybe tomorrow she'd go out to the cemetery and bury a picture of this house along with a copy of the deed.

There was no way a two-day marriage would have ever worked out. That was nothing but a fairy tale in the making. What she had, what she'd done for Andy, that was real. Bella Ames was just a fairy princess who would turn into a frog and disappear from his life. Sara had endured. So had Andy. So what if he'd taken a two-day flyer instead of a one-night stand?

If that two-day marriage meant anything, Andy would have had the nurses and doctors find Bella and bring her to the hospital where he was being cared for. He hadn't done that. And he hadn't cared enough about his precious Bella to do more than send Sara the paperwork necessary to provide for his new wife, which she had, somehow, never got around to doing by the time Andy had been killed. And then it was all over.

Putting all of the above aside, she knew she really didn't need any additional proof, what with the packet of papers the private detective Clint Aldrich had given her. Bella had been on her way to sign divorce papers the day the military informed her of Andy's death. Clint said he was not certain if Bella had signed the divorce papers or not. Nor was Clint certain if the divorce papers ever got filed in court by Bella's attorney. More likely not. Why bother? It would be such an ugly memory. It wasn't as if Andy had died the day Bella either signed or didn't sign the papers. Bella was *notified* of Andy's death on the day she was to sign the divorce papers even though he had died eight months earlier, and therein lies the difference, Sara kept telling herself. With that, she'd told Clint Aldrich to stop the surveillance and drop the case. She paid him his outrageous fee and tried not to think about what she had learned and what it meant in terms of her inheritance. Sometimes, ignorance was pure bliss.

One more thing to do and she could retire for the night. Tomorrow was another day. Tomorrow was a new beginning for her and all the wheels she'd put in motion. All she needed to do was follow through, and if there was one thing she excelled at, it was arranging details to make things work to her advantage.

Sara typed an e-mail to her new fertility clinic, saying she would be in at noon to discuss a matter of grave importance and settle her bill. "Settling the matter of grave importance" was going to give her such pleasure. She crossed her fingers in the hope that she would be able to achieve personal happiness the moment things were settled. She was giddy at the thought. She was still smiling to herself as she tidied up the kitchen table, checked the lock on the back door, turned out the lights, and set the alarm. Finally, she was ready for bed.

Sara hoped that when she slipped between the thousand-thread-count Egyptian cotton sheets and laid her head on the downy pillow that had once been on Andy's bed back in Tulsa, Oklahoma, she would dream about Andy. Still, to this day, she would from time to time, spritz a dab of his favorite aftershave onto the pillow. She loved drifting off to sleep savoring Andy's scent next to her cheek.

Sara sighed. Tomorrow was going to be a wonderful new day for her. She could feel it in every bone of her body.

Chapter 14

Avery Snowden slapped at the corner of his eye to ward off a nervous tick that had been plaguing him for almost a week. He hated it when the tick attacked him, because it meant he had failed and was returning to Pinewood virtually empty-handed. Until now, the word *failure* was not in his vocabulary. Unsuccessful. He and his team had been on the job for almost ten days by this time, and he had so little to show for his and his team's efforts that he wanted to smash something. Nothing . . . nothing at all . . . should be this hard. Yes, every case had its downside, as well as an upside, but this . . . this mess had only a downside. No upside at all. In his opinion. His team was just as upset and frustrated as he was. For all the good it was doing any of them.

Snowden pressed the button on his oversize SUV to lower the window, but he didn't enter the pass code that would open Myra's gate to admit him. He should be sitting here on top of the world with a briefcase full of information that would help the Sisters solve their case. Did he have a briefcase full of such information? No. He. Did. Not! Not even close.

A gust of damp autumn air slammed at him through the open window. For some strange, ungodly reason, he felt himself backing up the SUV, and he had no idea why he was doing it. *Fear? Anxiety?* Alien words to him. *Damn, what the hell is wrong with me this evening?*

Snowden leaned his head out the window but immediately pulled it back in. There were too many crazies out there to allow himself to be vulnerable. He didn't move the SUV forward, though. His gaze swiveled to the dense, well-tended forest that surrounded Myra's farmhouse. There could be a dozen crazies lurking in there, and he'd never know it unless he put on his tactical gear. He knew that someone could be hiding there, surveilling the farmhouse, because he'd done it himself.

Snowden leaned forward to stare out at the horizon. It was almost dark. In just about five more minutes, the world would be like black velvet. It was so easy to hide in the dark. The fine hairs on the back of his neck moved. Why weren't the dogs barking? Lady always knew when he was at the gate. Once she barked to alert the family someone was approaching, her pups took up the cry and started to yammer at the top of their lungs. The fine hairs on the back of his neck moved again. He sat still, rigid actually, as he wondered if Annie was creeping up on him, with the gun that she was never without, rock steady in her hands. It had happened before, so if it happened again, like now, he wouldn't be surprised. The Sisters wanted results, and ten whole days had gone by with him and his team acquiring little to no information. His stomach felt like it was curdling.

Of course, he wasn't returning here to Pinewood totally empty-handed. He did have reams of paper, forms, contracts, legal this and not so legal that. Everything in the military was either hurry up and wait or fill it out in triplicate, then in triplicate again because you were given the wrong forms the first time around. He had eleven banker boxes filled to the brim so tight he'd had to use duct tape to seal the covers. And that was just Sara Windsor's stuff. That woman had to be the busiest person in the universe. There were another nine cartons alongside Sara's stuff that related solely to Major Andrew Nolan. There were only two padded manila envelopes that contained information on Bella Ames Nolan, Major Nolan's widow.

Snowden shook his head to clear his thoughts. He was about to press in the four digits on the keypad that would allow the massive gates to move so he could drive through when his cell phone chirped. "Snowden!" He barked a greeting, hoping against hope that the call would contain some good news. He listened, his jaw dropping. Finally, he managed to get a word in to his operative on the other end of the phone. "Get here as soon as you can. Just tell me one thing. Are you totally, one hundred percent sure about all this? Because if you are, it means we've hit the mother lode?"

The voice on the other end of the phone assured Snowden the information he had was pure gold, and he was less than twenty-five miles away and would be there as soon as traffic would allow.

The old spy's shoulder's slumped as he sighed in relief at his operative's words. He squinted at the keypad before he pressed the numbers needed to gain entrance to Myra's compound. He drove through the open gate and waited until it closed completely before driving to the lot where guests parked. With the engine running, he spent ten full minutes staring into the mini forest with his special night-vision goggles that turned the world green. He saw no heat signatures, which meant that other than wildlife, there was no one there who was trespassing and surveilling Myra's farmhouse.

Snowden parked his SUV, climbed out, and made his way to the kitchen door, which opened just as he put his hand on the knob.

"What took you so long, Avery?" Annie barked. "Coffee?"

"I'm right on schedule, so don't try throwing a guilt trip on me, and you know damn well I don't drink coffee. Tea will do nicely, along with four sugars. If you're having a bad day, get over it, because until ten minutes ago, mine was probably ten times worse than yours. So . . . let's start over. I'm on time, I have good news and bad news, depending on your point of view. I could use the tea, like right now, if you don't mind. I also do not want to go through my report until my man gets here. He's the one bringing the good news. Does that work for you, Countess? By the way, where are the dogs? I didn't hear even one bark."

"They're at the clinic. This is the week they get their yearly physicals, so they all go at the same time. Takes four days from start to finish, and this is only day three," Myra said.

"Why are you so . . . grumpy, Avery?" Annie asked as she placed a cup of tea in front of the old spy.

Avery threw his hands in the air. "Until roughly twenty minutes ago, I was fit to be tied. I've had six operatives plus myself on this case for over ten days, and while I have a truckload of files, folders, contracts, you name it, I was bringing nothing here to help you on this mission. This woman . . . Sara whatever name she wants to go by, Major Nolan's . . . I don't even know what to call her. She's no blood relative, but she lived with the major and his family and was treated as a sister even though she was not a blood relative to anyone in the Nolan household and certainly not to Major Nolan. Her life is so muddied and mucked up that none of us could make sense of it."

"So what happened twenty minutes ago?" Isabelle asked, coming into the room. "I'm only asking because I've been trying to hack into her background, and I am about ready to pull my hair out. I don't think it's me. Even Abner, I'm thinking, would be having a hard time with this woman's background and her life in general. I've gone through reams of paper, printing out some of her trails. I got so bogged down that I had to stop because I didn't know if I was coming or going. We need to know the why of all this. She has hundreds of bank accounts, brokerage accounts, properties all over the country, not to mention a bunch of stuff offshore. I can't do it anymore. It's making me crazy. I'm not stupid, Abner taught me well. It's her. She . . . she . . . she can't be real and actually know what she's doing. I don't think a dozen people all working in tandem could figure her out and what she's up to. I know I sound like I'm babbling, and I am, but . . . this is . . . is crazy. I don't know what to do. I'm ready to ditch all of this."

Snowden got up and paced Myra's spacious kitchen. "Isabelle is right. Seven of us, myself included, are on my team, and we hit the same wall that Isabelle did. But . . . I think we'll have a better understanding of things once my operative gets here. Somehow or other, he managed, with the help of the other members of the team, to get something. He says it's our answer, so we'll just have to wait and see."

Kathryn looked around at the group and groaned. "And if it isn't what we need, then what do we do?"

"Start over would be my guess," Alexis said. "I'm sorry I got us involved in this mess. I should have minded my own business that day in the restaurant. Poor Bella."

"What's the game plan for her? I'm referring to the major's sister, or whatever she is," Nikki asked irritably. "She got everything is my understanding. Isabelle said high millions. Sara whatever her name is got everything, and Bella got squat. Supposedly, it was all legal. That should be the beginning and the end of it, but it isn't. Why?"

"The part I'm not getting is why did she steal Bella's eggs from the fertility clinic? Spite? Jealousy. Neither makes sense. Where are those eggs now? Is she going to sell them? What for? It's not like she needs the money. And the other thing is where is Major Nolan's, um, sperm . . . I don't know what to call it . . . deposit, donation, contribution? Who has it? Does she plan to match the major's sperm with Bella's eggs? Why? What for? I know nothing about stuff like this. Do any of you?" Yoko asked.

The Sisters looked at one another and admitted they knew nothing about how it all worked. "Why *don't* we know where the major's sperm is?" Maggie asked. "Did anyone ask Bella?"

"All she said to me was the major made the donation at a clinic, but she was never told the name of the clinic. We all assumed it was the same clinic in which she stored her eggs because the major recommended that particular clinic to her. The assumption is natural that it is the clinic he used, but there is no record of an account under his name," Alexis said.

"Maybe he used an assumed name. Guys are funny about stuff like that. At least that's what Ted told me. He said all college guys did it to make extra money. He said he did. Bella's explanation was he did it in case something happened to him while he was deployed that made him unable to father a child. If that happened, at least his sperm would be safe and frozen. If that was his frame of mind at the time, then of course it makes sense. But why would he use another name?" Maggie asked.

"Dear, we are not sure the major used another name. He might have used another fertility clinic. Avery, did you or your people check any of the other clinics?" Myra asked.

"In the immediate area only, in a seventy-mile radius to be exact. The major has been all over the country, so he could have made his donation or deposit, whatever you want to call them, in any state, not just here in the District of Columbia area.

"We came up with nothing, which just about convinces me that he used an alias. Again, I cannot tell you why. The sister might know. Or maybe it was his own private secret. I don't have the answer, but I think my people may have found it. They should be here in about ten minutes," Avery said, looking down at his watch. He held his cup up for Annie to refill.

"Anyone care to speculate?" Kathryn asked.

"I wouldn't know where to start. This whole case has been a mindblower from the get-go," Maggie growled.

"The sister is the key. I know it. I feel it," Annie said. "We just have to find her and take back all the money she claimed fraudulently and give it to Bella."

Alexis slapped at her forehead in exasperation. "Here we go again! It's not fraud if the major left his estate to Sara Windsor and also gave her his power of attorney. His parents died first. As I understand it, their estate, aside from a $5,000 bequest to Sara, all went to the major. That's all legal. There are no ifs, ands, or buts about that. The major died after the parents passed away, so his inheritance from his parents goes into his estate, which then goes to Sara because of his will and the POA. Unless the major made a new will or appointed someone else to hold a new POA. We all need to accept that all of that is legal even though we don't like it. This all rests on the major's shoulders for doing things the way he did. Of course, probably back then, he wasn't planning on getting married. And for sure he wasn't planning on dying. What that means is we have nothing. There is no case here."

"Then why impersonate Bella and steal her eggs?" Maggie mumbled. She hated it when something didn't make sense, and this did not even pass the sniff test of rationality as far as she was concerned. "The sister has money literally coming out her ears, so she doesn't need the money she could make by selling the eggs.

"Damn, I hate when I can't figure something out. And for sure, I want to know where the major's sperm is. I think that's paramount right now. I wonder if the sister knows where he stashed it. I think he shared that with her for some reason."

Nikki reared up, both arms shooting high in the air. "Hold on! Hold on!" she shrieked. "We're smarter than this! We're going about this all wrong! We're thinking about this all wrong, too! We need to stop right now, fall back, and regroup. Now, all of you, think about what I just said. *Sister!* Sara is not the major's blood sister. She's not any kind of relative of his. She's not even his stepsister. She's just a person like a neighbor. You following me here?" Nikki's excitement was at an all-time high as she paced and waved her arms about. "C'mon, girls, get with it here!"

"Are we talking unrequited love here?" Annie asked, excitement edging into her voice. "On the sister's part, not the major's. Can we start calling him Andy? I think that would be easier."

"I think so," Myra said, her eyes sparking with excitement. "Yes on calling him Andy. She, Sara, was infatuated or in love with Andy. He did not share her feelings, would be my guess. She's devastated and does everything possible to be around wherever he is. In order to do that, she needs lots of money, so she goes after men, marries them, lives with them, cleans out their bank accounts. All so she can be at Andy's beck and call."

"Meaning she'll take him any way she can as long as she can be near him. From what we've been able to figure out, the two of them were close and had a bond, different for each of them though it was, and that was good enough for Sara. I guess," Maggie said.

"The major had no clue. He didn't see her that way," Isabelle said. "Yes, yes, now it's starting to make sense. Over the years, Sara probably put the kibosh on any relationships he might have had. She'd find something wrong with them; they weren't good enough, trouble, baggage, that kind of thing. Andy was like a babe in the woods, would be my opinion. He'd go with his sis's worldly opinions and probably thanked her in the bargain for saving him from making a mistake. Until he met Bella."

"We know now that Sara followed him around to his different bases, set up housekeeping, met men, married some, lived with others, and managed to clean out all of their bank accounts so she could have a lifestyle that enabled her to chase after the major, hoping eventually he would realize that he loved her. That's sick!" Kathryn said.

"Where does that leave young Bella?" Myra asked. "This is beyond sad and unreal. What is that young woman supposed to do?"

Alexis screwed her facial features into a tight grimace of disgust. "Wouldn't you think the sister would share some of Andy's money with his widow? At least some of it. She's got millions. Bella can't even pay for the upkeep of Andy's beloved truck. This is so unfair. And yet there is nothing illegal we can pin on the sister. Before any of you can suggest it, I'm all for finding her, stealing all the money, giving it to Bella, and having Avery disappear her forever."

The Sisters hooted and hollered their agreement just as a horn sounded and Myra's gate opened. All eyes turned to the camera over the back door just as a cherry-red Jaguar roared through the open gates.

Snowden was off his chair and out the door before the Sisters knew what was going on. "This is Matt Spenser, my number one investigator. This better be good, kid, or your ass is grass."

"Mr. Snowden, sir! I have the meat!" the investigator said, making a joke from a commercial he was overly fond of.

Matt Spenser's feet left the floor, and before he could blink, the Sisters had him planted firmly in one of the captain's chairs at Myra's table. The women surrounded him as they pummeled him with questions, one after the other.

"I think he needs some air; you're all suffocating him. And I think he might like a drink. We have all night, ladies, so calm down." Avery shouted to be heard over the din of clamoring women.

"Maybe you do, Avery, but we don't," Annie said, as she jerked at Matt's arm. "Talk, Mr. Investigator, and talk fast. Someone make him a cup of coffee."

Matt Spenser was what Kathryn called a hunk. In other words, ripped. He was forty-three, dressed in jeans and a worn, comfortable T-shirt that said: SEAL TEAM 6.

"Ladies, ladies, you're killing me here! Don't get me wrong, I love the attention, but I really need something to drink. Like now would be good, or my tongue is going to fall out of my mouth." He grinned, showing a set of pearly whites that would make any dentist shout for joy.

Yoko poured a cup of coffee, handed it to him, and watched as he drank it in two huge gulps.

"Fan out, girls, give him air, and he'll talk," Avery said.

Spenser took a deep breath and let it out slowly. "I followed every silly, stupid lead we came up with, and let me tell you, we had hundreds. We started with the last husband, Steven Conover. While everyone referred to him as her husband, including himself, there are no records on file anywhere for a marriage, much less a divorce decree. Conover said Sara kept all the certificates, and he has no idea what happened to the divorce papers. He said he wasn't interested in looking at them. The only thing he knew for sure was that she stole all his money. After we got this information from him, it was a struggle every step of the way.

"But Duke Young, that's my partner, and I persevered. We were finally able to track the chick down, and let me tell you, she is one busy lady. She was not at all easy to find, I can assure you. She has so many aliases, I doubt she can keep them straight herself. We just lucked out because we refused to give up. She goes non-stop twenty-four/seven. I have her current address and her current cell phone number. They could be good for days or hours. This chick is a fast mover, as I said. She's kept Duke and me on our toes, that's for sure.

"I don't want any of you to get excited. One day she moved twice, and each move required a new identity. Right now she is in Kalorama in a very nice, very expensive house. She lives there under the name Nora Lewis. She moved there weeks after collecting Major Nolan's benefits. I've been trailing her for two days. I can't be certain she didn't spot me, but she hasn't relocated, so I think I lucked out."

"How do you know it's Sara Windsor?" Annie asked.

"Because she looks like the picture Avery handed out to the team. It was easy to spot her once the wig came off, the extra padding in her cheeks, stuff like that. She's pretty good at disguises if I do say so myself. The person who thought he was married to her helped quite a bit with insight as to what he thought made her tick."

"When you say she's pretty good at her disguises, what does that mean? How good is good?" Alexis sniffed. "Better than me?"

"No one is as good as you, dear," Myra said soothingly. "I'm sure Sara has nothing else to do with her time, so she works on her disguises. It's probably her life's work. She doesn't appear to have recently held a job. At least we haven't any indication she ever worked a day in her life. She's a con artist, so maybe that's considered a job in her world. What else do you have, Mr. Spenser?"

"Duke and I have been on her for a while. Actually, it seems like forever. At first, I wasn't sure it was her, but I stuck with it. Either she's sick, or she gets her jollies going to doctors. She went to five or six different doctors every day for a week. Sometimes she had two appointments on the same day, and yes I have the names of the doctors and the addresses."

"What does that mean?" Maggie asked.

Spenser shrugged. "I have no clue. No doctor or nurse was going to tell us anything, so we didn't even bother to ask. She did go to a fertility clinic twice if that means anything. She's on her phone a lot. Seems like more than most people."

As one, the Sisters pounced on Spenser and peppered him with questions. "Where? What's its name? Did you go in to check it out?" Those were among the dozens of questions they threw at him.

Yoko handed over a second cup of black coffee. Spenser drained it, smacked his lips, smiled, and kept talking.

Chapter 15

"I'm kind of hungry, ladies. Do you have anything to eat here? I hate complaining, but I haven't had anything to eat other than a protein bar since yesterday. Duke and I were afraid to let the woman out of our sight for fear we'd lose her. Cheese? Crackers? I'll settle for anything, and a beer would go really good right now. Icy cold. Look, Duke's on it, so my stopping long enough to eat isn't going to change anything. It would be nice if you could pack up some food for me to take to Duke when I leave here, too."

"Of course we can give you food, you dear, sweet man, and for your partner also," Myra said. "We're not usually this inhospitable, but we've been slowly going crazy here trying to sort this all out for Bella. Then you show up with actual results, so we're a little wired right now. I apologize on behalf of all of us. When Avery said you had answers to all our questions, we ran with it. Again, I apologize for all of us. One ham, turkey, and cheese with lettuce and mayo coming up. Pickles and chips on the side."

"And one icy-cold beer," Kathryn said as she pulled a Corona off the door of the refrigerator and took off the cap before she handed it to Spenser.

"Can you make two sandwiches for Duke? He's a big eater."

"Absolutely," Myra said, as she layered bread and cold cuts, while Yoko spread the mayo and layered the lettuce. Isabelle wrapped the two extra sandwiches in tinfoil and slipped them into a paper sack. At the last second, Nikki tossed in two Red Delicious apples.

Spenser propped his legs on a spare chair, his eyes dreamy as he wolfed down his sandwich and swigged his beer. It was as if he were on vacation.

The minute Spenser's jaws stopped moving, Annie said, "Can we get to it now?"

"Did you go inside the clinic?" Alexis asked.

"Did you at least try to bribe the help to find out what was going on with Sara at the clinic?" In your face and ever blunt, she said, "You know the rules, Mr. Spenser. Money talks and bullshit walks. Well?"

Spenser laughed out loud. "Ladies, this is not my first rodeo, nor is it Duke's. Just ask Mr. Snowden here. We can hold our own, but to answer your question, we do indeed have the meat. We paid out some large bribes, but we got what you need. Otherwise, I would not be sitting here, and Duke would not be baby-sitting Sara with a million names."

"What was she doing at the clinic? Do you know?" Annie demanded.

Spenser rolled his eyes. "Of course I know. She was claiming Major Nolan's . . . uh . . . sperm donations. She showed absolutely no interest in Bella Ames's eggs, which she had stored there earlier. When she left the clinic, she left with two of the major's . . . uh . . . donations. There was a man with her dressed in medical garb and he had a medical cooler of some sort. It had a big red cross on it. Our contact, the one we bribed, did not know who the guy was. She surmised he was some kind of medical techie, and that they were taking the sperm to a doctor's office."

"You followed them?" Myra asked.

"Duke did. I stayed behind with the lab tech I was flirting with and bribing at the same time. The major's donations were listed under the name Windsor Andrews. That's Andrew with an *s*. That tells me that the major confided in Sara with a million names, and she's known all along where the donations were. She has his power of attorney. That's how she was able to walk out with the major's . . . donations. My informant said there are eight donations total. Sara took two with her. That means there are six left to carry on the Nolan bloodline. So, unless your Bella has an updated POA, those donations belong to Sara with a million names. She can do whatever she wants with them."

"I got it! I got it! I know what she's going to do! She is going to get artificially inseminated, that's what she's going to do!" Maggie said. "One way or another, she is going to get her piece of Major Nolan. The guy is dead, she can never hope to somehow maybe get him to fall in love with her. Next best thing, bear his child. Make sure Bella never gets her hands on those donations to taint the major's bloodline. Andy Nolan belongs to Sara with a million names, and no one can do anything about it. She hasn't, as far as I can tell, done anything wrong unless you want to string her up for breaking and entering to get copies of stuff from Bella's apartment. But there's no proof she did that, no witnesses to any of that. She pulled it off. I have to say, I'm in awe, and I did not think there was anything in this world that could shock or awe me. But this takes the proverbial cake in my opinion."

The women looked at one another, and as one said, "Oh my God!"

"That was Duke's and my sentiment, too,

when we figured it out," Spenser said. "If there's nothing else, ladies, I need to get this food to Duke." He picked up the messenger bag he'd dropped by his chair and handed it to Snowden.

"Everything we got is in there. All the doctors' names, addresses, receipts, notes, our thoughts. We took a lot of pictures of the inside, as well as the outside, of the house in Kalorama. Oh, there is one other thing, Avery. We got the name Paul Montrose from Sara's husband or whatever he was to her, that guy Steven Conover. He said she was on the phone one day talking to her brother and he heard her mention that name. Conover said he thought Montrose was a member of the major's team, as well as a personal friend. We didn't have time to look into that because Sara kept us hopping. Montrose might know something. Check with the army. As far as I know, that name has never cropped up anywhere else."

The goodbyes were quick and curt. The Sisters started to chatter the moment the door closed behind Matt Spenser. Avery ignored the women as he started to sort through the papers he'd taken from Spenser's messenger bag. He did mutter that neither he nor any other member of his team had come across the name Paul Montrose until Spenser just mentioned him. In other words, a new, clean lead to follow up on.

"Someone call Bella and ask her if she knows who Paul Montrose is?" Annie said.

Maggie said she would do it. She fired off a text and waited for a response.

Maggie read her response. "'Colonel Paul Montrose was Andy's best friend. They were in the same unit. Andy said if they had the time to have a formal wedding, he would ask Paul to be his best man. I don't know anything else about him other than he is not married and was due to get out of the army soon. Then he was going to go to work for some big firm in Silicon Valley, and they were going to pay him scads of money. Andy pretended to be jealous, but he wasn't.' So where does that leave us?" Maggie asked when she had finished reading Bella's text.

"We need to find Colonel Montrose," Myra said.

Annie leaned forward. "I don't see that as being all that hard to do. We know now that he left the military and went to Silicon Valley to work. Maggie, use all your resources to find him. Isabelle, hack into whatever it is you hack into for the military and see what you can find out about him."

"And when we find him . . . ?" Kathryn demanded.

"Then we call him or have Bella call him. We either go to where he is or ask him to come to us. That's a no-brainer," Maggie said. "Bella doesn't know him; she never met him and only knows what Andy told her, which is not all that much. I think it would be good for Bella to meet and talk to one of Andy's best friends. I really want to help that young woman because I feel so bad for her."

"We all want to help her, but you heard Alexis, we can't just bulldog our way into the sister's life and take her out when she didn't break any laws. It's okay to not like someone—"

Yoko literally jumped off her chair and into the air to land on the kitchen table, a perfect ninja move as she put it. "People! Listen to me! What do you mean the sister did not break any laws, that it was all legal? All of you, look at me! Tell me!"

The Sisters and even Avery Snowden all started to babble at once. Annie did a double take and let loose with a sharp whistle. Translation: Quiet down!

"Thank you," Yoko said. "The sister impersonated Bella and stole her eggs! Doesn't that constitute breaking the law? She had them transported somewhere else. That guy Peabody is a witness to the transfer. So we do have a case against her. Nikki, Alexis, you're lawyers, do we or don't we have a case to go after her? It's a simple yes or no question."

Nikki and Alexis responded in unison. "Yes!"

Yoko hopped off the table. Annie patted her on the shoulder, and whispered, "Well done, darling girl. I was getting a little worried there for a minute." Yoko laughed out loud. She loved it when Annie praised her.

Snowden shuffled his papers, then stuffed them in his backpack. He looked around at the Sisters to see if he was still needed. Myra threw her hands in the air. "I guess you can leave, Avery. Things seem to be at a standstill until we hear back from Mr. Montrose. We need to remember California is three hours behind us. We will, of course, apprise you if we hear anything or need your expertise."

"Then I am outta here, ladies. I'll check back in later. I'm going to swing by the house in Kalorama just to see it with my own eyes. I do not trust that woman. Duke and Matt are seasoned operatives and both were Navy Seals, but this woman . . . she's something else. I could see her outwitting them. And as much as I hate to admit it, I think she could maybe bamboozle me in some way." The old spy shook his head in disgust at his own words.

The Sisters laughed. Nikki narrowed her eyes to slits and stared at the old spy. "Not to worry, Avery. Now that we have the skinny on her, she's toast."

Snowden shivered as he waved goodbye and left the kitchen, wondering what kind of devious punishment the Sisters were going to dish out to Sara with a million aliases. He gave himself a mental shake and decided he really didn't want to know. He shivered again in the damp October night as he recalled the look on Nikki's face. For one brief second he almost felt sorry for Sara.

Back inside the kitchen the Sisters sat around the table hashing and rehashing what they'd learned from Matt Spenser and Avery Snowden.

Annie raised her hands and waved them about to gain everyone's attention. "So in the end, this whole . . . super mess comes down to a case of unrequited love. Do I have that right, and do you all agree?"

The Sisters' heads bobbed up and down in unison. They all agreed that Annie was right and spot-on.

"What do you suppose Sara would have done if her brother hadn't died? This whole mess just fell into her lap in a manner of speaking. She never once sought out Bella other than to break into her apartment, and we aren't even a hundred percent sure she did. Would she have just stood off in the distance watching the couple, or would she have tried to ruin the marriage in some way? Personally, knowing what I know about Sara now, I think she would have eventually harmed Bella," Annie said.

"I can see her trying to undermine Bella. I'm sure she did it with Andy's other relationships, so why wouldn't she do it with Bella? As far as she was concerned, Andy was hers. He belonged to her and her alone. She didn't mind sharing him temporarily, but not for good. Marriage means children, family, the whole ball of wax. There would have been no room for Sara in that family. I only say that because I think Andy would have tried to include her, but she wouldn't have wanted any part of that. Being the aunt to the children of the man you love was not in the cards for Sara Windsor. Like I said, Andy was hers. She wasn't sharing," Annie said.

"I see it the same way," Maggie agreed.

"Me too. I could see Bella on an outing with Sara and Bella never coming back owing to some kind of cockamamie accident, arranged by Sara, of course," Kathryn said. Yoko and Alexis nodded to show they agreed with Kathryn. Myra, Annie, and Nikki just shook their heads as they tried to comprehend the lengths Sara would go to try to win Andy's love.

"Stop the presses, everyone. I have a text coming in from . . . drum roll, please . . . Mr. Paul Montrose!" Maggie cried excitedly. "Boy, that was quick!"

Everyone started to babble at once, drowning out what Maggie was trying to say. Annie shook the rafters with a whistle so shrill, Myra covered her ears. "You're worse than a roomful of magpies. Calm down, be quiet, so Maggie can share Mr. Montrose's text. The floor is yours, Maggie," Annie said so softly that the girls had to strain to hear her words.

Maggie cleared her throat and read the brief

text. "'I would be more than happy to hop on the red-eye tonight and appear on your doorstep first thing tomorrow morning. Just give me your address. There is nothing in the world I wouldn't do for Andy's widow and Andy's friends. I'll help in any way I can. I can stay as long as you need me.'"

"Sounds like a sweet man," Myra said. "First thing in the morning sounds really good to me. Will someone notify Avery and make sure he gets the message to his operatives who are surveilling Sara? We don't want her taking off on us since she seems to be such a getaway expert. Matt and Duke might be tired and need to be relieved. Nights are long, and it's easy to let your guard down at three in the morning."

"Done. Mr. Montrose said he is partial to pancakes and would see us for breakfast," Maggie said.

"Done. Avery said he'd pass the word to the boys," Isabelle said. "He also said the shift changes at eleven, so they're good for now."

"I just sent Bella a text explaining the current situation. I told her to be over here at eight tomorrow morning. Wouldn't it be nice if . . . if Mr. Montrose and Bella hit it off? He's single, or at least he was according to Bella," Nikki said.

"Ever the romantic, eh, Nikki," Myra said softly.

"Always and forever." Nikki sighed. "It's just

that Bella is so young to have gone through all that's happened to her. We're going to dump another load of misery on her when we tell her about Sara. How much is one person expected to suck up? She needs a break. So, yes, someone from her husband's past that she can talk to about Andy will do her a world of good. At least I think and hope it works that way. If nothing else, they become friends. His coming here is a good thing for all of us. If that makes me a hopeless romantic, then so be it."

"It's a good thing, dear. Don't ever apologize," Myra assured her.

"I think our biggest problem is who is going to cook breakfast tomorrow morning?" Kathryn said. "I'm not seeing anyone volunteering," she said, then giggled.

"Okay, okay, I'll do it," Maggie grumbled.

"Oh, you dear, sweet child, thank you, thank you," Myra gushed. "Bacon?"

"Don't get carried away, Myra. I said I'd do the pancakes, I didn't say anything about bacon. We need, like, three pounds for just our crew alone, and I bet that guy eats a whole pound himself," Maggie said.

Alexis raised her hand. "Since I'm the one who got us into this mess, I guess it's the least I can do. I'll do the bacon."

The Sisters clapped their hands in appreciation.

"Well, then, I think on that note we can tidy up here and head upstairs to bed. A good night's sleep will have us fresh and dewy-eyed when we meet Mr. Montrose for breakfast. I think if we agree to meet down here at eight, it will be good. I don't expect Mr. Montrose to arrive until around eight thirty, possibly nine o'clock. Let's say we call it a night, girls."

And that's exactly what they did.

Chapter 16

Maggie stifled a yawn as she made her way down to the kitchen using the back stairway. It was early, just two minutes past seven. She had awakened at six o'clock and couldn't go back to sleep, so she'd gotten up, showered, and was now going to start the day by cooking up a batch of pancakes.

Everyone knew she hated cooking, so she had no clue why she'd volunteered to cook breakfast for Paul Montrose. Especially pancakes. The girls all liked pancakes, which meant she was going to be making stacks and stacks of them. She figured each sister would eat at least four. Paul Montrose was probably going to be able to scoff down at least a dozen. Lordy, lordy, she'd be making pancakes till the sun went down. She giggled at the thought; then her thoughts went to Ted and how they would make breakfast on Sunday mornings, read the funnies, then hop back in bed. Those were some of the best days of her life. More days to come just like those if she didn't get carried away over one thing or another and make a mess of her relationship with Ted.

She loved Ted. Ted loved her. For now it would stay that way because to change things might endanger their strange relationship, and she did not want that to happen. Even though she didn't like to cook, she was actually a good cook and Ted loved, loved, loved her blueberry pancakes. She missed him and wished he and the boys would finish up their business in Seattle, which seemed to be taking much more time than anyone had thought it would. She was sure the other Sisters were wishing the same thing.

Maggie sniffed when she hit the bottom step of the stairway. Bacon! Coffee! She looked around. Alexis was already at the stove, wearing an apron. She was separating the bacon, which looked especially lean. "Wow! You're up early," Maggie said.

Alexis laughed. "Do you have any idea how long it takes to cook three pounds of bacon?"

"Actually, I do, so have at it. Do you have any

idea how long it takes to make pancakes for just our crew, and today we have two extra mouths? Why weren't we smart enough to suggest bagels. I would have run into town for them."

"Because you said Mr. Montrose said he liked pancakes. And we want to be nice to Mr. Montrose, so we can pick his brain while we try to arrange something between him and Bella. Or did you forget?" Alexis teased.

Maggie poured herself a cup of coffee. "Sometimes . . . actually, a lot of times, I get caught up in the moment and say something or volunteer for something that sounds so right at that moment, but when it comes to executing whatever it is, I wish I hadn't. Does that make sense?"

"Yep, happens to me all the time. To everyone, I think. What do you think he's like?"

Maggie didn't have to ask whom Alexis was referring to. Paul Montrose was, unfortunately for the Sisters, who all missed their men, the only male within miles on this particular day. "Probably tall, sandy hair, hazel eyes, good build, is a gym rat. Was he the one someone said was forty-three? Not married. Wonder how he escaped that? Maybe he's gay and has a partner. Bella really didn't know much about him other than that her husband considered him his best friend."

"A lot of men who make the military their

career don't want to get married. I read that somewhere. They say it's not fair to the family because they're gone all the time. I hear there are a lot of military bachelors out there. Bella said Mr. Montrose was a full bird colonel, but he got out. I assume that means he actually retired from the military. I guess if he's forty-three, he put in his twenty years and decided not to make the military his life, or was not promoted and had to retire. Now he gets a pension and he can have a second life and get married and have a family if that's in his plans. Maybe, if we're lucky, he and Bella will hit it off and become a couple. And if not, friends. He sounded really nice via his texts. My goal in life is not to be a matchmaker, so I'll just keep my fingers crossed," Maggie said.

The Sisters started to trickle into the kitchen one by one. While everyone was freshly showered and dressed, they all still looked sleepy. As one, they mumbled the word *coffee*, and in the blink of an eye, the pot was empty and Annie was filling it up again. "Whatever would we do without our morning coffee? I think I would just curl up and wither away. How did we ever get so hooked on something?" she asked.

"I don't know, and right now I really don't care," Nikki said as she looked up at the monitor over the door. "I think our guest just arrived. Hop to it, Maggie!"

"Bella isn't here," Myra said.

"That's because you told her to come at eight o'clock, and it's only a quarter of now. Mr. Montrose is also early. Whose turn is it to set the table?" Yoko asked.

"Mine. Oooh, look, he's getting out of the car. Now, girls, that is what I call a mighty-fine-looking specimen," Kathryn joked. "A pity we're all taken. If I weren't, he could park his shoes, or boots as the case may be, under my bed any day of the week."

"You harlot, you," Nikki teased.

Kathryn winked. "I'm just saying out loud what you are all thinking to yourselves, and don't bother to deny it. I really think someone should open the door. He's knocked twice now, and all we're doing is standing here ogling him. Helloooo."

Yoko sprinted across the kitchen and opened the door. "Mr. Montrose, please come in. Let me introduce you to your hosts."

Introductions over, Myra said, "Bella should be here in a few minutes. She's staying in my guest cottage. We were . . . um . . . concerned for her safety, so we thought it wise to . . . to keep her close by."

Nikki stared at the attractive man with the ramrod military posture seated at the table. She didn't think he could possibly sit up any straighter, but he did when he asked, "Is Andy's wife in some kind of danger?" He turned in his chair to stare at Myra and Annie, assuming they were in charge of the group.

"This might be a good time for me to ask you people who you are and how it is you're involved with Bella if she's in danger. Shouldn't you maybe at least think about calling the police? There are eight of you counting the newspaper person!"

"It's a long story, Mr. Montrose," Myra said. "We've just recently come into Bella's life. Alexis and Nikki are lawyers. They are working on Bella's case, and before you can ask, Alexis met Bella by pure chance at a restaurant and offered to help her when she saw her sitting at the table crying. We're simply trying to help her."

Montrose looked around. "So what you're saying is you're strangers to Andy's widow. I don't see Sara anywhere. Shouldn't she be included and be here helping Bella. I think that's what Andy would want. In fact, I know that's what Andy would want. If he thought his wife was in danger, his sister is the first person he would call to take care of her."

Kathryn stood up and stomped her way to the other side of the table. "And how is it that you know what Bella's husband wanted for his wife, Mr. Montrose?" Kathryn snapped.

The Sisters as one were on their feet, surrounding Paul Montrose. Yoko pressed her tiny hands down on Montrose's shoulders. In his life, he'd never felt such pain.

"Talk to us!" Alexis said.

"What the hell . . . who are you people? What's going on here? Where is Bella?"

"I asked you a question. Don't make me ask you again," Kathryn said, leaning in so close that she could smell the man's aftershave and minty breath. She nodded to Yoko, who grinned and increased the pressure on the retired colonel's shoulders.

The kitchen doorbell rang. Isabelle moved to open the door for Bella. "Right on time, good girl!" she said, and smiled at Bella. "Come in, come in, Mr. Montrose just got here, and he was just getting ready to tell us something about Andy."

"Good Lord, he looks . . . he looks like he's in pain." Bella's face registered shock at the scene before her at the table.

"He is," Yoko said cheerfully. She stepped back.

Bella watched the color flood back into Montrose's face. Her hand shot out. "Bella Nolan. It's nice to meet you, Mr. Montrose. I appreciate your coming to help us. Me in particular."

Montrose looked around. "I don't understand any of this." He homed in on Maggie and asked her directly for an explanation as he struggled with the pain in his shoulders, which was slowly easing up.

Maggie sucked in a deep breath and let it out with a loud swoosh of sound. She then let loose and brought Paul Montrose up to date. He looked stunned as he stared at Bella. He thought she was one of the prettiest young women he'd ever seen. He almost said so, but then he remembered she was his best friend's widow. Better he should keep his opinions to himself. For now, anyway.

"No, no, no, that can't be right. I mailed Andy's packet to his sister. In fact, because it was so important, I went to the FedEx office and sent it that way immediately after I dropped Andy back at the base. I can even prove it, since I'm sure I still have copies as well as the receipt. I kid you not, Andy made his flight with a second to spare. On his mad race to the cargo plane, he threw this manila envelope onto the tarmac and yelled for me to mail it for him but to make a copy first. I did what he asked. Then I deployed myself the following day. I never saw Andy again," he said with a catch in his voice. "I didn't even know he'd been killed until about two months ago, when I came East to a wedding for one of the guys. There were six of us from the outfit at the wedding. When it was over we all went to the nearest bar and got drunk, drinking toasts to Andy."

"We're going to need that packet and the receipt, Mr. Montrose," Annie said.

"What was in the manila envelope?" Myra asked. "Did you look at the contents?"

"I didn't read them word for word if that's what you mean. Andy did talk to me about it, so that's how I know. Andy drew up a new power of attorney for Bella. He made a will, and I witnessed it, and so did Zack Bradley. Andy said he left everything to his wife. I asked him about his sister, and he said she was rich and didn't need his money. There were some other . . . personal papers I'm not comfortable talking about in the envelope."

"You mean the sperm donations?" Kathryn barked.

Montrose flushed. "You know about that?"

"Andy told me," Bella said. "I've never seen or heard from Andy's sister. As Maggie told you, it was all such a horrible mess. I didn't know what to do. I didn't hear from Andy for months and months. I didn't even know he'd been wounded. I was told he never told anyone he was married, so any and all communications were with Sara, who took it all. His military insurance, his pay, everything. I never got a dime. If she knew about me, she made no effort to get in touch with me. She knew Andy was dead, and she didn't care enough to let me know. I will never get over that or forgive her for it. It wasn't the money, although things were tight, what with payment for his new truck."

Bella took a deep breath. "When I couldn't take it anymore I went to a lawyer and filed for divorce. I assumed Andy had had a change of heart and regretted our quickie marriage. Especially when the other wives I contacted told me that they had FaceTimed with their husbands at least once a week plus almost daily e-mails. I was making myself sick and could barely function, so I did what I thought I needed to do for my own well-being. The day I signed the divorce papers was the same day I found out that Andy had died. I tried finding Sara but had no luck. The army people had not had any success at that, either.

"Sara impersonated me and went to the clinic and helped herself to my eggs, and I guess she took the sperm donations, too. I didn't know where those were. Andy never told me, and I didn't ask. I don't know why I didn't ask. I think because it sounded so . . . so decadent."

"We've been on Bella's case for almost two weeks now. We've been searching for Andy's sister with no success until last night, when we finally found out where she is. Right now we are doing our best to try to figure out how to handle the situation and deal with this. We brought Bella here because we think Sara is deranged. We all agreed she might try to harm Bella if she found out that Bella was looking into this whole mess. By the expression on your face, it looks to me like you're still skeptical. You do know that Sara is not Andy's blood sibling, right?" Nikki said.

"What? No! Andy never alluded to that. He just referred to Sara as his sister. He loved her like a sister from what I could tell. He constantly said how great she was, how he trusted her. He told me he didn't think he could have gotten to where he was in his life without her and how grateful he was to her. The only thing that bothered him was she couldn't seem to make a relationship last. Other than that, in his eyes, she was perfect. He said she was on to the next man and then another one, looking for Mr. Perfect. Like she was searching for the perfect man and couldn't find him. He said he really couldn't fault her for that because everyone was looking for the perfect life partner. Andy simply was not judgmental the way most of us are. This is just blowing my mind.

"If all you say is true, and I'm not really doubting you, I don't understand how Andy could believe and love her the way he did and not see what she was all about. She would have to be damn near perfect to pull that off, and let me tell you, Andy Nolan was no fool. He was smart as a whip, top of every class we took, and we were together from the get-go. Even though I was older, it didn't make a difference."

Myra scoffed. "Some men are not particularly wise when it comes to women. They never look for some reason beyond the surface. What they see and hear is all they need to know for some reason. I don't doubt for a moment that Andy was smart, but Sara Windsor was, I don't want to say smarter, but she was calculating, manipulative, and downright sneaky. She wanted Andy for herself, but she was smart enough to know while Andy was what she wanted, she was not what Andy wanted. She had a plan and she made it work for her. The one thing she didn't count on was Andy's dying."

"And she didn't count on Andy's finding Bella and falling in love," Alexis added. "The tricks that had probably worked with other relationships Andy had had didn't work in regard to Bella. From what we understand, Andy more or less stopped confiding in Sara, so Sara knew almost next to nothing about her. Sara had to hire private detectives to search her out. One of our people discovered that. Most of this is conjecture on our part, but conjecture or not, when you piece it together, it makes sense. Andy Nolan was Sara's life. Period. End of story."

Paul Montrose slapped at his head, his eyes on Bella. "I just . . . It's just so hard to believe. Andy was so . . . so . . . enamored of his sister. He really did love her. But, *as* a sister. I believe what you're telling me, I really do. I'm just having a hard time accepting it for what it is. It's killing me, but I do believe you. Now, tell me what I can do. Whatever it is you need me to do, I can do. No ifs, ands, or buts."

"We need you to go back to California and send us that packet of papers Andy gave you to send to Sara. Nikki and Alexis, because they're our attorneys, will visit the army and the probate lawyers and take it from there. We have to be extra careful right now because we don't want to spook Sara. She has no clue, at least we don't think so, that we're onto her. She thinks she's safe. We do have two-man shifts surveilling her twenty-four/seven to make sure she doesn't skip out. It's uncanny how they tell us she can disappear, then appear across the country with a totally new identity," Annie said. "Our people are telling us she has dozens of aliases that she uses."

Montrose just sat there and shook his head back and forth, his eyes glassy. "I don't have to go back to California. I have a town house here in Alexandria. I bought it before my last deployment, when Andy said that when he got out he was going to buy a house in Kalorama. Neither one of us wanted our friendship to wither on the vine, so to speak. You know, a card at Christmas with the year's happenings penciled in at the end with a postscript. We talked a lot about going to Redskins games, taking our kids to football games, and enrolling them in Little League.

"I stored all my gear and everything I owned in the town house, which wasn't all that much when I deployed the last time. I liked the idea of having a place here on the East Coast. I thought about selling it when I found out about Andy, but somehow I just never got around to doing it because I was too busy making a new home for myself in California. My two brothers took me in as a full partner in a firm they started when I was in the army. I kind of like living there, but I'm partial to the East Coast for some reason.

"Andy must have told his sister that's where he was going to buy a house if you say that's where she's living now. Again, if true, it shows how much he thought of her and how he discussed everything with her. Like I said, she was everything to him. She was family, and family was important to Andy. Even though, as you say, she wasn't a blood relative. Obviously, he didn't care about that, and they were raised together.

"This is eating me alive. All this time . . . I wish I had known . . . I don't know what I could have done, but something. I would have . . ."

Maggie set a plate in front of him with a dozen pancakes piled high. Montrose took one look at it and shook his head. "I really and truly appreciate your taking the time to make those for me, but I don't think I could eat a bite of them. Suddenly, I just want to go running and breathe cold air. Would you all mind if I do that?"

The Sisters all looked at one another, shock and surprise on their faces. Maggie, on the other hand, just eyed the plate of pancakes.

"I think that's a really good idea. I feel the same way. Do you mind if I run with you, Colonel?" Bella asked.

Paul Montrose was clearly flustered. He nodded his head and headed toward the door, Bella right behind him.

"Just follow the path to the barn, and then you'll see our bike trail. Follow it. It's a three-mile run from start to finish. More than enough time to clear your heads. Perhaps when you return, you'll feel more like eating," Myra said gently.

When the door closed behind the stressed-out couple, Kathryn looked around and asked what they all thought.

"He's what he is—a good, kind, loyal friend. I saw him look at Bella every chance he could. I would say she's a subject of interest, and I do not think any of us need to worry about fixing them up. I think they'll do it on their own. And I say good for them," Isabelle added.

Annie's fist pumped the air. "We got her! Now we need to start thinking about how we're going to bring this to a conclusion and not spook Sara whatever the hell her name is in the process," Alexis said.

"Let's finish these pancakes. And then we can get down to work," Maggie said, as she dug into the stack of pancakes Paul Montrose had left behind.

Chapter 17

Sara Nolan. The name rolled off Sara's tongue like pure liquid silk. She was, according to the paper in her hand, officially as well as legally now Sara Nolan. Soon to be the mother of Andy Nolan's child. The gold seal on the certificate said it was so. That meant she was legally Sara Nolan, and no one walking the earth could do a damn thing about it. Her fist shot high in the air to signal her victory.

Sara took a moment to look upward, wondering if Andy was peering down from some fluffy cloud and seeing what she was holding in her hand. She realized how silly and stupid that thought was and laughed out loud. She knew, and that was all that was important. One of these days, she would go to the cemetery and sit down and have a long talk with Andy. One of these days.

Maybe she would wait till the baby was born to do that so she could take him or her with her. Yes, yes, yes, that was a better idea. That way, if there really was an afterlife and a spirit could look down, Andy would do so and see his firstborn. Sara grimaced, not sure if that idea was just as silly and stupid as her original thought or not.

Sara sighed. She had months to go till that could happen. Her doctor had warned her of the possibility of a miscarriage. She refused to allow her mind to even contemplate the warning. She would do everything possible, including bed rest if it came to that. She'd simply hire round-the-clock nurses to take care of her. Months of pampering was something she could live with.

Sara slid the paper she was holding into a glossy yellow folder and put it in a small cedar chest in the dining room. She'd purchased the chest to hold what she considered to be the most important documents pertaining to Andy Nolan. It was the only thing she ever took with her when she moved from place to place. It was hers and Andy's. She giggled when she thought, never leave home without it. Like that would ever happen.

The huge, six-thousand-square-foot house yawned around her. There were echoes everywhere because she hadn't totally furnished it. The reason for that was that she wasn't sure how many children she wanted. A house this big cried out for a large family. Andy always said he wanted enough kids to have his own baseball team. He'd laughed like a lunatic then and said that he would have the baseball team and she could have her kids be their cheerleaders. Though she'd laughed right along with him, she didn't think it was at all funny. Then he put his arm around her shoulder the way a brother would do, and said, "We'll always be side to side, Sara. Me and you against the world." There was no mention of where the mother of the baseball team and father of the cheerleader squad would be. She liked the way it all sounded, so she just kept smiling.

Sara looked around. She'd chosen well when she had picked this house. Andy had said he'd looked at it once when he was in town and said it was a perfect house to raise a family. He also said that the reason it wasn't selling was because it was overpriced. Andy was always frugal and looked for bargains, a trait he had inherited from his mother. Sara, on the other hand, never bothered to ask the price of anything. If it was something that caught her eye or she wanted it, she simply bought it, no questions asked.

Walking from room to room, she tried to imagine what the house would look like furnished from top to bottom. What would it be like with kids running around and sliding down the polished banister on the staircase? Add in a few barking dogs and a couple of cats, maybe a parrot and some hamsters to round out it all. In a word, a family. A family minus a dad. Sad but doable. Definitely doable. As she walked around the rooms, she crossed her fingers behind her back that the insemination would work. If not, she would keep trying until it did work. She didn't come this far to give up over an initial setback.

Sara walked into the kitchen and sat down at the counter. She longed for a glass of wine, but the doctor had said no drinking or smoking. A glass of ginger ale would have to do.

She noticed that her hand was trembling when she opened the refrigerator. She was antsy, jittery for some reason. Why? Everything was just fine; everything had gone off just the way she'd planned it. She was sitting pretty right now, so why was she feeling like this? She tried to define the feeling to herself so she could get a handle on things. It was as if she were waiting for the other shoe to drop, which was downright silly because the first shoe hadn't even dropped. So, then, what was it?

There had been no glitches. Her finances, which were beyond robust, were safe and secure. All her assets, of which there were many, were being cared for and had finally been cataloged and filed away. Her money manager was top-notch and worth every penny she paid him. So if all that was in order, what was it that was bothering her? The little widow? Was she going to cause some trouble? Of course she was, that was a given.

Sara eyed the ginger ale in her glass and decided it was flat. Apple juice would have been a better choice and, of course, healthier. If she wanted apple juice, she either had to go to the supermarket or call in an order, and that would mean she needed to make a grocery list.

Sara's acrylic nails drummed on the countertop. Her life, as she knew it now, was brand-new. No more chasing rich men to add to her assets. She bit down on her lower lip as she contemplated the changes she would have to undergo, along with the fear that Bella would somehow find her and rip everything away from her. All Bella had to do was find Andy's friend, Paul Montrose, and it would all be over. Maybe. She had to believe everything was as airtight as her lawyer said it was. Of course, she had not bothered to tell him about Andy's new will and the new POA paper Andy had had Montrose send her.

Possession was nine tenths of the law, and she had possession of the will and the new POA. She hadn't bothered to file anything. Why would she? She knew she would have to be extra careful going forward. She could not put herself out there for anyone to see. The name of the game now was hunker down and live the life of a recluse.

No one knew she was now legally Sara Nolan except her and her lawyer. Not even her doctors knew, and she planned to keep it that way. At least for now. The name change had been strictly for her own satisfaction. She had taken on a whole new identity after she had left Steven Conover and sent him the phony divorce papers. The deed to this house, the title to the Mercedes in the garage, and her brand-new driver's license plus three new credit cards were in the name of Nora Lewis. The little bronze plate on her mailbox also carried the name of Nora Lewis. All the utilities were in the name of Nora Lewis and paid ahead for a full year. All she had left to do was establish an account at the supermarket and drugstore, and she would have her new life all set up in a neat box with a big red ribbon on top.

Tears rolled down Sara's cheeks. All her plans were in place. There had been no glitches that amounted to anything. She was about to start living the life she planned.

Yes, she could live that life, but she wasn't happy. She wasn't happy because Andy wasn't here. Andy would never be here, and if he were, he would want to be with Bella, not her. There was just no way she could ever live with that. Some way, somehow, she needed to eliminate that woman. Now that she had her new life in order, she couldn't let that little snot ruin it.

Sara knew in her heart that Andy would never want her even if she was holding his baby in her arms. He'd snatch the child from her and give it to Bella. Maybe knowing all of that was the reason she was feeling so tense and jittery.

Maybe it was time to make a new plan. A new plan that erased Bella from her life. Her mood lifted at the thought. She turned on the stereo with a remote that was on the kitchen counter and proceeded to dance around the kitchen to Bon Jovi, Andy's favorite band.

One new plan coming up!

Paul Montrose held the door of his rental car until Bella was inside and buckled up. Once he was behind the wheel and the engine was running, he turned to Bella. "I don't know about you, but this feels . . . awkward as hell." He threw his hands in the air, and said, "And I have no clue why that is. I could talk nonstop for days about Andy Nolan and, suddenly, I can't think of a thing to say."

Bella smiled. "I can relate. I have a million questions to ask you, and right now I can't think of a single one. I think you probably knew Andy better than I did. That goes for Sara the sister who isn't his sister, too. Andy and me . . . it was so quick, so fast, not enough time to learn about each other. It was about us and the moment we were in. I guess we both thought we had the rest of our lives to learn about each other. I'm ashamed and embarrassed to admit right now that there are times I barely remember him. Our time was so short. I think if I could condense the hours into days that we were actually together as in face-to-face, it would be ten days, and that's probably stretching it."

"And yet you fell in love with each other," Paul said gently, as he backed up the rental car and drove through the gates of Pinewood. Outside the gates, he stopped just long enough to program the address of his town house in Alexandria into the GPS.

"I suppose. Right now, I'm not even sure what I feel or what I thought I felt. The truth is, this has been such a nightmare, I just want this all settled so I can get on with my life."

"How do you plan to do that?" Paul asked.

"Well, for starters, I'm relocating to North Carolina, where I have a distant cousin. I have no other relatives. Starting over. I can't do that until . . . until . . . the girls tell me it's safe to do that."

"Those women back there in the farmhouse . . . do you trust them?"

Paul's voice sounded so anxious, Bella laughed out loud.

"Oh yeah," she drawled, still laughing.

"What's so funny?" Paul asked, taking his eyes off the road long enough to stare at Bella. "What did I say that was so funny?" he repeated.

"You really don't know who those women are, do you?"

Paul shrugged. "Two are lawyers, two are older. One is a truck driver, one is an architect, and the Asian lady owns a plant nursery. And then there is the reporter for the *Post*. As a group, are they famous or something?"

Bella laughed again. "Or something. Remember a few years ago, when the Vigilantes hit the scene and turned things upside down?"

Paul took his eyes off the road again to stare at Bella, his jaw dropping. "Tell me you're kidding."

"Nope, and they're on my side."

"I'll be damned. Now that's something Andy would have gotten a kick out of. We used to talk about those women. All the guys in our company did. I mean those women kicked ass and took names later. We were all rooting for them. I know that's hard to believe, but it's true. We all respect a true warrior, and it doesn't matter if they're male or female. A warrior is a warrior. I don't think Andy's sister will be any match for them, do you?"

"I'm hoping not. I'm sorry to be doing this. I would have liked nothing more than to be friends with Andy's sister. Now, knowing what I know, I don't want to be within a mile of her. I can't believe she bamboozled Andy. Andy was so smart. How could he not see what she was?"

"Well, I believed everything he told me about his sister, too, so what does that make me? Because . . . he believed what he was saying, so there was no reason to doubt him. He thought the world of her, and I can tell you right now, he never thought of her in any way other than as his sister. Whatever she thought she had going on was on her side only.

"What's your game plan, or don't you have one? You know that I can stay on here as long as you all need me. My brothers told me to take as much time as I need. We're a close bunch, so in a way I can identify with how close Andy was with Sara.

"See that red brick complex up ahead? That's where my town house is. It took us forty minutes to drive here from the farmhouse where you were staying. That's not a bad ride, and we did hit traffic."

"Why did you pick this area to buy in?"

"It was what I could afford because I wanted to pay cash and not have a mortgage. I just wanted someplace to stay when I came back East. I'm not a fancy kind of guy, in case you haven't noticed. I'm not into possessions and putting on the dog. I'm just a guy who's making his way. Like I said, my family is pretty tight-knit. We're all alike, which means we share and share alike. Andy liked that. He met my family. Now, he did say his sister would never fit into our brood. I was okay with that.

"Here's the thing. I never met Sara. And yet I introduced him to my entire family. Everyone liked him, and he liked them. There were several times when Sara was in the area, and he could have introduced us. But he never did. Until now, I could never figure that out.

"That's my town house on the left. I bet there are six inches of dust on everything, so I apologize ahead of time."

"We could clean it. I don't have anything to do, no plans except to go back to Pinewood and watch television. Do you have any cleaning supplies?"

"Are you kidding?" Paul asked in awe.

Bella giggled. "Do I sound like I'm kidding?"

"You're blowing my mind here." Paul chuckled. "But to answer your question, I bought the place from a retired schoolteacher who was moving to Florida. She left the entire contents. She even left me a bottle of aspirin in the bathroom medicine cabinet. Everything was in excellent condition, no wear or tear, and she said she was going to buy new stuff to fit the condo in sunny Florida. It was win-win for both of us. I personally think I got the better of the bargain," Paul said, chuckling.

"Then I guess we're good to go. After we

check out the papers Andy gave you. That was pretty smart of you to make a copy."

"That was Andy's idea. I doubt I would have thought of it on my own. It was kind of wild that day. I think I told you that Andy made his flight with no time to spare. Truth be told, he almost forgot to give me that packet. He was so busy talking about you and the two days you had together. I really miss him. He was a truly great friend, one in a million. Everyone should have a friend like Andy," Paul said, his voice choking up.

Bella stared out at the busy parking lot of the town house complex. "This is really hard to put into words, Paul. I don't expect you will understand either because I don't understand it myself . . . I don't feel anything. I guess it was all those months of not hearing a word, hearing the other wives talk about the daily contact, the FaceTime. I made myself sick. At first I was crushed. I thought I was going to just lie down and die. I couldn't function. I didn't eat or sleep. All I did was cry.

"Then it all stopped. I was me again. It was like Andy was someone I used to know but not very well. Almost like he had moved away and forgotten to say goodbye. It probably doesn't make sense to you because I couldn't even figure it out. My feelings right now are all mixed up, and I blame it on Sara. I think I was jealous of her, in the beginning. Not now, though.

Now I am afraid of her. I mean that literally. I can't tell you how relieved I was when Myra asked me to come out to the farm so I would be safe. They were on the same page as I was, so I knew I had to pay attention. Sara whatever her name is means me harm. I am certain of that."

All Paul could do was stare at Bella. He wished he had a magic wand to wipe the misery from her beautiful face. He had to find a way to help her. Andy would expect him to step in and protect her. "Now that I know all that, I am not leaving here until all of this is resolved. I'll ask those ladies if I can pitch a tent out there near where you are staying. I won't let you out of my sight. Remember," he chuckled, "I've had combat training."

"Deal," Bella said, stretching out her hand. She was aware instantly of how hard and calloused Paul's hand was. What she wasn't prepared for was the jolt of electricity that raced through her whole body. Whoa, Nellie.

Paul Montrose felt his eyes glaze over when he clasped Bella's hand. Something he had never in his life felt wrapped itself around him as he struggled to take a deep breath.

Bella withdrew her hand and stared up into Paul Montrose's glazed eyes. "I . . . ah . . . um . . ."

Paul shook his head, and said, "Uh . . . ah . . ."

"I need some exercise. I'll race you to the door!"

"Now that's a hell of an idea," Paul said, in a voice that was so strangled that he barely recognized it as his own.

Chapter 18

Paul unlocked the door of the town house and stood back for Bella to enter. He quickly disarmed the security system, then walked around to open all the windows and rid the house of the musty, closed-up smell. "I covered everything with dust sheets the way the previous owner told me to. I have only come back East once since I bought this place, and that was to pay the bills ahead for a year in case I forgot or something went awry. It's comfortable, as you can see, perfect for a bachelor like me. What do you think needs to be done? Where should we start?" he asked, a hopeless expression on his face.

Bella looked around, relieved that they were

on a friendly footing again and not . . . *Don't go there,* she warned herself. "I guess we should start by washing all these dust sheets. I can do that while you search out Andy's paperwork. You do have a washer and dryer, don't you?"

"I do, it's outside the guest bathroom on the second floor. Soap and stuff is in the closet where the unit is. It's a stackable, one on top of the other to save space. Margaret, that was the owner's name, said for one person like herself, and now me, it was perfect. I'm going to turn on the A/C even though it's nippy with all the windows open. It might help to get rid of the musty smell more quickly."

Bella took off her denim jacket, rolled up the sleeves of her button-down shirt, and went at it. She worked quickly and efficiently, Paul noticed. Almost like she was in the military and knew all about precision. Once or twice, she called out a question while Paul rummaged through boxes in what had been Margaret's master bedroom. The small dressing room was Margaret's mini office and was around the corner from the kitchen on the first floor. He wished now he had marked the boxes with the contents, but he'd been in such a hurry back then. Now he might have to go through each and every one of them until he found what he wanted.

"Do you want me to plug in the refrigerator? Are you really going to stay here on the East Coast? If so, I will clean it out. In case you don't know this, it takes twenty-four hours for a refrigerator and freezer to reach the right temperature."

"Yes, plug it in. I told you I'm staying on until I'm satisfied you're completely safe. I'll go shopping later for what I need, so wipe it down and plug it in. Please," he added as an afterthought.

Bella smiled to herself. He was staying. The thought made her happy for some reason. *Some reason my foot.* She grimaced. *Be honest with yourself, girl. Admit it, if only to yourself, that you are attracted to this man. This man who was your husband's best friend. Good Lord, what kind of person am I turning into?* She felt her face and neck grow warm. A minute ago, she had been shivering.

She whirled around and whipped out a can of Clorox wipes from the tiny closet. She moved like a whirlwind, wiping down and then drying everything so she wouldn't have time to think.

An hour passed, then another, before Paul bellowed, "Enough!"

"That works for me. I'm done down here. All that's left is to put the sheets back on the furniture and close up everything. I think I could use some heat right now, so I'm going to turn off the A/C and close all the windows. Everything smells clean and fresh. Is that okay with you, Paul?"

"Yes. I'm going to order a pizza and some beer. You up for that?"

"I absolutely am," Bella said. Then she smiled when she realized she felt happy. Not just so-so happy, but genuinely happy. She couldn't remember the last time she had felt like this.

"So you found Andy's paperwork?"

"All in one place, too. Of course, it was in the last box and at the very bottom. Here it is," Paul said, handing over the packet of papers to Bella. She noticed the tremor in his hands but only because it matched the tremor in her own. She took a long, deep breath and looked Paul square in the eye. "Thank you," she whispered.

Paul nodded, not trusting himself to speak. He turned around, pulled out his phone, then plucked a magnet off the refrigerator with the name of a local pizza emporium, one he guessed that Margaret used. He called in his order and gave his credit card information. He was told a piping-hot pizza with all the trimmings would be delivered along with two Bud Lights in twenty minutes.

Paul looked over at Bella. He winced when he saw tears rolling down her cheeks. She looked up at him. She waved the papers at Paul. "I don't know if you believe me or not, but this is not about money for me. I just couldn't comprehend Andy's not taking the time to advise the military of his new status. I took it, right or wrong, to mean that I wasn't important enough to do all that, and he'd get around to me when he could. And then all those months with no word . . . part of me feels guilty for the way I felt, and another part of me feels justified. Right now, I don't feel anything in regard to Andy. I hate saying that. I really do because I do not understand how that can be. I know that doesn't say much for me as a person, but I can't help it. I'm starting to wonder if I was in love with the idea of love, and Andy just came along at the right moment. I barely knew him. I married a man I barely knew. That's so sad. Just from the little you and I have spoken, it is clear that you knew him better than I ever did. This is all so surreal. It's scaring me.

"These papers . . . He made a new will. I assume it's legal since you and Zack witnessed it. And here is a new power of attorney with my name on it. Andy was worth millions of dollars. I never knew that. All I wanted was enough money to help pay for his truck. If he had all that money, why did he buy a truck on time? It doesn't make sense."

"Sure it does. Andy wanted to be like every other guy on the team. We were all struggling. He inherited most of what he had. He told me once that made him feel dishonest. He also said that Sara invested his money. He didn't feel like it was really his. And . . . believe it or not, he had a game plan as to how he was going to give most of it away when he got out and was a civilian. You do realize that what you are holding in your hands supersedes anything Sara has, right? Doesn't matter whether she filed it or not. It's now a legal issue. Tomorrow, your lawyer can file these papers at the courthouse."

"It's strange that Andy didn't leave anything to his beloved sister. I know that sounds snarky, but it's how I feel. But in the end, everyone believed her, and she got it all. We need to go back to the farm and show all of this to the girls. We need to be on top of it, so she doesn't pack up and hit the road," Bella said. "I'm going to send a text off to Alexis so she can alert the men who are stationed out at Sara's house. Their guy might need to add more people, and he'll probably want to see all these papers with his own eyes before he does anything. Mr. Snowden was an MI6 agent. A superspy for the queen. He retired and relocated here to work for Charles, who is married to Myra. He was also a spy for the queen. Martin and the queen were childhood friends. Fergus is Annie's significant other. He used to head up Scotland Yard. The three of them worked together over the years and now work for . . . the ladies. Annie de Silva is Countess Anna de Silva, one of the richest women in the world. Myra, I'm told, is no pauper either when it comes to having money."

Paul whistled. "You do travel with some impressive people. I had no idea." His voice and his expression were so full of awe, Bella burst out laughing.

"That's how I felt when I found out. You'll get used to it. For the most part, all of the women are pretty normal and ordinary." She laughed again when she said, "Just don't ever turn your back on any one of them, even Maggie, the reporter."

Paul nodded because he didn't know what else to do. "But one of them said that the house Sara is living in is under surveillance by your people round-the-clock. If she gets spooked and takes it on the lam, they'll catch her."

"There are just two of them out there now. Front door, back door, side door, basement door. Various windows. From what I've been told, Sara is a remarkable escape artist, and she also excels at various disguises." Bella talked nonstop until the pizza arrived. They ate and guzzled until everything was gone. Then they cleaned up, checked all the windows and doors, set the alarm, and left the town house. Paul tossed the pizza box and the beer bottles in the Dumpster in the parking lot.

"Back to the farm, right?"

"Yes, we need to bring this to a close as soon as possible. Not us but the Sisters. You do understand there is no way we can interfere in any of this going forward. That's how they work. We can voice our opinions, but that's it.

Tell me you understand, Paul. Otherwise, I cannot take you back to the farm," Bella said.

Paul looked down at her anxious face. He wanted to cup her face in his hands and kiss her. He had never wanted anything more in his whole life. He jammed his hands in his pockets and looked down at his feet. "I understand. Remember, I'm ex-army. I'm trained to follow orders whether I like them or not. Right now, I'm just here to do whatever I can. I won't botch it up. I know who's in charge. And it is not me. Okay, let's go now that we have that all cleared up."

"You look upset," Bella said quietly. "You don't agree, is that it? I think we need to clear that up before we leave here, or there are going to be problems. Or is it that you resent taking orders from a bunch of women?"

"What?" The single word exploded out of Paul's mouth like a gunshot. "Good God, no! I . . . just . . . I'm fighting with myself here not to grab you and kiss you till your teeth rattle."

"Then maybe instead of thinking about it, you should do something about that thought." *Good Lord, did I just say that out loud? I guess so,* she thought, as she felt hot lips crushing her own.

Paul was the first to pull away. He stepped back to stare at the woman whose world he had just rocked out from under her. He needed to do something, say something, but he was frozen to the floor, his tongue glued to his teeth. He was mesmerized as he watched Bella lick at her swollen lips. She said, in a harsh whisper, "I think we should head back to the farm. Like right now would be good."

He followed her to his rental car. He really needed to say something.

"Looks like it's going to rain," Bella said. "I like a good rainstorm sometimes, but only if I'm safe inside. When I was a little girl, I would hide under the covers when it would thunder and lightning." Bella babbled away to hide the way she really felt and what she really wanted to say.

Paul swallowed hard. He joined in and started to recount his own boyhood tales of storms he'd weathered. *So that's how we're going to play it.*

That rock-my-world kiss never happened.

But it did happen. And they both knew it and were hyperaware of it.

"They're back!" Annie said, looking at the overhead monitor.

"And they have the goods, as the saying goes," Nikki said.

"I just got a text from Avery saying he is three miles out and will be here shortly. He said he has the house surrounded. Six operatives are on duty. Sara with a million aliases is not going anywhere. Well, she might try, but she won't get farther than the doorway," Myra said.

"Isabelle, how's it going with her finances? Do you have them all? Even the overseas ones?" Nikki asked.

"I have seventy-five percent of them. Abner's friend Phil is helping me. He said he'd have the ones that are off the beaten path shortly. He did say she is pretty smart, and that not many people know how to utilize whatever it is he uses to track . . . um . . . other people's illegal money."

Alexis's fist shot in the air. "The only thing that is important is we got her. We really got her. And all that lovely money. Bella, you are going to be a very rich young woman."

Bella held up her hands, palms outward. "Like I said, for me this was never about the money. All I wanted was enough to pay off Andy's truck, the tax on it, and the insurance. I didn't want him to go to his maker as a deadbeat who didn't pay his bills. I was expecting a little to help me with my move. Paul said Andy had some ideas of what he was going to do with his inheritance and his own personal fortune when he retired from the military. I'll do whatever it was he wanted. I don't need his money; I can support myself.

"I thought I would keep Andy's life insurance, and that would take care of everything. I really thought he would have left his money to his sister. Of course, that was before I knew what I now know."

"That's a lot of money to give away," Kathryn said. "If you factor in all the money Sara scammed from unsuspecting men, we're going to be busy distributing it to worthy causes, minus our expenses." The others agreed with Kathryn's statement but also agreed they would all be happy doing it.

"I also made another decision," Bella said, looking at Alexis. "I'm going to need your help, I'm thinking. I want the clinic to dispose of my eggs and Andy's donations. I want that done as soon as possible. I have a sick feeling that Sara already . . . I think she . . . I do not think Andy would want Sara to carry his child. He would think that was incestuous even though it wouldn't be since they aren't blood relatives. I want them destroyed," she said firmly.

"Nikki and I can legally take care of that for you," Alexis said. "And for whatever it's worth, I think you are doing the right thing. And from what we know of Andy, I think you are right about that, too. I do not think he would want Sara giving birth to his child. Better, he would think, just to let it fade away."

"Avery's here," Myra said, as she walked to the kitchen door to let the old spy in. He was grinning from ear to ear.

"We got her. She's not going anywhere,"

Avery said, as Annie thrust Bella's papers into his hands. Satisfied at what he was seeing, he started to laugh. "Okay, ladies and one man, what's our next move?"

"Everyone, head for the dining room, take a seat, get comfortable. Myra and I will make fresh coffee; then we'll join you all to decide our final move," Annie announced.

As the two women bustled about the kitchen, they whispered to each other.

"I have to say, this mission ate at me, Myra. I didn't think we had a snowball's chance of making this come out right for Bella."

"I agree. What we lost sight of was Andy himself. He was, according to Bella, a stand-up guy. He would have done the right thing no matter what. At the last second, yes, and on the fly, but he did do what was expected of him. We can forgive him that laxness, he just got married to the girl of his dreams, and that's all he was thinking about. I feel so bad for Bella. I'm sorry Andy passed. Life would have been so promising for them both."

"Annie, by any chance did you happen to notice anything different between Mr. Montrose and Bella?" Myra asked, a smile tugging at the corners of her mouth.

"I certainly did. That mouth of hers was kissed solidly for a very long time. Their eyes are glassy. I'm happy for them, but they're both feeling guilty and don't know what to do about it. That's the sad part."

"They'll figure it out and go on from there. It may take a while, but they both have all the time in the world now," Myra said.

"I agree. Coffee's ready," Annie said, picking up the tray.

Myra held the swinging door leading to the dining room open. "Just coffee, people, and we're fresh out of goodies," she said, setting the heirloom silver tray on the sideboard. "Avery, we're out of tea, so it's coffee or ginger ale."

"Ginger ale is fine. Okay, ladies and gents, let's get to it!"

Chapter 19

Kathryn waited until Paul Montrose raised the huge golf umbrella so that it covered Bella and himself in preparation to walking Bella back to the cottage, where Myra had invited him to stay before she locked and bolted the door.

Paul grinned. He didn't bother to demur. He simply said okay and squeezed Bella's arm in a show of protection. The little move did not go unnoticed by the Sisters or Avery, who smiled.

Love was in the air, and it was more than a little noticeable.

"Okay, people, time to head to the war room

and get this show on the road. Avery, what are your operatives telling you?" Annie asked, as she led the way to the bookshelf that would magically open to reveal the moss-covered stone staircase that led to the dungeons below and the war room.

"Reports have come in, but there has been no activity. They are picking up sound, human and either TV or stereo. It's doubtful Sara will venture out in this deluge. But, if she does, my people will be on her like fleas on a dog."

Myra turned on the lights, and the massive TV on the wall came to life to reveal Lady Justice in all her glory. They all shot off a snappy salute before taking their assigned seats at the table. Except for Nikki and Isabelle, who scampered up to the dais, where the bank of computers awaited them.

"We're up and running, so let's get to it," Nikki called out.

"Before we do anything, we need to decide what we're going to do with all of Sara's money. I'd like to get on this right now because Phil is waiting to help me, and I hate tying him up any more than necessary. Remember, I'm in training and need all the help I can get so we don't have to depend on Abner all the time," Isabelle reminded them.

"Okay, girls, let's run this up the flagpole and see what happens. Yoko?" Myra said.

"Let's start with Bella. She said all she wanted

was enough to pay off Andy's truck, plus the insurance and taxes. That doesn't seem fair enough to me. Maybe it's because I'm a woman, maybe not, but I keep thinking about all the pain, the misery, the unhappiness she went through all those months. I think she deserves to be compensated, and obviously her husband thought so, too, because at the eleventh hour, he came through for her," Yoko said.

"I believe Bella when she said she didn't want Andy's money. She certainly didn't marry him for it because she didn't even know he had any other than his military pay. I say Nikki and Alexis set up a trust of some kind for Bella's future. If she uses it, fine; if not, that's fine, too. She can donate it to charity," Kathryn said.

"I think three million dollars will do it plus a check for $75,000 to pay off the truck, taxes, and insurance," Alexis said.

"I think that will work," Avery said. "What about the fertility clinics?"

"Alexis and I are on that. We'll see that Bella's and Andy's ah . . . um . . . donations are destroyed since that is what Bella wants," Nikki said.

"That just leaves Sara with a million aliases. What should we do with her?" Annie asked, a tight edge to her voice.

"Even though we have liberated most of the assets that were in her name or any of the names we know about, we're going to have our hands full trying to sort out the rest of her false identities and the various bank and brokerage accounts into which she placed what she swindled from her boyfriends, fiancés, and the like. Let us not forget that she is an outright thief. She stole Andy's inheritance. She made Bella's life miserable. How could she not tell that girl that her husband was dead? How? She has to pay for that?" Nikki said vehemently.

"We can do most of that for you and give you a summary," Avery said. "Then, if you want, you could attempt to repay some of the men she stole from, like Steve Conover."

"All right, Avery, we'll leave that up to you. Just let us know when you're finished so we can wrap things up. Our big question right now is we have . . . Sara's punishment all set up, but now that we think, I say think, she might have gotten herself inseminated and could be pregnant, it kind of throws us into a tailspin. Does anyone have any suggestions?" Myra asked.

No one did.

"Hold on, people, I'm getting a text from Matt. Oh oh!"

"What? What?" The Sisters crowded around the old spy to see what he was seeing on his special sat phone.

"Matt and Duke are following her. She backed her car out of the garage and roared down the road. He said the weather conditions are horrible. Right now he has no clue where she's going. They're right behind her. Don't worry, they won't lose her."

"Something must have happened," Annie said.

"On a night like this? What could happen? She got spooked watching TV? What? Could she be coming here to harm Bella? Avery, call Matt back and ask him which direction she's going, this way or into D.C.?"

Avery did as instructed. He listened, then clicked off. "She pulled into a strip mall and parked in a handicapped space in front of an urgent care facility. Matt is right behind her. She's getting out. Oh, this isn't good. Matt said she's leaving a trail of . . . of blood. Someone is at the door helping her. That's it. She's inside and out of sight. Matt and Duke will go in in a few minutes and pretend to be a relative to see what they can find out."

"*No!*" the Sisters shouted as one.

"That will spook her, prove to her someone is watching her. They can't go in until she leaves. If she leaves. They might decide to keep her for twenty-four hours for observation," Annie said. "I'm thinking right now that we're all thinking the same thing. She is probably having a miscarriage. Avery is right, this is not good for her but might solve our problem," Annie said.

Kathryn jumped up. "Come on, girls, we

gotta go. This is the perfect opportunity to go to her house and go through it."

The girls raced to the stairs, leaving Myra, Annie, and Avery behind.

Myra looked over at Annie. "We'd just be in the way, Annie. They move a lot faster than we do."

"Like it or not, Annie, Myra is right. Why do you think I let the young bucks do all the heavy lifting? There's a lot to be said for standing on the sidelines and calling the shots."

"Oh yeah, name me one thing!" Annie shot back. "Just one thing, Avery!" There was such menace in Annie's voice, the old spy trembled.

"I was just trying to make you feel better. I hate it that I can't be in on the action anymore. I admit it, it's hell getting old. This is the next best thing, and as far as I can see, there are no other options."

Myra laughed.

Annie grimaced. "When you're right, you're right. I wonder what they'll find. Do you think we should tell Bella?"

This time Avery and Myra laughed.

"Ah, I see. You are assuming the two of them are . . . busy."

"I'm not going to pretend I'm a seer or anything like that, but I do not see Bella jumping into a romance. I also think it's a given that she is attracted to Paul Montrose and he to her, but they will fight their feelings. Bella has to come to terms with what she felt for Andy. I heard her talking to Yoko the other day. She was crying and saying she knew almost nothing about the man she married and was having trouble remembering what he looked like. And then there is that business of her signing her divorce papers the same day she found out her husband was dead. That's a lot of weight for that young woman to be carrying around on those slim shoulders of hers. I do think she'll be okay in the end; I really do. She has a good head on her shoulders, and I think Paul Montrose is a stand-up guy," Myra said.

Myra was stunned when Annie and Avery both said they agreed with her.

"All right then, we'll keep this to ourselves for now. Why don't we go upstairs and see about a late lunch. Those pancakes Maggie made were a long time ago."

"Weenies?" Annie asked hopefully.

"Spot on, sister." Myra giggled.

"I like hot dogs," Avery said.

"Then let's do it," Annie said, rushing to the stairs. "Boiled, fried, or grilled?"

"Grilled," Myra and Avery shouted at the same time.

"Three dogs coming right up," Annie shouted happily.

The girls sat in the *Post* van outside Sara's house in Kalorama. The rain was pounding down. "We'll be soaked before we get to the door, which means we'll be leaving puddles all over the house," Kathryn said.

"I don't think any of us care, Kathryn. Can you tell if the alarm is on? If it is, it will be glowing red. She left in a hurry, so hopefully she forgot to set it. I can pick this lock, but before we open the door, we need to know about the alarm. Look through the side window and tell me what you see," Nikki directed.

"It's green," Maggie said.

"Hot damn," Nikki said, working the pick-lock the way Annie had taught her.

"Move! Move! Move!" Kathryn shouted to be heard over the heavy rainfall. "Quick! Lock the door. Let's split up and go over this house with a fine-toothed comb. I know that's an old, tired cliché, but this woman is one smart cookie, and we do not want to miss anything. This house has to be at least six thousand square feet. Almost a mansion. If you let your mind jump ahead with seven or eight sperm donations, this would be a house for seven or eight kids."

"She hasn't furnished it all yet. It's giving off a kind of temporary feel to me," Yoko said.

"I'm picking up on that, too," Isabelle said.

"Considering her life these past years, I think this is how she lives. There is no permanency to this place, at least not that I'm feeling," Maggie added.

"Let's branch out. I'll take the second floor with Maggie," Nikki said.

"Yoko and I will take the kitchen and dining room. The family room is empty, no furniture, nothing on the shelves, no carpeting to rip up. Just closed blinds on the windows. Did you all notice that all the blinds are closed?" Kathryn asked. The Sisters all said they had noticed. Sara with a million aliases was a very private person.

"I'll take the makeshift office, which is here off the kitchen in this alcove. That's where her computer is," Isabelle said.

"I guess that leaves the garage for me," Alexis said. "Let's get to it, girls. For all we know, the urgent care facility could release her and just order bed rest. Maybe someone should turn down her bed just in case."

The Sisters hooted and hollered to show what they thought of that idea.

It took only an hour before the girls met up in the kitchen. "Let's hear it," Maggie said.

"Refrigerator is full of healthy food. There's a row of vitamin bottles on the windowsill over the sink. Prominent among said vitamins is a bottle of prenatal vitamins. Everything appears to be new. Nothing looks used. Very little in the way of pantry goods. No alcohol to be seen. Cleaning supplies under the sink. That's about it.

"The master bedroom is all girly and fancy, lots of ribbons and doodads. To me it looked like the bedroom of a seventeen-year-old. Lots of perfume bottles, lots of jewelry, looks real to me. All kinds of clothes, designer and off-the-rack plus rummage-sale items. She's ready for whatever comes her way. All the bedrooms are empty. All have bathrooms. Nothing. But there are paint and cloth swatches, both pink and blue, in one of the bedrooms. There was nothing on the second floor of any interest to us.

"Garage is clean as a whistle. You know, like someone just moved in who didn't have anything to put in a garage but a car. No paint cans, no Weedwacker, nothing. A lightbulb, that's it, plus an oil stain on the garage floor," Alexis said.

Isabelle held up Sara's laptop. "I can't crack this here. We have to take it with us. I'm going to need Phil's help. There are a few receipts in the cubbyholes in this little desk. All in the name of Sara Nolan. Everything I've seen says Sara Nolan. I wonder if she actually changed her name legally."

"Where's her stuff?" Maggie demanded. "Where's her life? You know, the stuff you never leave home without. Like my backpack. I would never leave that unless my house was burning down and I couldn't get to it. It's not here, so she must have taken it with her. Someone text Avery and have him ask his people if they saw her take anything into urgent care? If she didn't, have him tell them to ransack her car. And tell them to hurry it up."

"I'll do it," Kathryn volunteered. She started to tap the keys on her phone in a near frenzy.

Twenty-five minutes later, Kathryn received a text from the old spy. "She went into urgent care empty-handed. Her car is clean. The only thing they found was a box of tissues and a pair of sunglasses. Okay, girls, fan out and search every inch of this house. There's a bag or a box here somewhere with, as Maggie said, her stuff. For all we know she could have a built-in safe somewhere. Fine-tooth comb, inch by inch. Take your time and be careful."

The Sisters muttered and mumbled as they searched the house Sara with a million aliases lived in. Two hours later, they once again met in the kitchen, hands up in the air to indicate nothing had been found.

"I don't believe this. I don't think she'd bury it outside. Every time she wanted something, she'd have to dig it up to get it. Maybe she rented one of those oversize safe deposit boxes at a bank. But that is more or less like burying something outside, she'd have to get in her car, go to the bank, and get into the vault. No, it's got to be here. She's no fool. In fact, I think she's supersmart. Let's all just stand here, close our eyes, visualize all the rooms, and ask ourselves where you would hide your stuff," Kathryn suggested.

The girls did as instructed. Ten minutes went by, then another ten, before Maggie bellowed at the top of her lungs. "There is no place. She hid it somewhere else. We're beating a dead horse here!"

"No, we're not! I think I know where it is," Nikki said, excitement ringing in her voice.

"Where? Where?" the girls shouted.

"Look around, girls, what do you see?" Nikki asked.

"Well, since we're in the kitchen, a table and chairs and a bunch of basically empty cabinets. We went through them all. Canned soup, macaroni, cereal," Maggie said.

"What's under the sink? What did you see?" Nikki asked.

"Cleaning supplies, trash bags, dishwasher soap, dust mitten, duct tape. That's it. I have that same stuff under my own sink at home," Alexis said.

"How much duct tape?" Nikki asked.

"Maybe a quarter of a roll. There wasn't much left on it." To prove her point, Alexis opened the sink cabinet and pulled out the remains of a roll of gray duct tape. "So what are you saying? She taped something somewhere? But we took this house apart and didn't find a thing," she said.

"That's because we didn't look in the right place. Girls, grab hold of the kitchen table and be careful, it's solid oak and heavy, turn it over, and tell me what you see!" Nikki said, bubbling with excitement.

The expletives rang loud and clear in the cavernous kitchen as the Sisters stared at all the ziplock bags duct-taped to the underside of the table. They ripped at them in a frenzy. "I always put my roasts or a big chicken in this size ziplock bag and put them in the freezer so they don't get freezer burn," Nikki said.

"These bags sure are jam-packed," Nikki added. "Sara what's her name was one busy lady. Just look at this stuff. Quick, let's fold it all up and get out of here before she gets back here. Make sure the table is in the exact same spot so she doesn't see anything amiss."

"If she even suspects something, she's going to take off. But considering the circumstances right now, she might not be in any condition to go anywhere but home to bed," Alexis said.

"We need to make sure we're not leaving any signs we were here. Check for water in the foyer, we did drip when we got here," Kathryn said.

"I cleaned it up," Yoko said, "but Kathryn is right, fan out and check everything you might have touched and didn't put back in the right place."

Ten minutes later, the Sisters were at the

front door. "It's still pouring rain. If anyone is looking out their window, they'll be hard-pressed to identify any of us. Everyone, make a mad dash for the van; keep the door open and the engine running for me. I have to lock up," Nikki said.

The girls followed Nikki's instructions.

Within minutes, Maggie was careening down the road, her horn blasting for no reason.

"Why are you blowing your horn?" Kathryn shouted.

"I don't know, Kathryn, I just felt like I should. You know, success and all that. It was a dumb thing to do, I admit it."

"A text is coming in from Avery," Isabelle said. "Sara is still inside urgent care. He said Matt said they have a lot of emergencies right now. Mostly car accidents. He said Duke went inside and looked around and tried to talk up one of the aides. He said he was trying to find out if a buddy of his was brought in. And then he did a bit of flirting and learned that prior to the sudden rush, only one patient came in and her condition wasn't life-threatening. He said she would be discharged shortly. Duke thinks it's Sara. He now has a dinner date for Saturday night with the nurse's aide."

The girls burst out laughing. "At least some good came out of this little caper," Nikki said, and giggled. "And we got the brass ring in the bargain."

"We need to decide what we're going to do from here on in. As soon as we get to the farm, we'll let Avery go through all these ziplock bags while we decide if Sara deserves the punishment we had planned for her. We have to keep in mind that she did not physically harm anyone. Yes, she's a thief. We're going on pure instinct when we say we think she was going to harm Bella. I do believe that is so, and for that reason I'm still okay on the punishment. We all agreed that she literally stole Bella's eggs and Andy's sperm. Obviously, the first insemination didn't work. Who knows if the other six or seven will work. Regardless, Bella gave us our marching orders. She is the legal custodian of her husband's donations and she wants them destroyed. Now, having said that, once Sara realizes the jig is up, if we don't intervene, she's going to go after Bella because there is no one else for her to blame," Nikki said.

Myra, Annie, and Avery clustered around the rain-soaked women. Nikki handed over the ziplock bags, and the group ran up to the second floor to put on dry clothes.

"Is it all you thought it would be? Is it enough, Avery?" Annie asked anxiously.

"Enough plus more. I assume you want my people to continue with the surveillance. By the way, Matt just sent a text saying that Sara is on her way home, and they're right behind her at a safe distance. Obviously, she's going to be fine. If you no longer need my services, I'll take my leave of you all. I'll have my people stay on surveillance until you notify me otherwise."

"One more thing before you go, Avery. Is there a way for you to jam Sara's phone around seven o'clock this evening? Better yet, make it six o'clock," Annie said.

"Not a problem. Does that mean I should be ready with my people for the send-off?"

"Eight o'clock will be fine," Annie said primly. "We will call you. You can see yourself out while we retire to the war room. Thanks for your help on this mission." The Sisters all echoed Annie's thanks.

Yoko locked and double-bolted the kitchen door.

The mad scramble to the dungeons left the Sisters giggling hysterically. They had prevailed. Now all they had to do was finalize the plan, and Bella's world would be right side up again.

Each of the women snapped off a crisp salute to Lady Justice before they took their seat at the table. Myra called the meeting to order. "Girls, this is going to be one of our shortest meetings on record. So, let's get to it so we can all go out for some surf and turf and a barrel of margaritas. I guarantee all of us a safe ride home."

"Hear! Hear!" the girls shouted.

* * *

"It's all packed in the van. It's almost six, girls. We should be on our way. Avery said he would jam Sara's phone at six, so we can break and enter at will. Does anyone have any questions?" Alexis asked.

There were no questions.

Ten minutes later, Maggie had the van on the road and they were on their way to the house where Sara with a million aliases lived.

When they arrived at the house in Kalorama, Maggie backed the van up to the garage doors and hopped out as Kathryn, with her steel-toed boots, kicked in the front door.

"I was going to pick the lock, Kathryn," Nikki grumbled.

"Takes too long. Look, it's open! Let's go, girls! The prize is standing right there in the kitchen. Let's make this quick."

And quick it was. Yoko did her whirligig dance, and before Sara could blink or demand to know what was going on, Nikki and Alexis had her tied and were dragging her to the garage, where Kathryn decided to pick her up and throw her over her shoulder. She marched to the van and dumped Sara in the back.

"I closed up everything. We were never here," Isabelle said.

"What time is it?" Alexis asked.

Annie looked down at the Mickey Mouse watch that was her prize possession, and urged,

"Drive faster, Maggie, we only have seventeen minutes. Don't worry about speeding."

In the back of the van, Sara started to scream. "Who are you? This is kidnapping! That little snot sent you to kill me, didn't she? She's sick and deranged. She put you up to this. I know she did. Let me go, I'll pay you whatever you want, ten times whatever she paid you."

The Sisters laughed. "Impossible," Isabelle said. "We already took all your money. We found all your stuff under the kitchen table. You sure did use a lot of duct tape."

Sara started to curse at the top of her lungs. She didn't stop until Nikki whacked her across the face with the back of her hand.

Sara started to cry. "Who are you crazy people? I just got out of the clinic. I'm sick. How can you treat me like this?"

"Oh, it's easy," Kathryn said.

"We're here with nine minutes to spare," Maggie said, careening into the parking area near the beach. "Timing is everything, girls, move it!"

And they did. It was a precision drill. First, they assembled the oversize dog crate. Maggie and Kathryn carried it to the beach. Nikki and Alexis half carried and half dragged Sara through the sand to the dog crate. Yoko cut her bonds as Annie and Isabelle shoved Sara into the crate and locked it.

"High tide is in six minutes!" Myra shouted.

"Our work here is done!" Annie said, as she followed the girls back to the van. Off in the distance, if anyone was looking, Avery Snowden and his operatives were laughing like a bunch of lunatics.

"Anchors away, mates!"

Epilogue

Twenty months later

Bella looked to the horizon and smiled. A perfect day as far as she could tell. And, it was the first day of summer, June 21. *How pristine everything is,* she thought. How green. Did they measure with a ruler to make sure all the crosses lined up so perfectly? She should know the answer to that question, but she didn't. But then how could she know? She had never been here before. Well, she was here now, and the answer really didn't matter. Not now.

Bella dropped to her knees and laid the single yellow sunflower at the base of the cross that said that Major Andrew Adam Nolan rested here unto eternity. Because she didn't know if flowers were permitted on the pristine grounds, she'd only brought one sunflower.

"It's me, Andy. Bella. I'm sorry I haven't been out here to . . . to visit. I just couldn't make myself come here, knowing I couldn't handle it. I stayed away on purpose. Forgive me, please.

"I came today for several reasons. I've had a rough time, Andy. I met a group of wonderful women who helped me. I wouldn't be here talking to your . . . ah . . . spirit if it weren't for them. Truly, I owe them my life. I don't know if I will ever be able to repay them, but I am going to search for a way. I learned from them that it isn't about weathering the storm but learning how to dance in the rain. I did it. I can now dance in the rain.

"I'm not going to go into all that went on with your sister. I think, wherever you are, you know. And I don't want to ruin this visit."

Bella rummaged in her bag and pulled out a mini recorder. "I brought something with me that I think will sum up my visit. Remember when you kissed me out on that pier, and we could hear the music from the bar. It was so romantic. They were playing that song Dolly Parton wrote and Whitney Houston sang and made famous, 'I Will Always Love You.' You kissed me and said you would always and forever love me even though we had just met. I cried the way I'm crying now, and this song is saying what I feel. Andy, a part of me will always love you. *Always.* I had to come here to tell you that.

"Paul Montrose came to help me when those wonderful people I told you about asked for his help. He stayed on. We got to know each other. We were friends, and that friendship went further as time went on. He asked me to marry him. I didn't give him my answer because I wanted to talk to you first." Out of the corner of her eye, Bella noticed a flash of pale blue. A tiny blue hummingbird was sucking at the nectar on the sunflower. She smiled.

"I'm going to go back and tell Paul that my answer is yes, Andy. By the way, I scrimped and saved and the mechanic felt sorry for me and gave me a good deal so I got your truck fixed, painted, and worked over. And then I gave it to Paul. He loves it as much as you did. I just don't get that whole truck thing. I guess it's a guy thing. Somehow, deep in my heart, I thought you would want Paul to have your truck. He's a great guy, Andy, and he loved you like one of his brothers. He flew here when he came to help, but we're going to pack up my stuff and put it in the back and drive cross-country. Paul works with his two brothers in a high-tech company in Silicon Valley. They made him a partner. He has a big family, and I can't wait to be part of it. I want to belong, Andy. I *need* to belong to someone.

"Which brings me to the real reason I came here today. I came to say goodbye. I won't be coming back here to . . . to . . . visit. It wouldn't be fair to Paul. It has to be all or nothing or it won't work for us. I hope you understand. But . . . I think it's okay for you and me to have a secret. I know you aren't going to tell anyone, and I will never, ever admit that one small part of me has been carved out and saved, the part of me that will always love you. So this is goodbye, Andy," Bella said, as she put her hand over her heart and placed it on the pristine white cross. She looked down at the tiny hummingbird still feasting on the sunflower.

Bella was on her feet and about to walk away when she turned around, and said, "Hey, Andy, it would be nice if you could somehow give me a sign that you're okay with all of this." When nothing happened, Bella swiped her hand across her eyes to wipe away the tears. She walked away but turned back once to wave.

"Remember what I said, Andy, our secret, part of me will *always* love you."

Six weeks later, in a small white church in California, the Montrose family, which numbered thirty-five, and what they called the East Coast family, eight Sisters and their menfolk, all clapped when the minister said, "I pronounce you man and wife. You may now kiss the bride."

And the groom did exactly that.

And then they were all outside, laughing and throwing popcorn instead of rice. Bella turned when a little girl who looked to be around ten years old held out a sunflower. "That man over there said to give you this. He said if you hold it long enough, a hummingbird will come."

Bella whirled around. "Where? What man? Where is he?"

The little girl pointed to a tree across the road from the church. "There was a man wearing a white suit. I don't see him now. I asked him why he didn't give it to you himself, and he said he had to get back. It's a pretty flower, Miss Bella."

A smile that rivaled the bright sun washed over Bella's face. "Well, okay then, Andy. Message received."

Keep reading for

a sneak peek at

the next novel in the Sisterhood series,

BITTER PILL,

coming soon from

Fern Michaels and

Zebra Books!

London—present day

Charlotte Hansen peered closely into the magnifying mirror on her vanity. "Why do I keep having these fog-like moments?" she whispered to her reflection. Looking down at the array of prescription bottles, she could not remember which pills she was supposed to take next. *These were supposed to help me, but I feel like I'm getting worse.* She had numbered the white caps of the green bottles to make it easier but had forgotten to replace the caps when she took the first three pills. She wrung her hands in dismay. *I simply cannot tell Maryann that I've messed up my routine again. For sure, she'll have me put under observation. And what would they observe? A sixtysomething woman losing her memory? Nothing too odd about that.* She heaved a big sigh and decided to skip the rest of her morning routine of taking twelve different pills. *What difference will one dose make?*

Unless her daughter, Maryann, was counting the pills. With that thought, Charlotte flushed what was left of her morning dose down the toilet. She splashed water on her face, took another deep look in the mirror, and decided she could fake it for the day if necessary.

Charlotte thought a visit to London to see Maryann and her grandson Liam would raise her spirits, but instead she seemed to be in a downward spiral. She would discuss the matter with Dr. Marcus at her next appointment. Checking her desk diary, she noted she was due to see him the next day. Charlotte didn't care for him very much even though he was effusive and turned on the charm. But he had been recommended by her new personal physician in Aspen—who insisted she have a doctor on hand, particularly in a foreign country. Apparently, Dr. Marcus and her new doctor, Dr. Harold Steinwood, who had taken over the practice of her long-time physician, Dr. Robert Leeland, had studied together in Switzerland, and when Charlotte had told Dr. Steinwood that she would be traveling to London, he insisted that she get in touch with his classmate, Dr.

Marcus. In time, she would reevaluate this "miracle doctor" and his "cure" for mental acuity and longevity, but for now she was content to get dressed and prepare for the rest of her day.

Sag Harbor

Dr. Raymond Corbett strolled around his two-hundred-square-foot walk-in closet, deciding which cashmere blazer he should wear to the party. It was finally going to be his big night in the Hamptons. After years of being overlooked by almost every yacht club and country club in the South Fork of Long Island, he had persuaded the Longboat Yacht Club to allow him to become a member. The membership came with a very high price tag. Apparently, one could buy his way into the stodgy organization that catered to old-money and the nouveaux riche. One either had to own a yacht over eighty-three feet, be a power broker, or be some sort of celebrity. He was none of those. He was merely a physician who specialized in longevity wellness. Yes, he had been treating patients for almost a decade now, prescribing placebos and mind-altering drugs to women of a certain age—mostly rich widows, to be precise.

He took one of his Tom Ford designer blazers from the rack and frowned at the brass buttons. They needed to be polished. Now. He pressed his finger down on the house intercom. "Henry!" he bellowed. "Meet me in my dressing room. Now!"

A soft voice replied, "I will be there right away, sir."

Corbett tossed it on the bed and then chose an Armani blazer to wear. He thumbed through his new collection of striped, button-down shirts and picked a shirt from one of his favorite designers, Brioni. Recalling the $820 price tag, he snickered. Yes, he would almost look like a million bucks. Almost. The jacket, shirt, Gucci shoes, and Audemars Piguet Royal Oak Concept 44mm Titanium watch totaled almost $160,000. He'd leave the pinky ring home. No sense being ostentatious. He snickered to himself again. Tonight was the night he would reveal to the members of the yacht club that he would be displaying a painting at a private exhibit: one by Marc Chagall once thought to have been stolen and burned by the Nazis. He had made arrangements to acquire it at a private sale brokered by Christie's. Tonight, he was having a party, basically in honor of himself, at the yacht club. Once he had possession of the Chagall, he would hire a private security company, which would cost a small fortune, to deliver the artwork and keep guard over it during the gala he would hold at the club, then take it to a special locker at the Museum of Modern Art. He had made arrangements for them to borrow the painting in the fall. He wanted to spend his summer being known in the Hamptons as a great art connoisseur.

Yes, his group of "longevity" doctors—who claimed to have a new protocol to moderate the progress of aging—had brought him and his two partners the wealth to live an extravagant lifestyle, something he was enjoying immensely. He had a co-op in Manhattan and now this modest home in Sag Harbor.

Corbett knew that he and his partners would have to retire soon—before the world learned the truth. There were two old biddies who could ruin it all. Lorraine Thompson had died of an accidental overdose, and Margorie Brewster had an incident that sent her into convulsions, the treatment for which put her in a semiconscious state. Even with the waivers and nondisclosure agreements their patients had agreed to, those incidents would eventually pop up on someone's radar. They had been lucky enough to fly under the radar for a good long while. These were simply a couple of mishaps. He, Marcus, and Steinwood had made a killing. He smirked. *No pun intended.* But enough of that. He picked a silk ascot, which added an additional $300 to his already ridiculously expensive ensemble, and left for the party.

Connect with

Us

Visit us online at
KensingtonBooks.com
to read more from your favorite authors, see books
by series, view reading group guides, and more.

for sneak peeks, chances to win books and prize packs,
and to share your thoughts with other readers.

facebook.com/kensingtonpublishing
twitter.com/kensingtonbooks

Tell us what you think!

To share your thoughts, submit a review,
or sign up for our eNewsletters, please visit:
KensingtonBooks.com/TellUs.